REMEMBER

REMEMBER

Patricia Shanae Smith

Copyright © 2019 by Patricia Shanae Smith
Cover and jacket design by Mimi Bark

ISBN 978-1-947993-68-6
eISBN: 978-1-947993-91-4
Library of Congress Control Number: 2019949098

First trade paperback edition October 2019 by Agora Books
An imprint of Polis Books, LLC
221 River St., 9th Floor, #9070
Hoboken, NJ 07030
www.PolisBooks.com

In Loving Memory
of My Mom & My Nana

Chapter 1

"My name is Elizabeth Smith. I'm here to help you. I am not going to hurt you."

She said it slowly, like she was talking to a little kid. I didn't think she was going to. I just kept staring at her distracting pair of high heels. I'd never met her before, but she looked familiar.

"So, do you know why you're here?"

I shook my head. I also didn't know where *here* was. I didn't remember how I got here. I had been with my dad but I didn't know where he went. According to what I'd seen on television, I was either in jail, the hospital, or a mental institution. The room was normal-looking enough, with a big chair and a sofa. I could tell by looking out the window I was a couple stories high. There was a video camera on a tripod in the middle of the room.

"Whenever you're ready, I want you to tell me what happened."

"Where's my dad?" I didn't feel like talking. "I need my dad."

"He's not here, Portia."

"Okay, well, I'm not talking without him. I don't really know what you want me to say, anyway."

"Is that why you need him here?"

"Are you even allowed to talk to me without a legal adult?"

"I'm not a police officer, and you *are* a legal adult. You are twenty-two years old. Do you know that?"

Why would I not know how old I am?

I nodded as I stared at the door.

"Your dad is not coming through that door."

"What do you want me to say? The faster I say it, the faster I can see him, right?"

"Start from the beginning. Tell me about your sister's play."

Five Years Ago

Piper had been cast as Beatrice in *Much Ado About Nothing* and tonight was opening night at Cypress High. The play was the only thing talked about in our house for the past three months. I was proud of her, she was the only sophomore who had gotten a lead role. But that didn't mean I wanted to go. Being a senior was hard enough for me without all these outside activities.

Although Piper was my whole world, I hated social situations even more than I loved her. Piper understood, though she was the complete opposite of me. Her world was makeup, attention, boys, parties…I, on the other hand, didn't want to leave my room, and I didn't have any friends. Only partners on school projects.

Though I hadn't gone to a single party in my four years of high school, I often picked her up from them. Piper was so popular, she was always invited to everything. Our parents didn't care. Mother was way too obsessed with the advertising company she owned. Dad was too obsessed with football and being a stay-at-home dad.

One time, Piper had been too drunk to come out to the car. I sat outside and waited for her for over an hour. Biting my lips, shaking my legs, tapping my fingers against the steering wheel, I kept whispering, "Come on, Piper," over and over again. Piper finally called me, crying, asking me to come inside and get her.

She told me exactly where she was.

She told me exactly what turns to take.

She reassured me that I wouldn't have to speak to a single person.

My little sister was in there, drunk, alone, helpless, and I was stuck in the car, heart racing. No matter how messed up she was, she still knew what she was asking of me was big, and danced around her words delicately, knowing how crippling my anxiety was. She promised to stay on the phone with me the entire way. It was her sobbing that got me out of the car.

I still can't believe I did that. Now I'm standing in her doorway years later, watching her curl her hair listening to Britney Spears.

"Mom is making me go tonight," I said, already dressed and ready. With my anxiety, I had to get up two hours before everyone just to get myself to school on time.

"What? We already talked about this. Dad is recording it for you." She threw down the curling iron. I shrugged my shoulders. "Portia, I'm sorry. Mom can be such a bitch sometimes." My mom didn't understand my problem. She refused to get me help, but I didn't care. Piper was more concerned about me than I was.

Piper raced downstairs, me trailing behind. "Dad, does Portia have to go tonight?" Oh God. Leave it to Piper to start drama. Leave it to Piper to stand up for me even when I didn't ask her to.

"It's fine. Don't worry about it. I'll see you tonight." I rolled my eyes and headed for the door.

"I thought she wasn't going. I was going to order her a pizza," Dad said, pouring a little bit of brandy in his coffee. I smiled at him. He never questioned me. He didn't really know about disorders and problems, but he knew *me* better than anyone. He knew there was no way I was going, even though we'd never talked about it.

"Well, I think she should support her sister. This is a big deal. I really want her to go." My mother looked at my father like she was about to stab him in the eye.

"She's standing right there, Carol." Dad came over to me and put his hand on my shoulder.

"I don't *want* her to go, how about that?" Piper snapped.

"I'm going to school." I stormed off, slamming the door. I knew the three of them were going to have a fight as soon as I left.

They always fought over me.

REMEMBER

Three Years Ago

"Hon, babe, sweetie, are you up? Can you get up?" Something nudged me gently. I could smell gross morning breath overlaid by beer. My dad and alcohol had become even better friends since my mother and my sister died.

It was just us in the house.

It was just us in the world.

We had both started drinking, smoking, and watching television almost twenty-four seven. At least I was taking online classes at UCLA. That had always been part of my plan. Once I graduated high school, I had never wanted to actually *go* to school again in my life.

"Dad, I have a test today and I feel like shit. I'm super hungover and need to rest."

"Okay, well, need a beer? I'll get you one. I'm going to be watching the game."

"The game? What time is it?"

"Two o'clock, honey."

"Oh shit." I'd missed my test. My first semester had been easy compared to this year, and now I was going to have to take this class over again. My dad and I had been living off of my mother's advertising company money. Susan, Mom's best friend, had taken over after she died. Susan always made sure we were doing okay. I felt like I was letting her down, between the drinking and taking care of my dad, I was failing.

I always wanted things to get better…tomorrow.

My dad plopped down on the couch and lit the last cigarette.

"We bought that carton for the both of us to split."

"We *are* splitting it."

"No, you've been smoking more than me. I want a cigarette, too."

"Here, have this one."

"No."

"Take it, we're also out of beer."

"I guess that's what I get for sleeping all day." I was annoyed, but understood. I had lost my mother and my sister, he had lost his wife and his daughter. And he got left with the daughter with the problems. My guilt numbed my anger toward him. I went over to the couch and he put his arm around me.

"I'm sorry. I knew you were going to have a rough morning so I thought I'd let you sleep," he mumbled in my ear.

"It's fine. I'll go to the store tomorrow, okay?"

For the last year and a half, I'd had to step up. I'd had to get over my social issues, well, not get over them, but push their boundaries. But I was struggling. Dad wouldn't go out in public. We'd basically switched roles.

Even though I'd lived on the same street since I was born, everything looked different after the accident. It was almost winter, no kids were playing in the streets. Even the neighbors looked different, changed somehow. Walking to the store was pleasant, in spite of the occasional stares. I was the girl whose family had died, the one with the father on the edge. If I had been with Piper, she would tell them all to fuck off and mind their own business. I kept my head down and kept walking. The store was only two blocks. I usually did it in ten minutes.

That day was different.

That day there was a man standing outside the liquor store smoking Marlboro Reds and looking at me. He was cute—dark hair, dark beard, deep, icy blue eyes, rough. I stared back. For the first time, I had something in common with a cute guy, even if it was a bad habit.

"Would you like one?" he asked, offering the pack. It was the first time in over a year that someone besides Larry and Joseph, the cashiers at the store, had said something to me. I froze for a second, then kept walking. My heart was starting to race. I felt like I was about to have a panic attack.

"You okay?" Larry greeted.

I nodded, staring outside. The man was still looking at me.

"Is he bothering you?"

I shook my head.

"I got your carton ready; you're out of beer, too?"

Larry had known my father for years. He told me how my dad would come in and always talk about me. How he told stories about my mother and Piper too, but talked most about me. The first time I came in here alone, Larry made me feel comfortable. And Joseph was quiet like me; that's why I took to him.

"Tell your father I said hello and I miss him."

"I will."

"And hey!" he called out. "You're a pretty girl, Ms. Willows, you're going to have to get used to guys hitting on you outside dirty liquor stores."

I giggled and stepped back out into the afternoon light. The man wasn't there anymore. I walked home, forgetting about it altogether, until I saw him ahead of me, going into the house across the street.

What the hell? No. No.

There was no way he lived there. I knew who lived there. It was a retired doctor. I didn't know exactly who it was but I did know it wasn't this guy. Then he saw me and started walking over.

Jesus! Why?

"Hey," he said. His voice was softer this time. He was more of a boy than I'd thought. He didn't seem intimidating like he did outside the liquor store. I could see he was wearing an SMC shirt underneath his red flannel. He was only two inches taller than me.

"I'm sorry about earlier. I didn't mean to scare you." He looked down at my bag. "Do you need help?"

I started to lose my grip. I thought I had gotten used to carrying a twelve-pack of Budweiser and a carton of Marlboro Reds. I shook my head as I struggled. He rushed over and grabbed it out of my hands.

"May I?" he asked as he took it. He smelled so good, like an Abercrombie and Fitch model or Hollister. I didn't know the difference. Piper would have been able to tell me. Relieved, I smiled and nodded. He looked up at my house and took a deep breath. I frowned—I should be more nervous than he was. My house was a mess. *Why was I letting him in?* I didn't know if my dad was even dressed. The kitchen was really close to the front door. My dad was in the living room. There was no way he would see him but he might hear him.

"Wow. This is a nice house!" He looked around.

I smiled for some reason.

"Can I ask you something?" he said.

I nodded as I started to put the beer away.

"Do you live alone? I'm just saying, it's a big house. You seem really young." His anxiousness relaxed me.

I shook my head.

"Oh…okay. That makes sense. I live with my father. Do you know him? My parents are divorced. I was living with my mom in Florida and then after high school, I decided to go to college out here. Nice neighborhood. Do you go to school?"

It wasn't that nice of a neighborhood, but whatever.

I nodded.

"Okay, well...my name is Ethan. It was nice to meet you."

I smiled and walked him to the door. I mumbled, "I'm Portia. I live with my dad, too. It's nice to meet you." I shut the door behind him.

What had just happened?

Chapter 2

I couldn't stop thinking about Ethan. I wondered why he had helped me. Piper always told me boys only want one thing, and once you give it to them, they get mean. But when she had gotten her first boyfriend, she took it back. I wanted to see Ethan again, but I had no idea how. I guessed I could stare out my window and wait for him to come outside, but that would be weird.

"You don't like this movie, do you?"

"I have class, Dad. I'm trying to study."

"We'll watch it when you're done."

"Dad...I don't really care about *Rebel Without a Cause*."

"Your mother never liked it either."

"Well, at least we had one thing in common."

"You guys had a lot in common."

"Like what?"

"You reminded her of the things she didn't like about herself. But those things were the very things I loved about her."

"Is that why she hated me so much? I wish every day that she could have loved me for at least a day before she died."

"She loved you. She loved Piper. She loved me. But she didn't know how to show it. She didn't express her feelings to any of us. You weren't the exception. Well, you were always the exception to me."

"I love you, Daddy."

"I love you."

He never said, "I love you, too." He felt like that meant he loved me less, or that he only said it because I said it first. He loved me the same as I loved him.

There was a knock at the door. We both jumped. There hadn't been an unexpected knock on the door in years. Grandma came by sometimes, but I always knew about it ahead of time so I could help her out of the car.

I ran upstairs and looked out my window.

It was Ethan.

I stood there for five minutes hoping he'd go away, even though I wanted to see him. Realizing my mistake, I ran down the stairs, mustered up what little courage I had, and opened the door just as he started walking away.

"You *are* home!" His smile lit up his entire face, and I swear it made his eyes sparkle. Remember, I don't get out much. I stuck up one finger and nodded. He smiled again.

Oh my God.

I went to grab two beers and a pack of cigarettes.

"Uh, for real?" he asked as I held up a beer. He didn't stop smiling and I could not stop staring.

We sat on the swinging bench Piper and I used to play on when we were kids. I had never wanted to go to the park. I had never wanted to play with the other kids or leave the house. Mom would make me go outside once a day, but I refused to go past the porch. Piper always made sure I wasn't alone.

Sitting on the bench without her, I felt like I was about to cry, but tried to hold it together. My throat was closing. I sucked down my beer so I could breathe again.

"Your dad lets you drink?"

I nodded. I liked his voice. I could just listen to him all day.

"*My* dad would kill me. He's very strict."

I cast a worried look at his door. We were outside. His dad could see him.

"Don't worry. He's not home. I got kind of lonely, thought I would ask if you wanted to come out and play." We both giggled.

"You should smile more."

I immediately put my hand to my lips.

"I'm just saying. You don't have to."

My heart started to race and I chugged more beer. I should have gotten us more.

"Budweiser, eh?"

"It's my dad's favorite," I said. "I hated it when I was a kid. I hated the smell when he would kiss me goodnight." I was about to tell Ethan a story but he was staring at me weird. "What?"

"I like the sound of your voice."

"I like the sound of yours."

"I can get annoying."

We both laughed.

We talked for what felt like hours. I told him a lot about Piper, and he told me about his family. His dad was a retired psychologist who worked at my old high school as a counselor.

"Do you miss your mom?" I asked.

"Sometimes, but I call her every day."

I nodded as I looked down.

"How long has it been?"

"A year and nine months and twelve days. I miss Piper more than anything. I miss my mom...sometimes. I think what I miss most is their voices."

"The voice is the first thing everyone forgets about someone after they pass."

"Not me. My mother yelled at me way too much for me to ever forget her voice. Piper still gives me advice in my head all the time, mainly on how to take care of Dad."

"What would Piper say about me?"

"That you would make a great first...friend."

"I don't know why I'm so intrigued by you."

"The whole neighborhood talks about me. I know your father wanted to talk to me when I was in high school but I never went, so I can't even imagine what you've heard."

"You're the only other person near my age on this block, plus you're pretty."

"Pretty?"

He nodded. "Yes. Is that weird for me to say?"

"Are you trying to get in my pants?"

"No. I mean. No. I'm sorry!"

"It's okay, I was just making sure. Do you want another beer?"

I had never talked so much to someone who wasn't family. Once I started, it seemed I couldn't stop. There was so much relief. I loved talking to my dad. This was something different. Piper would have been so proud of me. I wanted her to be there to scream and ask me a million questions until I would tell her to calm down.

Seven Years Ago

"Portia! Portia!" It was eleven on a Saturday night. Dad was out at a bar with his friends. Mom was away on a business trip. I had been sleeping. Piper had been out with her friends. I woke up in a panic.

"Are you okay? What happened? What's wrong?"

"I kissed a boy!" She had been twelve years old.

My first kiss wouldn't be until I was nineteen.

"*What?*"

"It was amazing. I did it and then he stuck his tongue down my throat." She started laughing.

"Gross," I said.

"It was, kind of, but when he did it, I thought I was going to choke so I told him to stop."

"How old is he?"

"I don't know…he's in the eighth grade."

"And he shoved his tongue in like on TV?" My eyes widened.

"Yeah, I told him I didn't like that. So we kept kissing but without the tongue."

Disgusted, I couldn't hear any more.

"Mom and Dad are going to kill you."

"They'll never know. It was so much fun."

"Piper, you're twelve, you're just a baby."

"No, I'm not. I'm a woman now. I feel so much older and more experienced. I can't wait to tell everyone at school."

"You'll be really popular."

"I know! I'm going to text everyone, you can go back to sleep."

"I'll do my best."

She giggled and walked out of the room.

After that, I started to look up to her. She was younger than me. She was a sassy little thing, but I wanted so badly to be her. She inspired me. I tried to get out there. I tried to change for her. When I couldn't, she never said anything, but I saw how it affected her, and it hurt. She never knew the guilt I felt for not being the sister she'd always wanted.

Three Years Ago

"Who's your new friend?"

"Ethan. He lives across the street. We only had a few beers."

"It's good you're making friends, but I swear, Portia, if you're making more runs to the store than usual, he's going to have to chip in. Beer is not cheap."

"Dad. Relax. It was one time. I'll probably never see him again."

"Why do you say that?"

"I don't know. Maybe I'm too busy taking care of you...speaking of, what's for dinner?"

"Spaghetti. I don't think I did it right, though."

I went into the kitchen and froze: the sink piled high with dirty dishes. A box of pasta was half-spilled onto the table. Dried sauce stuck to the stovetop. Empty beer cans scattered haphazardly around a stack of unopened mail. Somehow, there was red sauce on my shirt.

"Dad—"

"Yeah, I gave up. There are some TV dinners in the freezer; just pop one of those in the microwave and bam, four minutes later, dinner."

"Cool...but pasta is not as cheap as it used to be." I winked at him.

"We should clean the house tomorrow."
"Yeah."

Dad and I lived a pretty boring life. Fall television season was starting, my favorite time of year. We had something new to watch every single night. On Saturdays, we would watch a movie. During the day, he watched sports and I watched Lifetime movies. That was it.

Between the two of us, we smoked a pack and drank six beers a day.

I missed my sister and my mother, but this became a comfortable, familiar routine. I felt no pressure to go out and meet people. I was going to school, which I loved—online classes Monday through Wednesday, from one to six. I could understand why outsiders might be worried, but at the end of the day, it was none of their business.

Still, I was struggling. I needed to get the book for a class I was barely passing; I thought I would be able to get through the class without it. But getting it meant going to UCLA in person. I was dreading it. But I had an idea.

I invited Ethan over.

"I need your help with something," I said, grabbing him a beer.

"What is it?"

"I go to school online…"

"SMC?"

"No. I thought about it, but my mom had a trust fund for me and then when she died, my dad wanted me to use most of the money on school, so I go to UCLA"

"What? No way. You got in?"

"I got in a few places. Piper wanted me to pick UCLA mainly because she heard the guys were hot." I giggled. "Anyway, I always

24

knew I was going to do online classes."

"So, you *only* do online classes?"

"Yes."

"That's cool. Now I know you'll always be home."

"Or at the liquor store." I giggled.

"How can I help? I only go to community college. You are obviously *way* smarter than me."

"Don't say that. I just need a book from school. In situations like this...before, Piper would help me."

"I don't get it."

"I can't go to campus. There's no way. I can barely go to the convenience store. I can walk a block but I can't..." I started to choke up. I had to stop talking because I didn't know how to explain my problem. I'd never had to before. My family just *knew*. My family did the explaining for me. I hated this. Embarrassed, I chugged the beer.

"I'll be right back." I went to get another. I opened the fridge and stuck my head in, taking deep breaths. I got down on my knees.

"Are you okay?" He startled me.

"Yeah, sorry." I popped up and shut the fridge.

"I can get the book for you if you want. I can even pick up some beer and smokes for you guys—you know, make an errand out of it?"

"Why would you do that?"

"I don't know...I thought that's what you were getting at."

"I just need help. I can't explain why I can't do it on my own."

"You mean like a ride?"

"Sure, yeah, that's what I mean."

"You want to go right now?"

"After this beer..." I wanted to down two more before we left, but my dad would notice.

Chapter 3

The last time I'd been in a car, it had been my mother's and Piper's funeral. I just remember clinging to my dad. He'd made sure no one talked to me, made sure everyone stayed away. It must have been so hard for him to take care of me when he was going through so much pain himself.

"I know it's not the fanciest car in the world but—"

"It's fine. I don't care what kind of car you have. I just appreciate you taking me."

"It's okay. I like your company." He put his hand lightly on my thigh. "Seriously, I'm happy to help."

I smiled as we drove off.

We lived about thirty minutes away from the school. If I had been a normal girl, I thought, I would be making this drive every day. I would go to class. I would get called on. It was impossible, though. I was just thankful I could take online classes.

"What are you thinking about?"

I hadn't said a word since we'd gotten in the car. He hadn't either. He played music—country. It was soothing.

"My dad likes country."

"Yeah?"

I nodded.

"Who does he like?"

"Randy Travis. George Strait. I don't know. Kenny Rogers. Just the other day, we were listening to 'Alice's Restaurant' by Arlo Guthrie. That's our favorite song. It's always on. You would think I would get tired of it but it's just background music to me now."

He laughed. "What about you?"

"What about me?"

"What do *you* listen to?"

"I listen to newer stuff like Luke Bryan, Blake Shelton, and Hunter Hayes."

"Okay, so pop country."

"But I like my indie electronic, too—The Knife."

"Hmm. What do you do for fun?"

I had never been asked that. I would have never ever thought I would be in a situation where someone would ask me that.

"What? Is that a stupid question?"

"I hate talking about myself and I don't want you to get angry and not take me to get the book."

"I'm pretty sure whatever you have to tell me won't stop me from taking you. Come on, we already talked a lot about me, and I know everything about Piper. Tell me something about *you*, Portia."

I looked out the window and lit a cigarette. "Do you mind?"

"Nah, I smoke in the car all the time. But don't change the subject."

"I have a social anxiety disorder. I was ten when I got diagnosed. But my family didn't know how to deal with it. My sister was the only one who tried to get me help. It felt nice to know there were other people out there like me, but it also sucked to know that I would never get to meet them."

He stared blankly into my eyes and then onto the road. It felt like a whole two minutes before he began to speak.

"That's what you meant when you said you needed help?"

I nodded.

"I thought you just needed a ride. Wow. Okay. That's cool."

"It's not."

"A chick that smokes Marlboro Reds and can down a six-pack in thirty minutes." He looked over at me. "That's fucking cool."

"You think so?"

"Doesn't matter what disorder you have, I like you."

We were pulling into the parking lot of the university. This one was bigger than the one at the high school, and it was full of people. I hadn't been at a school in two years. The last day of high school had been the best day of my life. I thought I would never have to do that again, but here I was, at UCLA. I braced myself for a panic attack.

He parked. I couldn't talk. I couldn't move. I just sat there staring. There were so many people. My body reacted like I was about to get attacked by each one of them. Any minute, all those people were going to surround the car.

"Whenever you're ready."

He should not have said that.

I didn't think I'd ever be ready. I shook my head and started looking for my phone. There *had* to be a way he could just get the book for me.

"I have to call...I have to..." I was rocking in the passenger seat. It was so hot. I started to roll down the window but then I heard everyone outside and quickly rolled it back up. I turned away from him, not wanting him to see me like this. I would have never asked him if I knew it was going to be this bad.

"Let me find where the bookstore is. I can try and get closer." He pulled away. I started to relax.

"I'll just drop this class. I don't really need it. It's the only class that requires a book. Just take me home."

He ignored me and kept driving around the school.

"Just take me home!" I screamed.

"Okay, okay..."

"Wait. I'm sorry. I'm going to call the bookstore and see if you can just go get the book for me." I needed to relax. I made this guy drive all the way over here. He was being so nice to me. I could do this.

"I can go in with you, Portia. I can talk for you. I can do everything for you. I won't leave you." He put his hand on my thigh again. "Just breathe, let's take a minute. Let's just find the closer parking lot. Sit in the car. Smoke another cigarette. Talk, relax, and if you want to go home, then I'll take you home."

Why was he being so nice? What was in it for him? We had talked about his life. We had talked about everything. He didn't have any problems. He was a normal guy. I didn't understand why he was being so nice to me.

I wanted to get this over with. He pulled over. He was looking at the map on his phone. I was trying to call the bookstore.

"Hi," I began, "my name is Portia Willows. I'm a student. I was wondering if I gave a friend my student ID if he could buy the book for me."

"Hang up. Hang up," Ethan said.

"Uh, never mind, I guess." I hung up and looked up at him, puzzled.

"Look, we can see the bookstore from here. It is a little bit of a walk but there's not a lot of people around, see?"

"Uh-huh, but what if class lets out or something?"

"We'll be in and out in five minutes. You know the book?"

"Yes."

"Let's go."

He got out. *Holy shit. Is this really happening?* He opened the door for me. I looked around. I took one foot out of the car. He reached out his hand to me.

"Grab it, it's okay." I took his hand. "Do you think you would feel more comfortable if my arm is around you?"

"Nice one. Let's go." I jokingly pushed him away and walked ahead of him. I was confident for all of two seconds. The quad didn't seem too terrifying. It was extremely quiet. I heard the birds in the trees. I felt fine. I could do this. Where we had been before, though, was intense, a bunch of kids with backpacks walking the streets. It was near the hospital too, so there were crowds and crowds of people. I looked down and kept walking, all the way to the bookstore.

"How long have you been going here?"

"For about a year in a half. I came once with my grandma and I never looked back." I opened the door. The noise almost knocked me down. No wonder no one was out there. *Everyone* was in this bookstore. I immediately turned around, but Ethan blocked me. He put a hand on each shoulder and turned me back around.

"Don't leave me," I cried. He put his arm around me, which I needed. I put my face into his chest. It was warm and comforting. I knew I would have a panic attack if he let go of me.

"I'm not going anywhere," he whispered in my ear. "Do you know where the book is?"

"I think so."

"Just focus on where you have to go, get it, walk to the cashier, and then out." I felt his beard on my ear as he spoke.

"Okay."

"Don't make eye contact with anyone. Don't look at anyone. Don't worry about what anyone else is doing. I'm right here. We're good."

I found the aisle. I got the book, I stepped away from him. He looked at me and smiled.

"There's a long line to check out," he said.

"Can we stay in this empty aisle until the line goes down?"

He laughed. "I wish that was how lines worked."

"I don't do lines."

"No one does lines. You don't need a disorder to hate lines. If you want a couple minutes, that's fine, but the line is not going to get shorter the longer you wait; it will only get longer." He was right. I was the one who went to UCLA and he went to SMC.

I was acting like an idiot.

"Let's just go. I wish we could steal this book. We should just make a run for it."

He put his hands on my shoulder and massaged them gently. "You're doing great," he whispered.

Standing in line, my heart was pounding. I was just looking at everyone. *Everyone* was in this line—Asians, Caucasians, black people, Latinos. There was so much diversity in this one line. The whole world was like this. I'd been stuck in my room my entire life. This was what other people were used to. I saw my sister everywhere. Every girl who would talk to another girl reminded me of her.

"All these girls…Piper would have loved this school."

"Can you imagine what Piper would say right now?"

"Let's say she was at home and I was here and I called her, she would be screaming and jumping around the entire room. She had enough energy for the entire family. She sucked up all of our energy. She was so small and so free." He was smiling. "Sorry, you're probably so tired of hearing about Piper."

"Never. I'm just glad I got you talking."

"You got me waiting in line."

He hugged me. I was scared at first. Then I was comfortable. For the first time I felt completely okay. I didn't want him to let go—until it felt like everyone's eyes were on us, like I was doing something wrong. I wiggled my arms, so he let go. I was looking down but I felt his eyes on me.

He was trying to figure me out.

As soon as we paid, I made a beeline for the car.

"Race ya?"

He started to run. I was pretty sure he let me win.

"You know how many people are staring at us right now?" He laughed.

"Because you're so slow. Hurry, slowpoke. Get in the car." We hopped in the car, laughing.

"Drive. Drive. Get the hell out of here. Oh my God," I said, smiling. I couldn't believe it. I was so happy. I couldn't wait to tell my dad, but I also couldn't wait to be back in my comfort zone. This was the craziest thing I'd ever done.

"Breathe. We did it." He smiled at me.

"We did it. Thank you, I have no idea how to thank you, like, *no* idea."

"Hang out with me again."

I would have—should have—said no. He was too nice. He was too into me. There had to be something wrong, but I thought back to that hug while we were in line.

"Piper would have loved you. My dad is going to love you. What you did for me today is a really big deal. I hope you know that. Thank you from the bottom of my heart."

"Sounds like you're trying to get rid of me."

"No, no, of course not." I touched his arm.

"When do I get to meet your dad?"

The air got cold. My chest got tight. The way he looked at me was like he never wanted to leave me.

I liked it. It scared me.

"Whenever you want. Eh, not really. I'll let you know when he's in a good mood."

He nodded as he continued to drive.

Chapter 4

Five Years Ago

Monday through Friday, at six forty-five a.m., I woke up in a panic. You'd think I would have gotten used to it after seventeen years. Instead, it just got worse. In the shower, I would try to get my bones to stop feeling numb. My hands would shake brushing my teeth. Makeup was out of the question. Getting dressed was a process. I didn't mind too much about what I wore—it was one step closer to having to enter my nightmare. Piper started sneaking me Mom's anti-anxiety medication because she thought it would help. It did, and Mom just doubled her prescription once she found out. Mom would never have allowed me go to therapy—that would have meant admitting she'd raised a fucked-up child.

I walked to school with headphones on. It was a normal day for me. At lunch, Piper met up with me in the library. It was the opening night of her play. I thought for sure she would be going around telling everyone about it, even though she didn't need to. Everyone was going. Everyone loved Piper. They would have gone just to see her.

"Hey."

"What are you doing here? It's the library. You have to be quiet."

"I am being quiet," she said loudly.

"See…you think you are because you're not aware of your own voice. You naturally have a high tone so you have to try *extra* hard to be quiet."

"Okay, shut up. I came to tell you that after you left we all agreed you don't have to go tonight."

"Really? I can go, Piper. Mom has made me do worse things. This isn't the worst."

"That's not the point. The point is that Mom needs to respect your decisions. Anyway, I'd love to spend all of lunch with you, but…I don't think my voice tone will allow it." She smirked and I giggled at her silliness. "After school, I have to go straight to hair and makeup, then dress rehearsal…"

"So, I won't see you until tonight, I know. Good luck." I was so proud of her, truly.

"Love you. Dad is buying you the good pizza, save me a piece." She kissed my forehead. I pushed her away because people were starting to stare. I really wished I could go. I mean, I wished I could do a lot of things I couldn't.

Not being there for her that night was the only one I was going to have to feel guilty about for the rest of my life.

No one was home when I got there—just the way I liked it, but I wondered where Dad was. I was fixing myself something to eat when the door flung open.

"Anyone here?" Dad yelled.

"Just me," I yelled from the kitchen.

"Oh good, my favorite." He kissed me on the cheek and handed me the mail.

"You have to stop saying that."

"What? Piper knows how much I love her."

"College brochures…great." I rolled my eyes as I flipped through all the different UCs.

"Mom will probably be working so I can take you to any campus you want."

"I'm good. What time are you guys leaving tonight?"

"The play starts at eight. I don't know. To be honest, I don't think your mother is going to make it…"

"Is that why she wanted me to go so badly? So it wouldn't look awful that she'd skipped? Jesus, that woman." I loved my mother, I really did, but sometimes I hated her. No, I hated the way she acted but I loved her as a mother. She spent so much time judging me for my issues that she didn't look at her own. She didn't appreciate my dad as much as she should. Sometimes, it felt like she loved her job more than us. We all noticed, and I really didn't think she cared.

"I don't care. You're not going. *She is*. I don't care if I have to pick her up from her office myself and drag her out of there. Is there any beer?"

Three Years Ago

"Look in the fridge, Dad."

"Why?"

"Ethan bought us a twenty-four pack…"

"Why? What did you do? Has he been in your room, Portia Willows?" he said, getting fake angry.

"Dad, grab a beer and calm down."

"I'm just saying, I only bought women beer when I was…"

"Ew. Gross. Dad…I can't right now. I haven't even hugged a boy. Why would you think…?"

I smiled to myself since this was actually a lie.

"I know. Just be careful."

"You should be nice. We're not doing too well with money. We're paying all the bills but the mortgage is a struggle."

"I thought Susan dealt with all that."

"Susan has five kids and a cheating husband. Remember how hard Mom worked? She only had two kids. Can you imagine?"

"What do you want me to do, babe?"

"Cut down. We both should, actually. It's been over a year. We can't use this as an excuse anymore."

"Oh. Was that what we were doing? Because I thought I was living my life the way I always have, except this time I don't have anyone nagging me about it."

"Before you were a functionally great alcoholic father," I laughed, "because of Mom, now I'm just making you an alcoholic." At the end of the day, we both needed Mom. Dad needed her more than I did, but I was barely functioning without Piper. It was all so sad that we just had to laugh about it.

It was so much easier studying for class with an actual book. I started looking into other ways to do better, but the only thing I could find was study groups—fuck that. Sometimes teachers held study groups on campus. They were only four times a semester, around test time. I didn't think I'd be able to do that. Plus, I hated driving.

"Do you want to go to a bar tonight? Like a dive bar?" Dad asked. Ever since the accident, my dad had lost all of his drinking buddies. It had hit him pretty hard. He was literally stuck with me. Part of me knew it was a rhetorical question, but I also knew this was one of those moments when he was really missing his friends.

"If you really want to…" He was walking into the kitchen. I heard the footsteps stop.

"What?"

I was really hoping he wasn't going to make me go, so I kept reading and taking notes.

"Did you just say *yes*?" Dad came back and plopped down on the couch next to me, messing up all my papers.

"Dad! Watch it…"

"You want to go to a bar, Portia?"

"I said if you really want to go…"

"Wait…I keep thinking you're twenty-one, you can't go."

"You used to take Piper and me to bars all the time when Mom was on business trips."

37

"That's because you guys were under ten and I worked there. You guys drank cranberry juice." He smiled at me while tucking a strand of hair behind my ear.

"I remember being on my knees, looking over and watching the cranberry juice squirt out of the gun. I thought that was the coolest thing in the world."

"You stayed next to me and watched everything. Piper…I couldn't get that girl to relax. She played with everything and everyone."

"The only reason she kept it a secret from Mom was so you'd take us again."

"I thought she was going to grow up to be an alcoholic." We both laughed. Neither of us was going anywhere and he knew that, he just liked to talk about it to seem normal.

Ethan and I were on the porch again. I suddenly realized how old the bench looked. There was nothing romantic about this. Did I *want* it to look romantic? I wasn't sure. I found myself putting way too much thought into us hanging out on my porch with a couple of beers and smokes.

"I was thinking…I want to take you to the beach," Ethan said, grinning like he was wasted but he'd only had two sips of his first beer.

"It's September…"

"The beach never closes, Portia."

"It doesn't?" I'd never really thought about it before.

"Are you serious? You've never been to the beach?" His eyes widened like he couldn't wait to take me.

Yeah, not happening. "I don't like being around people, what makes you think I'd like being around people half naked?"

"What about Piper?"

38

"She only went during the summer."

"I guess coming from Florida, I went to the beach every day."

"That sounds nice. Were you happy?" I was trying to change the subject.

"I don't know. I mean, I had fun. I went out every day, but I don't miss anyone besides my mom. It just makes you think…"

"You think you'd miss me if I died?" It just came out of my mouth. For the first time I'd said out loud what I was thinking. I'd only ever done that with my dad and Piper. I hadn't even done it with my own mother. He stared into my eyes and I looked down, mortified.

"This is why I don't talk."

"It was a legit question." He still seemed taken aback by it. "We barely know each other and yet I feel closer to you than I felt to any of my friends back home that I've known my whole life."

"Why is that? We don't do anything."

"We talk, and there's literally not one distraction between us." He looked around. It was a ghost town. The only thing we could hear was my loud television coming from inside the house and the birds chirping. It was a nice day.

"What do you mean?" I knew what it meant but I wanted to hear him say it. I needed validation.

"It's just us. All you see is me and all I see is you. There's no social media, waiters, friends, parents…"

"I can tell that your parents' divorce affected you a lot." I wanted him to tell me more about his past.

"You're so random." He shook his head and smiled.

"And you really don't like talking about it," I said, hoping to get him to open up.

"I just wish my family was whole…"

My eyes started to water because no matter how bitchy my mom was to me, I missed her judgmental looks. I missed our family dinners even though I had hated them. We had been together—not a lot of people got to have that. That stupid accident had ruined everything. It broke us apart. Now we would never all be together ever again. The more I thought about it, the more I broke down crying.

"I'm so sorry…" I said, wiping my tears.

"No, I'm sorry. Come here." He grabbed my shoulders and put my head on his chest. I was so weirded out by the touching that I stopped crying. I wanted to get up but didn't. We just swung in silence.

"Is your dad going to come out here with a shotgun?"

"He doesn't own a gun, and he definitely doesn't know how to use one."

"Well, that's good to know."

"But he is worried that you only want one thing…" I said.

"I *do* only want thing…"

I jumped up.

"…for you to be happy," he finished.

"Are we friends?" I mumbled.

"I hope so."

"Good, because I look at you like I want to kiss you, but I don't know what kissing means. I don't know…a lot."

"Why do you want to kiss me?" He backed away from me, just a little.

"I don't know, but Piper would know, so without her, we're just friends." *Yikes*.

"If Piper was here, what do you think she'd say?"

"She'd tell me to stick my tongue down your throat and grab your junk." We both busted up laughing.

"She was forward."

"*So* forward. She lost her virginity at fifteen, and Mom put her on birth control for her sweet sixteen. You're the only boy I've ever hugged," I said.

"I like hugging you." He smiled as I hugged him.

I wondered why.

For dinner, Dad made chili with Parmesan cheese, salsa, and crackers. It sounded disgusting when he was explaining it to me in the kitchen, but it actually wasn't that bad.

"What do you want to drink?"

I looked at him, super confused. We always drank beer. Breakfast, lunch, and dinner. "What you want to drink?" was never a question.

"We've got to cut down, right?"

"Do we even *have* anything else?"

"Water."

"Ugh."

"I know. Your idea."

"Pour me some water, Dad." There was nothing on television so we ate at the dining room table. We hadn't sat there in a while. It was awkward. He sat in his usual spot and I sat in mine. I kept staring at Mom's and Piper's chairs. Piper would have been texting. Mom would have been talking on her phone while slamming down the dishes.

"Drinking this, I feel like your mother is here," Dad said.

"Let's not have it for breakfast. Like, as soon as we wake up, maybe we drink orange juice, or just coffee?"

My dad stared at me. He stopped eating, stopped drinking.

"Does it really sound that bad?"

"No, you just suddenly reminded me so much of your mother."

I put the fork down my throat and gagged.

"You know, you didn't always hate her. There was a time when you wanted *only* her. I couldn't make you stop crying. She had the special touch."

I hated talking about the past.

"I came out of her vagina, Dad. Every mother has 'that special touch'. She always had it. She just…didn't know how to use it." I finished my plate and got up.

"Hating her may be helping you grieve for her, but she was still

41

my wife. I miss lying next to her every night."

"Yeah, but I bet you don't miss having sex with her because it never really happened."

Dad slammed down his water. "That's enough, Portia!"

I grabbed a beer. Fuck it.

I went into my room and cried for hours before I took out the box of letters—I hadn't looked at them in six months. When Piper and Mom died, I didn't know what I was supposed to do. I couldn't feel anything. I couldn't feel tears. I couldn't feel like they were actually gone. So I wrote them letters. I wrote one every single day for a week. Then Dad introduced me to beer and cigarettes. Suddenly, I didn't need to write letters anymore.

Dear Mom,
I can't believe you're actually gone. I refuse to believe it.

Actually, I'd rather be drinking beer than reading sad letters. Actually, I'd rather be hanging out with Ethan. So, I texted him. I saw that his name had jumped up above Piper's in my message list. I freaked out and deleted it. I went downstairs. A few minutes later, there was a knock at the door.

"It's pretty late, Portia."

"Now who's sounding like Mom." I went into the living room—Dad had had five beers. "So much for cutting down." I grabbed two from the fridge.

"Don't you have a friend at the door?" he said as I rolled my eyes.

I went to the door and saw Ethan, his hands in his pockets. He didn't have a jacket on.

"You okay? It's late." He sounded worried.

"Let's go to my room." I grabbed his arm and took him upstairs, glaring at my dad. He just continued downing the beers.

"How many have you had?" Ethan asked.

"Just one." I threw him on the bed.

"Portia…what's all this?"

I had left the letters on the bed. I grabbed them, threw them in the box and then threw the box in the trash. His facial expression never changed. He just looked confused.

"What?" I snapped.

"What happened? Where's your dad?" He still had this puppy dog look on his face.

"You didn't see him in the living room?"

"He was in the living room?" Ethan raised his eyebrows at me.

"It's okay. He doesn't care you're here."

Ethan got up off the bed. "Let's talk."

"We talk all the time. What else do you want to talk about? The weather?"

"Yeah…it's really hot today. It's like it's summer. You wanna go to the beach?"

"It's cold." Ethan was acting so strange that I just decided to drink. I opened another beer.

"I don't think you should have another one." Ethan grabbed my beer. I looked at him like he was insane.

"Do you know how much beer I drink in one day?" I said. I was being myself, I was being open. I was letting this guy into my life—into my room. And he honestly thought I was drunk.

"I know I'm acting weird. You've never seen this side of me. No one has. I'm not drunk. I'm just letting you in." I put my hand on his thigh. People did that in movies. It seemed appropriate. He looked at the box and then he looked at me.

I kissed him.

I did it.

It was slow. There was no tongue—just four lips that somehow fit together. I stayed pressed against his lips, wondering how this was working scientifically. He moved, and I moved mine as well. I didn't get it. Why did this feel nice? His lips were so soft—mine were chapped. I could smell my beer. He put his hand on my cheek. It literally felt like everything was happening in slow motion. I stopped and touched my lips.

"How was that for your first kiss?" he whispered, inches away from my face.

"My heart is racing." I put my hand on my chest.

"Let's just relax." His other hand appeared on my shoulder and he laid me down. He was right next to me. We talked for a while but I couldn't remember anything we talked about—just the way we kissed.

I woke up to a familiar smell, but it was a forgotten one. It was eight a.m. I was getting ready to roll over and go back to sleep but thoughts of what happened last night kept clouding my brain. I got up and peed and then I heard someone downstairs. There was a smell coming from my kitchen. It was so quiet, but I heard pans clinking.

"Dad?" There was no way my dad would be up, especially after how hammered he had been last night. I went to his room. He was knocked out.

It was Ethan.

Cooking.

In my kitchen.

"Sorry, I didn't mean to scare you." He said it so nonchalantly.

"What the hell do you think you're doing? My dad is upstairs."

"I was hoping I could meet him…and the best way to impress a girl's father is with food."

"That's a *lot* of food. You cooked enough for my whole family, but they're dead," I said sternly.

"Well, we don't have to eat it all. Is your dad still sleeping?" Why did he want to meet my dad so badly?

"Yeah, he got pretty messed up last night. Look, um…I know you probably just got here, but I need you to go. I don't want my dad to get the wrong idea."

"Portia. I spent the night." He dropped his spatula or whatever utensil he was using and turned off the burners. I looked at the French toast, the eggs, the pancakes, the coffee. He'd spent the night? And then he made my family breakfast? Where the hell was Piper? She would be having a field day.

Then I remembered again. I put my hand over my eyes and my heart constricted.

"Portia…Portia…I'm sorry. I overstepped. We didn't *do* anything last night. We fell asleep. I got thirsty this morning, and when I went to get water, I saw you guys didn't have any food in the house. I thought…I'm stupid. I shouldn't have stayed."
I tried to get myself together while he talked.

"Thank you. My dad and I will eat all of this, but you really need to go."

He nodded. I walked him to the door and watched him walk across the street. In the middle, he looked back at me.

I walked away and looked at all the food. Who the hell was going to do all these dishes? I grabbed as much food as I could and put it on a tray. I made two coffees and grabbed one beer—just in case.

"Daddy?" I gently kicked his door open.

"Mmm…" I put the tray at the edge of Mom's side of the bed and crawled over to him.

"Dad…wake up, wake up."

"Who died? Good morning." He pinched my cheek like he used to when I was five.

"I made you breakfast." I got out of the way so he could see. He looked at it, and then looked at me. I was trying so hard not to laugh, because if it wasn't so early, he would have never believed that I cooked.

"There's even more downstairs."

45

"Who made this?"

Darn.

"Um, Ingrid brought it over." Ingrid was our neighbor. When it all first happened, Ingrid made everything for us. Then she stopped. It might have been because of me.

"Well, that was nice of her. I thought she hated you."

"She probably does, but she always loved you."

He started scarfing down the food. I took my coffee and walked downstairs.

"I haven't been up this early in so long," I yelled up at him.

"Go back to sleep. I am," he yelled back.

By the time I finished cleaning the kitchen and the house, it was time for class. I never had so much trouble focusing as I did today. I kept thinking about why Ethan had stayed and if I snored. I kept thinking about what if my dad came to check on me while I was sleeping—he used to do that. I needed to set boundaries with Ethan. I should never have let him in my room.

My dad came downstairs.

"How's it going?"

"Fine."

"Are you seeing your friend today?" he asked.

"No, I saw him yesterday. I have a lot of work to do today. I'm going to take a nap before *Lethal Weapon*."

"I'll make sure I wake you up in time, unlike Sunday when you let me sleep through the first five minutes of *Preacher*." He giggled.

"I couldn't wake you up to save Mom's life."

We both laughed.

Chapter 5

Six Years Ago

"Willows." I looked up. It was drama class. I hadn't known what elective to take. My mom thought this was the perfect class for me. I didn't fight her on it because I didn't know that drama meant *acting*. I thought it was like film, dramatic arts. I'd had no idea what I was getting myself into.

It was the first day of my junior year. The teacher called on everyone, asked them to tell a joke and then tell the class something about themselves.

I panicked.

"Can I pass?" I mumbled.

"No. This isn't homework, Portia. It's just for fun."

"I know...but can I pass?"

Everyone was staring at me. My hands got sweaty and I felt dehydrated. Uncomfortable would be an understatement. I started shifting in my seat.

"Okay, no joke, then. Tell me something about yourself."

"I don't like talking in front of people."

Everyone started whispering.

Tears started to form in my eyes. I hated high school. I knew I was almost done, but I really felt like I was ready to give up. I wanted to go home and never come back. My mom was just going to have to disown me. My father would bring me cheese while I lived underneath the freeway.

"This is drama class—all you will be doing in here is talking, acting, and being vulnerable in front of people. Not just people—your peers, your classmates. We're a family in this class."
I coughed and started getting my stuff together.

"What are you doing?" she asked.

"I'm in the wrong class."

"Your name is on my roster."

"Definitely a mistake."

I walked out while all the kids were talking. I walked off campus to a nearby park, then lay in the grass and texted Piper. I lay there until the bell rang.

Family dinner that night was awkward. Piper wouldn't shut up about how amazing her day was and how excited she was about it since the school was also a block away from the mall.

Mom was all smiles.

Dad wanted to hear something else, anything else.

"Portia…anything worth mentioning about your day today?"

I took a sip of my water and a deep breath. Mom was smiling at me. She never really smiled, so I remember every time she did.

"I dropped out of a class because the teacher wanted me to tell a joke."

Her smile disappeared. The intense stare I was so scared of surfaced.

I just looked over at Piper.

"What?" she asked.

"First, it's drama class. Why would you sign me up for drama class?"

"I thought it would be good for you. And you don't just drop out of classes. This is *high school*, Portia."

"I get to pick my electives," I argued.

"You were okay with drama."

"*Dramatic arts*," I defended myself.

"What the hell is the difference?" She was screaming now.

"Why are you getting so mad at her? What's the big deal if she doesn't like a stupid class?" Piper yelled.

"Both of you, relax. It's just a class. I got humiliated and I left."

"How'd they humiliate you? Was it bad? You want to report it?" Dad was truly concerned.

"Are you kidding, Rich? Report *what*? Our daughter walked out of a class." Mom turned her anger on him.

"I left and went to the park, not to go do drugs in the bathroom."

"People are doing drugs in the bathroom?" Piper asked, intrigued.

"Can you just put me in a different class, Mom?" I pleaded. I wanted this to be over.

"No. You need to make friends. You need to be more social. Frankly, I think you should audition for the play with your sister."

Piper laughed.

"Fuck. You." I picked up my plate and threw it on the ground.

Mom let out a weird cat scream.

Piper's mouth dropped.

Dad went to clean up the mess.

I just ran upstairs and locked my room door. I blasted Asking Alexandria and did all my homework in one hour.

"Sweetie, it's me. Daddy…"

I turned down the music.

"Happy?" I yelled.

"No. Why would I be happy?" he asked through the door.

"I turned it down. What else do you want?"

"To come in."

"Fine."

He climbed onto the bed next to me. I was not in the mood. I just wanted to go to bed and start this shitty life all over again.

"Portia…Portia…Portia…what am I going to do with you?"

"I have an idea."

"Hmm?"

"Chop my body into pieces, grab the trash bags from downstairs, and you might as well get your gloves from the garage. Put my body parts into the trash bags and then put it in Mom's car."

He didn't say anything.

"Make sure you're not messy because you know Mom would be more upset that you got blood on her seats than the fact that her daughter is chopped into pieces."

"See, this is why she wanted you to take drama class, because you're dramatic as hell." He kissed me on the cheek. "Just one more year, Portia, just one."

Three Years Ago

Dear Piper,

I was thinking about high school and how much you loved it and how much you loved life. You didn't just love me, Mom, and Dad, but you loved the carpet in our living room just the same. You loved being around people. You brought everything to life. Remember when Ingrid's husband died when we were little, and you brought her flowers from her own yard and ruined her garden? Mom was so mortified. Ingrid started crying but then laughed. Apparently, her husband hated the garden. You just got away with everything. You get that from Dad. His charm and his manipulation skills. It sounds bad, but God, was I envious of it.

I lit a cigarette while I was reading. I was so over being sad. I had been so fucking sad then. I was glad I didn't feel that way anymore. I missed them every day but at least wasn't crying over them every day anymore.

There was a knock at the front door.

It could only have been three people: Ingrid, Susan, or Grandma. Or Ethan. I had already forgotten about Ethan. It had been two weeks since I'd seen him.

He had called and texted every day, though.

"Hey." It was Ethan.

I instantly smiled. I had almost forgotten what he looked like. He had shaved.

I liked it.

He looked more innocent.

"I got you guys some beer. Can I join you for a smoke?"

I grabbed the case and brought it to the kitchen. He stayed outside.

"You can come in." I smiled.

"You smoke in the house?" He took out a cigarette.

"I do whatever I want in the house." I tossed him a lighter from the dining room table. We had an ashtray in the middle. There used to be flowers and a tablecloth. Now it was just wood and ashtray.

"How have you been?" He sat down.

"Same. You?" I lit my cigarette.

"Thinking about you."

I threw him a beer. He seemed different, like there was something on his mind.

"What's wrong with you? Usually, I'm the anxious one," I said.

"I'm just wondering if you're mad at me."

"Why would I be mad?"

"You barely spoken to me in two weeks. I was worried about you."

I smiled and shook my head. "I just didn't feel like it."

"Right," he said, looking around. Did he want a tour? It wasn't a mess. I would have never let him in if it were. "Are you good now?" he wondered.

We weren't acting how we usually were with each other. We were uncomfortable.

"Sure. Yup."

"Good," he said. I was trying to read him but his soul seemed blocked.

"How's school? Did you get your grade up in chem?"

"No. My dad wants to hire a tutor."

"That's smart. I would love a tutor. A lot of students have tutors."

He smoked his cigarette slowly. "But you're so smart," he said.

"With online classes, it's tough. It's nice to have another person there. I just...you know."

"I want to meet your dad," he said randomly.

"Is that why you keep looking around? Are you looking for him?"

"No. We just never hung out inside your house like this. I would feel more comfortable if I met him, ya know?"

"Good point."

"But I get it. I spent the night. Does he think we had sex?"

"No, he knows me better than that. He's happy I have a friend," I told him. I really didn't know what I wanted. I didn't feel like introducing him just yet.

"Is that what we are?" he asked. "Friends?"

I didn't know how to answer that question, so I just shrugged.

"You know, you kissed me."

"And you kissed me back."

"You should come over for dinner. I'll show you my place. You can meet *my* dad." He smirked. I giggled as I put out my cigarette.

"I'm not going to spend the night and cook you breakfast for twenty the next morning."

"No, I just...I don't...is this me overstepping again?"

"Do you have books?" I wondered.

"Books?"

"One thing I do miss about Cypress is the library. I would read during snack and lunch."

"Come over tonight and you'll see. I have lots of books. It'll be fun," he said, trying to convince me.

"Whenever Piper said 'it'll be fun,' it was a disaster. You know what fun is?"

"What?"

53

"Watching *The Bad Girls Club* with a cinnamon raisin bagel with two pounds of cream cheese on it and a bag of hot Cheetos. You eat both at the same time so you have enough cream cheese for both."

"Cream cheese for both…sides of the bagel?"

"And the hot Cheetos."

"You're ridiculous." He smiled.

He was beautiful. I wanted to kiss him again, but I had learned from my mistakes.

"Do they do that in *Bad Girls Club*?" He was still laughing.

"No, idiot," We both started laughing.

The more time went by, the more nervous I got about going over to Ethan's. I wanted to bring my dad so badly. I asked Ethan and he said it was okay, but Dad was not down.

"Just make sure you bring leftovers. I'm so tired of chicken noodles, canned tuna, canned chili, tortilla chips—let alone fucking rice neither of us can fucking make right."

Tell me how you really feel, Dad. Or maybe do it yourself sometimes.

"I really don't want to do this." I wanted to be home but I knew Piper would want me to take advantage of this opportunity.

"It's worth it for the food." Dad tried to convince me.

"*Dad*. If you want real food so damn bad, I'll go over to Ingrid's tomorrow or call Susan."

"No and no. I don't need their help to take care of my daughter."

But he'd take Ethan's help, apparently. "Right." I just wanted to drop it.

"You're right across the street. What's the worst that can happen? I'll be able to hear you scream. Remember the Fourth of July when you were three and we'd just gotten Pipes to sleep when a firecracker went off but she still slept until *you* screamed like you were getting murdered by Barney?"

"I hated Barney."

"Exactly."

I decided to make an effort with my hair and makeup. I didn't look like the grieving child anymore.

I knocked on the door and it was opened by his dad. I recognized him. I'd seen him like a hundred times before but I didn't think I'd ever said a word to him.

"Portia Willows," he said, and I smiled. "Come on in."

"Mr. Torke, I remember you."

"Call me James."

"I don't know that I can, Mr. Torke. My mom would talk about you sometimes."

"Hopefully good things," he said. We walked through the house. It was a lot different than mine. I didn't know why I thought it would look the same. The first thing you saw when you opened the door was the spacious living room. They had a red rug that matched the red pillows on the off-white sectional. The sectional took up a lot of space. There was no television, just shelves filled with books. It was almost like a library. Now I understood why Ethan had smiled when I asked if he had books. There were pictures of him and another girl. His sister? He didn't talk about her much. I could tell there was no way he had grown up in this house. He grew up in Florida, and now he was interested in the traumatized loner girl. But there was something strange about Mr. Torke. It wasn't my anxiety—from the moment I walked in it was as if they were hiding something. I didn't know why, I just felt the energy in the house.

"Mom wanted me to come see you," I admitted.

"She would ask me how to help you. I couldn't tell her anything since you weren't my patient." I didn't say anything. "I just gave her whatever advice I could…you know, she was a lot more worried than she had to be…."

What the hell? My mom worried about me? Yeah right. She was worried about her reputation, not me. I'd known she'd asked the guidance counselor what to do with me—but hearing it from him was just disgusting, especially since she was dead now. I didn't know what to do or say.

I was here for Ethan, not a lecture.

There were abstract paintings on the wall. I stared at them, trying to figure out what they represented while Ethan and his dad mumbled in the kitchen. There was one that I particularly liked. It had a square in the middle, shapes and chaos lines were all around the square and going through it. I related to that square. I had been the square my entire life. I didn't talk.

The dining room was in a completely different room—I'd only ever seen that in movies. We sat down at the dinner table. He'd made pasta with shrimp and there was a salad. I could have finished the whole bowl. I ate while they talked and stared off into the distance. I wasn't paying attention. I just kept eating. I knew I should stop so I could bring some home to my dad. I scraped off my plate anyway. While I was chugging my water, everything went quiet. I put it down.

"My dad had wanted me to bring some back for him," I mumbled.

"Of course. I'll put the leftovers in a container for you." Mr. Torke wouldn't stop staring at me as he got up. I smiled at Ethan. Mr. Torke came back in and handed me the container.

"Thank you. This was great. My dad is going to love it too," I told him.

"I'm glad. I can't get this kid to eat my cooking. It's not like his mom's, that's for sure," Mr. Torke joked, looking over at Ethan.

"Just different. I have to get used to it," Ethan said.

"You know, your father was more than welcome to come. I didn't know he was…uh…you know?" Mr. Torke looked at both of us.

"What? Living with me? Not sick?"

I wondered what he'd heard about us.

"I still haven't officially met her dad, so I didn't invite him. I want to make sure Portia was ready before she introduced us," Ethan said.

"Yeah, he's not sick. It's just that we all grieve in different ways."

"Interesting. Did you guys ever go to grief counseling?"

"Dad…" Ethan put his arm around me. It was fine. I just didn't understand the question.

"I've heard that term, but don't know what it is. Is it like a class to learn about grief? I don't know what it is."

"No, it's to help you grieve properly."

"There's a right way to grieve?" I didn't think so, but he was the doctor.

"Everyone is different, but these groups—I'm telling you, they work wonders. I know so many people—"

"I get what you're saying. My dad definitely needs counseling. I'm really just following him. When he cries, I cry. When he laughs, I laugh. If he goes to counseling and gets better, I'll get better." I smiled at Ethan, who looked pissed.

"Smoke?" he asked.

I nodded.

"When we get back, I can help you with the dishes," I offered.

"Thank you, Ms. Willows, but it won't be necessary."

We sat on the front steps.

"He wasn't so bad. I could have gone and seen him I guess." I lit my cigarette.

"You think you would be different now?"

"No. Not really, but I feel bad being rude and giving him the cold shoulder for four years."

"It's so weird. You've seen my dad more than I have." Ethan looked off into the street.

"I guess, but we didn't even talk, and he's your father."

"He wants to help you. I mean, I want you to be happy too, but I already fucked up so much already…" he said quietly. I didn't know what he meant by that.

"What do I need help with? Besides school, but I've got that handled. Help taking care of my dad? I do have help. Susan, my Mom's partner, and Ingrid, who lives next door. My grandma comes down from time to time. I know what it looks like, Ethan. I know what everyone is thinking…"

"Do you?"

"Yeah. No one has seen my dad because he won't leave the house. *I* barely leave the house. I'm about to be twenty years old and I drink beer like a country singer and smoke cigarettes like a sailor…I don't fucking know, but I know it looks bad. But we've been like this for over a year and we've survived. We'll keep surviving. It's not the norm, but I have it under control. Tell your dad not to worry about me, but he's so sweet for caring." I kissed him on the cheek. "If that's what all that was…" I said holding up the pasta. "I'm going to go home now and take care of my dad."

Chapter 6

Present Day

I still couldn't figure out exactly where I was. I was willing to say anything to see my dad. I was sitting on the sofa now. Knees glued to together. Toes quietly tapping the white tiled ground. My hands gripped my knees. Eyes down.

"Portia...what's the last thing you remember about the accident?"

"The police," I mumbled.

"Were you at the scene?"

"I would have been dead, too, if I was." I looked up with a glare.

"Okay, so the police?"

"I saw pictures, though..." I glanced down again, remembering. My mom's crushed skull, her eyes wide open. Piper had so much makeup on—she looked really good dead.

"I heard you refused to look at some and you didn't identify them."

"I didn't need to. Someone else did."

"What did the police tell you?"

Why was I talking about something that happened five years ago? Was my family murdered? Did my dad have something to do with it? Was my dad in jail right now? *Holy shit.*

"No. I'm not doing this. No. I want to see my father. I have the right to see him." I got up and walked to the window and looked outside.

"As soon as we're done, you'll get to see him."

I didn't recognize the street I was on. I'd been here before, though.

"Do you know why you're here?"

"No. What are you investigating? My father? It was an accident." I was looking out the window. "It was an accident," I said again, and put my hand up to the window. There was dried blood. It had mostly been washed off but the outline of the stain was still there.

I couldn't remember how…

"Who are you?" I demanded, turning around.

"Elizabeth Smith. I'm a forensic psychiatrist. I was hired as a consultant for this case. I'm on your side, Portia."

"What is so fucking complicated about a car accident that happened five years ago where my little sister died at sixteen and my mother at forty-two? It had been an *accident*. My dad blamed himself for months, but the police reassured him that it wasn't his fault." I started crying.

"That's not the case that I'm talking about."

I looked at my hands.

Blood on my kitchen floor.

I tried to remember more. *What the hell had happened?*

"Sit down, Portia."

I had done something.

Something really bad, but I had no idea what it was…

Three Years Ago

My dad and I were cleaning the house like maniacs because Susan was coming over with her kids. That meant all the blinds open, air fresheners, all the trash and clothes in my or his room. The kitchen needed to be full and clean. I was upstairs getting ready.

"Dad, are you dressed?"

"We have an hour."

I went to his room. He was lying in his bed watching TV with a beer.

"You're going to have beer breath."

"Is she bringing the kids?"

"Yes."

"Get your old toys from the garage."

"You should get a shower." Upstairs looked a mess compared to how well we had cleaned downstairs. I rushed downstairs, and through my living room window noticed Ethan coming back from a run without a shirt. I decided to open the garage door and walked outside to see if he'd notice me. I crossed my arms and smiled at him. He nodded and ran toward me.

"Hey, Portia, what are you up to?"

"My mom's best friend is coming over to check on us. It sucks. Her kids are coming, too. We had to clean up the whole house. I can't even drink a beer. I just want to get it over with."

"Would it help if I was there? I'm sure if she saw that you made a friend…"

"That would be awesome, but you'd have to put on more clothes and you'd have to deal with kids." I looked at his body. Jesus, there wasn't one unattractive thing about him. It wasn't like he had a six-pack or anything, but it was just perfect.

"I love kids." He started jogging in place. I gulped and looked away.

"You're crazy." I smiled as he ran back over to his house. Then I realized Ethan would have to meet my dad. This would be interesting.

After I brought the toys in and saw my dad dressed to a tee, I was excited. Everything was going to work out. He looked like my old Dad, my mom's husband.

"Dad, look at you."

"I do *not* want to do this."

"I want you to meet Ethan. He's going to come over. Ethan and I will distract her while you go do whatever you want."

"I don't want to meet Ethan and I don't want to see Susan. Can you just tell her I died?"

"Dad. I'd get taken away, idiot." Would I though? I was over eighteen.

"No, you won't. You're an adult."

Ethan knocked on the door. Dad started to run away but I grabbed his arm—there was no way he was going to look this nice ever again. He was meeting Ethan *now*.

I opened the door with my dad right by my side. I kept looking at him. He was acting like a five-year-old boy, quiet and just smiling.

"Daddy…this is Ethan. Ethan, this is my dad, Richard."

Dad half smiled.

"Come in," I told Ethan.

"It's great to finally meet you," Ethan said. They shook hands.

Dad didn't say anything.

"Dad, don't be rude, say hi."

"Hi," he mumbled.

"You see where I get that from," I giggled.

Ethan looked around. "The place looks nice."

I was pleased he noticed. "Thanks, we cleaned it together. So, Susan is on her way. We definitely have time to down a beer." I grabbed three beers from the fridge. Dad and Ethan were just staring at each other in silence.

"Let's do this fast. Cheers." My dad and I were chugging. Beer was getting everywhere. Dad was making stupid faces. I started laughing and sprayed beer everywhere.

"Stop. You're making me make a mess." I laughed at Dad. Ethan didn't find it amusing.

"I got it," Ethan said as he went to grab napkins.

"You're just embarrassed because you couldn't finish the beer," I said to Dad as I grabbed his.

"Uh, you guys got this," Dad said. "I'm going to go upstairs. If Susan wants to see me or the kids, tell them to come up." He walked upstairs. "It was nice meeting you, Ethan," he called.

"He said it was nice meeting you," I repeated.

"It was nice meeting you too," Ethan yelled back.

I rolled my eyes.

"What?"

"Nothing. Thank you for cleaning that up and for being here."

Finally, I heard the kids. I opened the door and Stefan, the oldest at fifteen, came in followed by Cassie, who was ten. Then there was McKenzie, six, and the twins, Joey and Jesse, who were three. They instantly ran all through the house.

"The toys are in the living room," I yelled to them.

Susan hugged me for the longest time. She and my mom were a lot alike, except Susan was blonde with hazel eyes. They had the same style—blazers, pencil skirts—but today she was wearing blue jeans with black pumps and a low-cut long-sleeved blouse. If you're wondering how a mom with five kids could wear pumps, you didn't know Susan. She was more insane than my mother. She did what she wanted when she wanted—kids or no kids. She was skinny, just like my mother. They both wanted to be young—go out for drinks after work, lie to their husbands about where they were. At least my dad only had to deal with Piper and me. Susan would leave Gary with five children. No wonder he cheated.

"Sorry it's been so long."

"This is Ethan Torke, he lives across the street."

"Oh, nice." She gave Ethan a hug. Ethan couldn't help but look at her cleavage. I giggled.

"Water, juice, anything?" I asked.

"Do you have wine?"

"Uh, I think so…"

"Do you want me to watch them?" Ethan asked me.

I shook my head, thinking, *Why would you offer to do that?*

"Would you please? Oh my God, I like him already."

I poured both of us a glass of wine and we sat at the dining room table. She drank half of it in one gulp. Like I said, what she wanted and when she wanted—kids or no kids. To be honest, she already seemed a little buzzed. Whenever Dad had raised concerns about Susan's lifestyle, Mom shut them down completely.

"It's been a long day. Gary has been on an extended business trip with that whore from his legal department and the babysitter went to an out-of-state college. Why would she do that to me?"

"I'm sorry."

Susan talked and talked, or more accurately, she complained and complained. I went in and out of listening.

"Stefan's stupid teacher made me leave the office to come get him just because he threw a fucking muffin. Are you kidding me? It's a goddamn *muffin*. If he threw a knife, call me. A muffin isn't going to hurt anyone. The twins, they were sick for two weeks straight. I thought they were going to die, and between you and me, I wasn't going to be that mad, but then they got better and it was the happiest moment of my life."

Holy shit, I thought, *I really hope Ethan isn't hearing all of this.*

"I almost left Gary, but I didn't. Do you have a cigarette?"

I got up to walk to the kitchen drawer where I had the cigarettes and took out two for each of us.

"Do you want to go outside?" I started walking out of the kitchen.

"No, I smoke in front of them all the time."

I sat on her other side.

"Mom, can I have one?" Stefan asked. Stefan looked twenty. He was as tall as me, with long dark hair that went over his eyes. He always wore a beanie, black sweatshirt and skinny blue jeans. Not to mention, he suddenly had a deep voice. I remembered the first time I saw him after puberty, I had jumped when he said hi to me.

Ethan was playing with the kids, looking over at me. He threw two thumbs-up. I mouthed, "I'm so sorry," to him. I felt so bad for him, but he was the one who wanted to come over.

She gave him the cigarette and lit it for him. I nodded at Ethan to join us. I could tell Ethan was about to say something about Stefan smoking, but I shook my head at him. It wasn't worth it.

"Are you guys, you know...?" Susan waved her cigarette between us.

"No. I mean, I don't know," I told her.

"No, we're not," Ethan said. He knew what she was talking about. Right now, I was feeling overwhelmed and weird.

"I'm going to check on my dad. I'll be right back."

He was sleeping. I climbed on the bed, waking him up. "I feel like she got crazier," I whispered.

He got up and smiled. "She's as crazy as crazy gets."

"I don't understand how she and Mom were best friends."

"There was a side to your Mom you girls never knew..." I over-

heard a bunch of mumbling and kid screams. It seemed like Ethan
was having a conversation with Susan, so I didn't rush down there.

"Between us…it was her better side," he whispered.

"Her better side was her crazy side?" I asked.

He nodded. "She was so focused on being a mother with a career
that she didn't spend much time being herself. I fell in love with a
wild child who loved to party, drink, and make bad decisions."

"That explains why she loved Piper more."

"No. She just didn't want you to grow up without experiencing
life and all of its opportunities." Dad was getting teary-eyed.

"Why didn't she ever tell me? I just wanted her to talk to me
more…"

"She never got the chance." My dad broke down and I started to
cry. He coughed and pulled himself together. "How's it going down
there? It sounds like a madhouse."

"We really owe Ethan one."

"He's a quiet one. I like him. I see why you do, too."

"I think he was just really nervous. I'm going to go get rid of
her and maybe he and I can watch a movie or something. Is that
okay?"

He nodded.

I went back downstairs.

"Okay, Susan, Stefan…Ethan and I have to get to school," I lied.

"We do?" he asked me.

I nodded.

"Yeah, well, we have to go anyway." Susan started to get her
kids together.

"Well, it was nice meeting you, Susan. Maybe we can talk again
soon?" Ethan asked.

I smiled.

"Yes, of course…come here." Susan hugged Ethan. It was a
long hug. I looked at them like there was something going on between them, then she hugged and kissed me on the cheek.

After they left, Ethan asked, "Do you need a ride to UCLA, is there something we have to get?"

"No. You like that? You want that? Five kids? You want your fifteen-year-old smoking cigarettes?"

"Whoa. Whoa." He held his hands up in mock surrender.

"I just don't get it. Is it that she's older?"

"It sounds like you're a little bit jealous." He came close to me—really close. I looked down and shook my head. He took his finger and placed it under my chin, lifting my head up. We were inches apart. I moved in, staring deeply into his icy blue eyes.

"I'm not jealous."

I could tell he wanted to kiss me, but I shoved his face away and giggled. "Want to watch a movie?"

"I should flirt with older women in front of you more often." He sat down on the couch and I sat on the other end. He smiled. I put my feet toward him. He looked at them and then I put them down.

"What's going on with you?" he asked.

"Nothing. I felt bad that you were stuck with Susan, but little did I know you were getting a hard-on the whole time," I said.

"Piper would be so proud of you." He smiled.

"Because I said hard-on?"

He crawled closer to me. "No, because you have feelings for a real person and not a character on a television show." He kissed me on the cheek. I couldn't understand why anyone would want to be around Susan, the kids, or me for that matter. It was that moment that I realized he really liked *me*.

"My mom would be proud, too." I grabbed his face and kissed him on the lips, but not like last time. This time was harder. Intense. This was for Piper.

I pushed him off of me. "We're just friends," I said, and smiled. I cleared my throat and crawled back to my side of the couch.

Present Day

"I don't remember anything. I mean, I remember the finger-printing, being naked, being brought water. I don't know how blood got on my kitchen floor or on my hands. Is my dad okay?"

"I want to work up to what happened last night."

"Last night?"

"Let's go back to the night of the play. You saw your sister at lunchtime and that was the last time you saw her."

"It was a normal school day. I went home…I had a lot of home-work. Dad had ordered pizza. I reminded him to record the play because I wanted to see her as Beatrice, but I didn't want to go."

"Why didn't you want to go to the play?"

"I didn't want to. I didn't even want to go to school. I was terri-fied of being in public. Piper told me it was social anxiety disorder. She understood and didn't mind me staying home."

"So, you were at home the entire time everyone was at the play. Did you see your mom before the play?"

"No, Dad picked her up from work. I watched television. It was nice," I choked. I remembered being happy it was just me in the house. It was like I'd secretly wished for this to happen.

"No one saw you? No one called you or texted?"

"Nope."

"Then there was a knock at the door at twelve twenty-five

a.m.?"

"I didn't realize how late it was or I would have called my dad first. Piper probably went to a party so I didn't expect anything from her, but it was strange because Mom had to go to work early so she should have been in bed already."

"You know, Portia, I want to try something with you. You're doing great, but I want you to sit back, close your eyes, take a deep breath, and think back to the exact moment there was a knock on your door."

I did as she asked, but I didn't think back to that moment. Instead, there were flashes.

My dad.

Blood on his hands.

A baby crying.

Blood everywhere—all over the baby, Dad and I in the living room against the couch.

I screamed and opened my eyes. I started hyperventilating. I screamed again. I couldn't stop.

Chapter 7

Five Years Ago

There was someone knocking on the front door. I opened it slowly. I was still chewing a piece of pizza I had just put down on the dining room table on top of a napkin.

It was two policemen. "Portia Willows?" one of them asked, and I nodded, still chewing. They took off their hats. I knew something was wrong, so I kind of just went into a zone. I heard them say Carol Willows and Piper Willows were confirmed dead at the scene and Richard Willows was in critical condition at the hospital. They wanted to know if they could take me to the hospital. I just stared. I didn't even realize they had asked me until one of them put their hand on my shoulder.

"We are sorry for your loss."

"Dad," was all I said. I followed them to the police car and sat in the back. I didn't cry. I didn't ask what happened. I just sat there, swallowing the rest of the pizza that was in my mouth.

When we got to the hospital, I ran up to my dad. His heart was stable. I lay next to him the entire time.

He was in a coma for a week. I didn't move or leave his side. Everyone we knew stopped by. I got flowers, letters, everything. Grandma said her goodbyes even though I knew he was waking up.

I was in the middle of writing one of my letters, waiting for him to wake up.

Dear Mom,
They want to know what to do with your body. I told them to make it alive again. I don't know what happened. I don't want to know. I know the facts. Dad is here and you're not. At least you have Piper and Piper has you. I'll take care of Daddy, I promise...

"Whatcha doing, buddy?" Dad mumbled from the hospital bed. My heart could have stopped. My whole world changed. My daddy was back. I just cried and hugged him so tight. I didn't want to let go, ever. The nurses had to come peel me off of him.

"I knew it. I knew it. I knew he was going to be okay," I said, and ran out of the hospital room. I was so happy I wanted to call someone, anyone, to tell them the good news. But everyone whose numbers I knew was dead.

"Portia Willows, I'm so sorry for your losses, but we need this paperwork signed."

I felt guilty for being so happy my dad was alive that I put my mother and sister's deaths on the backburner.

"I'll sign the papers, but we'll meet with the funeral directors once my dad is in recovery," I told the woman, and gave her the paperwork.

Someone called Susan to pick me up.

REMEMBER

Three Years Ago

"Dad?" I was in the living room brainstorming an essay I had to write for school while watching TV and smoking a cigarette. Dad had come downstairs to grab a beer from the kitchen.

"Yeah?" He sat next to me on the couch. "Are you watching this?"

"Eh, not really."

He changed it to the Discovery Channel. "What's up?"

"Grandma hasn't called in a while."

"Yeah…well, did she ever *really* call? We only saw her once every two years. If your mother and Pipes never—"

"I know. I just think she would at least call you or me, unless there was something going on between you two."

"I'm sorry. I know you miss her. It does get kind of lonely around here."

"Don't be sorry. I don't care, she's *your* mother. And lonely? After having Susan over and being around Ethan all the time, lonely is nice."

"So…you two…just friends?"

"Dad, don't even *think* about having the talk with me."

"Did we ever give you guys the talk?"

"Nope, it was never necessary. Piper would just ask Mom questions. I tried to leave the conversations, but she always told me to

72

stay because I should hear the answers, too."

"What were the questions little Pipes was asking?"

"I've tried hard to forget."

"Eh…I guess I don't want to know either."

Later that night, I was having a movie marathon by myself. I watched *A Walk to Remember*, *Remember Me*, *LOL*, and *Stay*. I was feeling super romantic. I didn't want to be just friends with Ethan. I wanted to be something more, but I didn't know what exactly. I guess I wanted to be his girlfriend. I wanted us to be a thing. I just didn't know where to even start or where his head was at. Thinking about it made me think of Piper. I looked up articles on how to be a girlfriend. I knew it was something I was capable of, but the more I read, the more nauseated I became. I wished there was someone I could talk to about this besides my dad. There had to be *someone*.

I didn't get much sleep. All I thought about was Ethan. I wanted to be with him constantly. He was always so busy texting me where he was at and where he was going. I always wanted to be with him, but I couldn't, and even though he never pressured me, I felt inade-quate. He even went to the store for me. He did so much for me and all I'd done was give him beer.

I went into Piper's room. I hadn't been in here in a while. I had stopped when it stopped smelling like her. It was more artistic than my room. She had painted the walls lavender when she was ten years old. She started to hate the color when she got older, so she covered it up with posters that she got from *J-14*, *M*, and *Seven-teen* magazines. Her desk was still covered with the play script and the homework she had been supposed to start weeks before her death. I sat on the edge of the bed, looked around, and took a deep breath. She had a collage of pictures above her bed. I crawled to the headboard and placed my fingers there, tracing all of her different memories.

"Piper…tell me what to do."

Maddie, her best friend, was in most of the pictures. She lived across town. I wondered how she was doing. I hadn't seen her since the funeral.

I lay on Piper's bed to try and take a nap, but instead I just thought of her and everything we had done together. Starting with the day she was born. I was so excited. I wanted to be with Mom the entire time, but Mom didn't want me in the hospital for that long, she was in labor for over twelve hours.

After lying there for about an hour, I decided to do something I never thought I would do. I grabbed Dad's keys.

"Dad, I'll be right back," I said as I was putting on a jacket.

"Where are you going with the keys?"

"For a drive."

"Portia, you haven't driven since you first got your license when you were sixteen."

"Actually, there were times I had to go pick up Piper. You guys didn't know."

"Well, what are you doing? Going to pick up Piper?" he said sarcastically.

"Kind of. I'll be back soon."

I couldn't believe I was driving. I'd only ever driven to Maddie's house and a few other houses in the area, always with or because of Piper. It was early, but it was Saturday. Maddie could be sleeping, but I didn't know. I had no idea what her life was like—it'd been over a year. She never talked to me when Piper was alive.

She lived fifteen minutes past Cypress High. It was a nicer neighborhood. There were a lot more people around walking their dogs. I was anxious but felt safe inside the car. I pulled up to her driveway and smoked two cigarettes before I got the courage to knock on the door.

It wasn't like how I remembered. There used to be high trees bordering the yard, but now the front yard was like a garden with a pond near the door. There was even a fake bridge going across it. It was cute.

I got out and slowly walked up the steps that went in between the yard. I knocked softly on the door. After two times, I swung back and forth and convinced myself this was a really bad idea. I walked back to my car and banged my head on the window in frustration, when I heard a voice.

"Portia?" It was Maddie's mother. She was a lot older than our mom. A lot more old-fashioned, too. I always liked her but I never could talk to her. I turned and smiled a little.

"Oh my gosh, the spitting image."

I didn't know what that meant, but she was looking at me intensely. I gave her a small wave and she ran up to me and hugged me. I didn't hug her back.

"Come in. Would you like some tea?"

I just nodded. I had completely forgotten what I came there for and instantly regretted it. Inside, the house hadn't changed at all. It was small but they had nice things.

It was bright.

Really bright.

Sky-blue walls, light grey sofas with knitted blankets over them. There was a floral tablecloth on their dining room table. She led me into the kitchen where the stairs were. I didn't know what to say or where to sit.

"Maddie? Honey? Come downstairs, guess who's here." I started shaking. Her mom sat the tea down on the table. "Have a seat, sweetie."

I sat down. I could barely pick up the teacup. Maddie was walking slowly down the stairs, texting. She was wearing tight black jeans, barefoot, with a *Twilight* shirt and a jean jacket over it. She had short brown hair and was wearing thick black eyeliner and really dark lipstick. She looked so grown up. I guessed she must be eighteen now.

"What, Mom?" She always had an attitude. She looked up, saw me and dropped her phone, then picked it up.

"Oh my God. For a second I thought you were her."

I'd never really noticed the resemblance. Our personalities were polar opposites, so neither of us mentioned anything about it. Neither did Mom or Dad. She sat down next to me and I cleared my throat.

"It's good to see you. I wanted to call or visit but…" She wouldn't look at me. She just looked down at the table. Her leg was shaking, and it was distracting me. I watched her mom look at her like she was worried. I hoped me being here was not causing them more pain.

"It's okay. I was just in her room looking at pictures. There was something I wanted to talk to her about and you told me if I ever needed someone to talk to…" I stuttered.

She turned to her mother. "Mom, can you give us a minute?"

"Of course. Let me know if you need anything, Portia."

I nodded and smiled. She walked upstairs, looking back at me.

"What did you want to talk to her about?" She finally made eye contact.

"You guys were like the same person. I remembered that in her room."

She smiled.

"I know, it's weird. We never talked besides that one time, but you're the closest person to her and you're still alive." I started tearing up so I took deep breaths.

"Take your time. I'm going to get a cup of tea." She quickly got up. I tried so hard to relax but I couldn't. I wanted her to be, but she wasn't Piper. It would have been so easy for me to talk to *her*.

"What is it, Portia? You can tell me. I always kept her secrets."
She took a sip and sat back down.

"It's not really like that. I just think I like a boy."

She sighed and started laughing with her head down. Then she started to cry.

"Are you okay?" I asked.

"Yeah…it's just…Oh my God. She always wanted you to get out there more and she wanted you to hang out with us, and she always said that even if you got yourself a weird boyfriend, it would be cool."

I started crying, too. I knew Piper wanted more from me but she never said it out loud. It sucked hearing it from someone else.

"I wanted to, but I just felt like I had the whole rest of my life, you know…"

"Yeah, it's okay. So, tell me about this boy."

"His name is Ethan Torke. He lives across the street."

"Wait…the guidance counselor has a *son*?"

"He was living with his mother but he moved in with his dad to go to school out here."

"Oh, okay. What does he look like?"

"Nothing like his dad. He has icy blue eyes, longish dark hair, and he has a little bit of scruff. He's very tan. He loves the beach and stuff like that, but he likes me, too. He does stuff for my dad and me."

"Has he met your dad?" She seemed concerned.

"Uh-huh. And he's met Susan, my mom's best friend. He's my only friend, but we kissed…"

"Oh really? Your first friend becomes your first *boy*friend. Wow, now I miss Piper even more."

"I don't know if I should take it to that level and that's why I went into Piper's room. I wanted answers. I wanted to know what I should do."

"She would say to follow your heart. Do whatever you feel like doing and don't worry about the consequences."

"What are the consequences?"

"You know, getting hurt, getting pressured into something you don't want to do."

"Like go to the beach?" I said.

She giggled. "She did say you were pretty funny when you did talk."

"Yeah, I just don't want to end up spending too much time with Ethan when my dad still needs me, like, twenty-four seven."

She sipped her tea. "You can do both, especially if he's already met him."

"Would you like to meet him someday? I really would like to know if Piper would think he's cute."

"Girl, Piper wouldn't care what he looks like. She would just be stoked that you kissed a boy."

Just then, my phone rang. It was Ethan. "Speak of the devil."

"Answer! Answer!" She was so excited she bit her bottom lip and smiled. Now *that* was Piper.

"Hello?"

"Hi. Where are you?"

"Uh…Piper's best friend's house. Maddie's."

"You drove?"

"Uh-huh."

"Okay, well, I was just worried."

"I should have told you, but I'm on my way back now."

"Drive safe."

"I will."

"See you soon."

"Yup." I hung up.

"Oh my God. You guys are already boyfriend-girlfriend." She was smiling. She had stopped shaking and I could tell she was getting more comfortable with the fact that I was there.

"What?"

"Only boyfriends call asking where their girl is."

"My situation is a little different. I haven't left my block in over a year besides to go to school and he took me." I started to get up.

"Well, it was good to see you. Bring him next time."

"Tell your mother thanks." I was walking towards the front door as she followed behind me.

"I will. It was good to see you. Bye, Portia."

"Bye, Piper…" I left. I didn't realize what I said until I got to the car. I looked back. She was still standing at her door. I was embarrassed, so I hopped in and raced home.

Chapter 8

"I'm so tired of being the girl with the dead family. I just want my dad and I to live a normal life." Ethan and I were doing our homework on my bed when I started talking out loud.

"What? Where did that come from?" Ethan put his pen down.

"It just seems impossible with my anxiety and his drinking problem."

"It's understandable," Ethan said.

"No. The thing is, we were like this *before*. They were keeping us together. They were keeping us normal." He just stared at me, so I said, "I don't know. Do you need help?" His homework looked so much easier than mine.

"Eh."

"Give it…" I grabbed his book and his assignment. "Do you have to type this or write it?"

"I was going to write the answers down and then type it later."

"Okay, just type what I write…"

"Wait. Are you saying what I think you're saying?"

"Yeah, I'm done with mine. I was just doing extra work because I was falling behind."

"See what not drinking does to you?"

"Makes me boring."

"Sure…"

I did his homework in ten minutes. It was a joke.

"So, what's your price for doing my homework?"

"I don't know. I have a question, though."

"What is it?"

"Do girlfriends do their boyfriends' homework?"

He started laughing but I was completely serious.

"It's just a question."

"If they're smart like you, I guess."

I shrugged and caught him staring at me.

"What?" I asked.

"Can I tell you a secret?" he asked, and got really close and put his ear to my mouth. I covered his ear with my hand and knocked him over. He almost fell off the bed but he grabbed my left arm. I held onto him.

"Stop, you're going to take me with you." I laughed as I pulled up and pulled us to the middle of my bed.

"What's the secret?"

"I don't know if you noticed, but I think I like you a lot." He brushed my cheek with his fingers. I took a deep breath.

"I asked Piper's best friend if I should make my first friend my boyfriend."

He frowned and pulled his hair back.

"That was stupid. I know. Just because we kissed. I'm new at this."

"What did she say?" he asked.

"To follow my heart."

"What does it say?" He placed his palm on my heart. The bottom of his palm was sitting right on top of my breasts. It made my heart beat faster.

"I don't understand it." I put both of my hands on his one hand. I didn't want him to move it. My heart was talking to me and I was listening.

"Try me," he said as he scooted closer to me.

"I don't think that we're meant to understand it all the time. I think that sometimes we just have to have faith."

He kissed me. It was perfect.

"Nicholas Sparks. *A Walk to Remember*," I said, and smiled.

"Seriously?" He smiled. We both started laughing.

For that moment I wasn't thinking about my dead mother and my dead sister. I was just thinking about us. This was definitely going to change me for the better.

I was really quiet during dinner. Dad was making chili spaghetti. Well, pasta with chili. He put four beers on the table and gave me my plate. I wasn't really that hungry but I did want to talk to him about Ethan and Maddie.

"What's going on, kiddo? You've been getting busier and busier every day."

"I was falling behind in school. I've just been busy doing schoolwork and trying to catch up."

"So you went to school today?" he wondered as he popped open his beer.

"No, I went to see Maddie."

"Who?"

"Piper's best friend."

"I remember her. Why?"

"Advice about Ethan."

"Why can't you ask *me* about Ethan?" He seemed offended I didn't want to talk to him.

"I can. What do you think of Ethan as my boyfriend?" I couldn't believe those words were actually coming out of my mouth. I wanted to take them back. I chugged the beer instead and didn't really look at him. I shoved my face with spaghetti and glanced at him under my eyelashes. He was eating, too. He cleared his throat and took a sip of his beer.

"Boyfriend? Like you guys, um…uh…" He sipped his beer.

"I barely know what that means. We're going to take it slow. He knows how inexperienced I am."

"Well, I don't really know what to say." He was onto his second beer. I had to catch up. I started downing my first.

"You never could keep up with me, babe." He smiled. He was trying to change the subject and I was okay with that.

"I don't have any schoolwork this week. I just have class. I'm pretty caught up."

"Nice."

"So do you want to go do something? Instead of being cooped up here?" I asked.

"I have the perfect idea. Let's camp in the backyard, just you and me." He put his beer down.

"Deal," I said, and held my beer up, "but you're doing all the work."

Ethan and his father invited me over for dinner, which was when I planned on telling him I would be spending a couple days alone with my dad. God, that probably made me the worst girlfriend ever. But it was important to me to let my dad know that he was my first priority and always would be.

I came over and there was a girl sitting on the couch. I recognized her from pictures in their house. Ethan put his arm around my shoulders.

"Sarah, get up, please."

Sarah. The imaginary sister.

"This is Portia. Portia, this is my estranged sister, Sarah." She looked like Ethan, but as a chick. She had long, thick, deep brown hair. *Huge* boobs. There was no way I couldn't look at them. She was short and had resting bitch face. She was wearing stockings with high-waist shorts and combat boots. Then I noticed her Cypress High sweater.

"What does 'estranged' mean?" she asked. I'd heard that questioning tone before. The sweater, the voice. Holy shit, *she'd been in the play*. Dad had showed me the tape as soon as he had come home from the hospital. She was in it. She was one of the last people to see my sister alive other than my parents. I didn't say anything.

"I knew your sister, Piper, she was cool," she said, and then she walked away. I couldn't stop staring.

"Sorry, I didn't know Dad invited her."

I had so many questions. She looked so different. Where had she been this entire time? Piper had never mentioned a Sarah to me, especially a Sarah who was in the play. I felt so out of the loop.

"I never talk about her because we were never close and she blamed my mother for the divorce. It was ugly. I just don't like talking about it," Ethan explained.

"It's fine."

"Are *you* okay? You seem thrown."

"Yup. I'm good."

We were all sitting at the table. I swear on my mother's life I was the main course. Everyone was staring at me. I started sweating. It got really hot all of a sudden. I didn't want to eat anything. I didn't want to pick up anything, I knew I'd drop it I was shaking so bad. My heart was racing. I just stared at my plate. Ethan had his hand on mine but it didn't help.

I wanted to get the fuck out of there.

I needed to know ahead of time if a stranger was coming.

Everyone knew that.

Ethan should have known better.

I was angry.

Since now I was his girlfriend, I had to sit here. I had to sit here and try my hardest not to stab my eyeballs with the fork.

"Just relax, babe," he whispered to me as he caressed my thigh like it was *so easy*. I pushed his hand off. He was only drawing more attention to me and making it worse.

"Can I address the elephant in the room?" Sarah asked. I didn't care, at least someone was talking.

"Do you have to?" Ethan rolled his eyes. He really didn't like her, I could tell. I still didn't understand why he'd never mentioned her, though.

"I just want to know what happened. How did the accident happen, you know?" Sarah stared at Ethan with a smirk. "She was really excited about the after party. It's too bad."

They had been going the opposite direction of home. When the police told me where the accident happened, it hadn't made any sense. For weeks, I tried to figure out why they were driving the opposite direction of home.

It finally hit me: they were dropping Piper off at the afterparty.

"Why didn't Piper go with any of you? It's just not like Piper to get a ride from my parents, especially to a *party*. She would be too embarrassed. She had enough friends who were in the play who could have taken her," I said, my voice had an edge.

"Sarah, stop. Why are you bringing this up?" Ethan slammed down his water.

Mr. Torke finally spoke. "Sarah, if you wanted to ask these questions, you could have asked years ago. It didn't seem to be bothering you when you decided to skip out on college and move in with your hipster boyfriend in New York."

"I'm sorry," she said.

"Don't be sorry. None of you be sorry. I mean, you both knew if you'd told me she was here, I wouldn't have come. You know my issues and you *still* put me in this position. Now that I *am* here, I want closure from the one person at this table who saw my little sister last, especially if I'm going to be forced to sit across from her."

"You're not forced to do anything here," Mr. Torke reassured me.

"Thank you," I said, and grabbed my purse.

"This is why I never leave my house." I glared at Ethan as he put his head down.

I ran home and grabbed a beer and a cigarette. I sat outside on my porch and saw Ethan walking over.

"I want to be alone, Ethan."

"I'm sorry. We've just been talking so much lately. It felt…"

"Normal. Like *I* was normal. Did you forget about the stuff we talked about? I'm not taking any medication for this. My problem is still there, no matter how comfortable I am with you."

"I want you to be comfortable with my family, too."

"I can't do that. *You* don't even like your sister. If you can't accept me for who I am, that's fine, Ethan. Seriously, leave me before it starts to hurt."

"Stop it. Stop it right now." He rushed up to me and grabbed my chin and looked at me.

"I want you. I want you just the way you are."

I looked away.

"No, I'm not done. I'm Ethan Torke, and I'm your boyfriend now, meaning it's my job to take care of you. You're so busy taking care of your father. I need to be there for you and I need you to be your best self, your most healthy self."

"What are you talking about?"

"I want my dad to help you. I don't need you to go to a bunch of parties or go clubbing. I just want you to be able to go to school, get a job, and mainly I want you to be able to walk across your graduation stage…"

"I'm camping in the backyard with my dad for a couple days. After that, we can talk, but I don't want to see your sister ever again." Sarah wasn't ever going to make me feel any better about Piper's death. If anything, she would only be a painful memory.

Five Years Ago

"Portia Willows. Your Godmother is here to take you home."

"I don't have a Godmother." I looked at Dad. "Who the hell is my Godmother?"

He shrugged. He was in horrible shape. I knew I was going to have to take care of him. I was just happy they didn't take everyone away from me.

"I'll see you soon," I said, and kissed his forehead.

"I love you, buddy," he whispered.

"I'll have a beer waiting for you."

Susan and her husband Gary were standing there with Stefan. All had blank faces. I got in the car. It was raining and really quiet. I noticed we weren't going in the direction of my house.

"Where are you taking me?"

"I think you should get some rest tonight and tomorrow, we'll get your stuff."

"Why? For what?"

"You're going to be living with us, sweetie." Susan sounded so sad and depressed.

Well, her best friend had just died.

"Fuck that," I blurted out.

Stefan started laughing.

"You can't stay on your own, you're still a minor."

"For a month, then I'm eighteen. But Dad is going to come home soon. Unless we can't afford the house and then we're *both* living with you." All these thoughts and changes were flooding my head painfully. Tears poured out like waterfalls and I was choking, my throat trying to close.

Stefan was just staring at me with his headphones in. "You okay?"

I looked at him with swimming pool eyes and nodded.

We got to Susan's. Their place was hoarder central. Toys were scattered all over the living room. Cartoons were on the TV. It looked so small because of how much furniture they had.

I couldn't stay here.

I sat on the couch while Susan made me a cup of hot chocolate. She couldn't stop crying. Gary couldn't stop stressing out.

"Look, both of you guys need to calm down. Let's think about this—we're not living here. I'm going home. I need to get the house ready for Dad. I have to be strong for him."

"Your mother and your sister died less than two hours ago. We need to think about this," Gary said.

"What's there to think about? You guys have nothing to do with us, with me. You're my Mom's friend, and she's dead. Let me go home."

Susan looked at Gary.

"Can you give us a minute?" Gary asked me.

I nodded and went outside.

"There's something really wrong with her…" Gary didn't even wait for me to shut the door before he said that.

I made a run for it.

No one followed me.

Three Years Ago

My dad was really excited about camping. He was bringing everything out—tent, wood, gasoline, air mattress and a sleeping bag, flashlights, even a lantern to go inside the tent. I was sitting on the back porch steps with a beer, smoking a cigarette, watching him.

"No cheating, you can't go inside once we start camping. No getting up in the middle of the night. No sneaking across the street to see your boyfriend."

"Well, you don't have to worry about that anymore."

"What happened?"

"Nothing, let's just focus on spending this quality time together."

After we got everything set up, we played card games and reminisced about Mom and Piper.

"What do you think they're thinking?" Dad asked.

"I think Mom is shitting her pants right now looking down at us, but at the end of the day, she knows that we're happy because I still have you and I didn't lose everyone. As far as Piper, she's also shitting her pants but in a different way. She's proud of me. I know she is, for a fact." I smiled. We were both on our backs inside the tent. It was Los Angeles, it wasn't like you could see stars and hear nature. It was mostly sirens and cars on the freeway and it barely looked like it was the middle of the night since the sky was lit up by all the streetlights.

Dad turned to me and said, "*I'm* proud of you, kid. I never thought you would get out there and have your life, which, as your father, I loved. You could be my little girl forever. Piper, I knew she was going to grow up and grow apart from us. But you, honey, you were going to be my quiet little girl who would never forget about her daddy."

I didn't want to cry. This was a camping trip, it was supposed to be fun, but Dad was getting teary-eyed.

The next day, I started getting bored around three in the afternoon. I kept thinking about Ethan and what he was doing. He lived right across the street and I was stuck in the backyard with no phone and no computer. I kept looking out the side gate to see if I could catch a glimpse of him.

"Dad, can I at least go inside to pee?"

"No. Pee in the bushes."

"Is that what you've been doing?"

"That's camping, baby."

I shook my head and laughed.

We did the same thing on this camping trip we would have done inside—drink and smoke. I was zoning out into the sky while we were sitting on lawn chairs facing our own trees in front of a fire.

"You really like him, don't you?" Dad asked. I hadn't really been thinking about him, but I kind of was.

"I guess." I took a swig of my drink.

"So what's the problem?" Dad asked.

"Do I really want to change who I am? Do I want to start putting myself out there more? No, I don't, but for some reason, he seems worth it to me."

He giggled.

"What?"

"You're your father's daughter. That's how I was, except your mother was *extremely* different, you know. I didn't think we could ever actually make a family and I wasn't always sure I wanted to with her because I never wanted to grow up."

"I remember you guys fighting about that a lot when I was younger."

"I didn't want to be an adult, but I would have done anything to make sure I didn't lose her. She was worth every change I made."

I looked down.

"Go."

"What?" I didn't want to forfeit the camping trip.

"Go," he repeated.

I smiled as I hopped up and gave him a kiss on the forehead.

I ran across the street to knock on Ethan's door. I was nervous. I didn't have anything planned. It was him when the door opened. I was speechless. I just backed up as my mouth opened a little bit.

"Portia?" Ethan came outside and closed the door behind him.

"I'm sorry. I really like you and I'm willing to do whatever you want me to do." My voice was shaking. "If you want me to get help, I'll do it." I stopped and he was just staring at me. I had no idea what he was thinking. Without warning, he rushed over and held me so tight. It wasn't a hug. It was like he was trying to push me inside him. It was tight but it was also perfect. I put my hands around his head as I began to kiss him. He ran his fingers through my hair.

"My dad's home, but you're more than welcome to come inside," he mumbled while still kissing me.

"Let's go to mine." I pulled him across the street with me. We went straight to my room. Dad was still camping. We lay down on my bed. It felt so nice to be in his arms again. I never wanted to let go. I didn't want to stop kissing him.

"This whole thing is so weird to me," I said, my head on his chest as he caressed my arm with his soft fingertips.

"What is?"

"You, me, this. I never thought it would ever happen to me. If it did, I thought Piper would have paid someone to do it."

"Oh, she didn't tell you before the play? She *did* pay me," he said as he hugged me tighter.

I got on top of him, smiling. He grabbed my butt. No one had ever touched my butt. I wanted to be uncomfortable, but I wasn't. He stared deeply into my eyes and moved my bangs behind my ear. He tried to kiss me but I backed away, and he smiled. We teased each other for an hour until he couldn't take it anymore. He started taking off my clothes.

"Can we go slow?" I whispered.

"We *are* going slow…" He kissed me.

It felt great but I was incredibly nervous. Now that my clothes were off, I was really anxious about my dad calling my name and having to get dressed fast. I kept looking at the door.

"I can lock it…" He got up.

"Wait. Let me just check on him really quick." I put on pajamas and looked at Ethan before I left my room.

"Were you just staring at me?" I asked.

He nodded.

I went to go find my dad outside passed out in the sleeping bag. I smiled at him. I went to get a fresh beer ready for him when he got up. I kissed him on the cheek and ran back upstairs.

"How is he?"

"Sleeping." I jumped on top of Ethan and started making out with him again. In all honesty, I wanted to do *everything* with him. I wanted to give Ethan my all. I wanted it to be like the movies, but Piper told me it never would be. It was hard to have this confidence but be scared shitless at the same time.

"You think you're ready?" He climbed on top of me and grabbed my underwear, basically asking me to take them off. I shrugged. "I guess…" I whispered.

"Why do you want this?" he asked me as he was grinding on

93

top of me with his boxers on.

"Because I like you and it feels good...I think..."

"You *think* it feels good?" he asked.

I nodded.

He slowly put his hands on my thighs. At first, his hands were freezing cold, so my legs jolted.

"You okay?" He smiled.

"Yeah, your hands are just cold. Is this weird for you?"

"No...is this weird for you?"

"No," I laughed. He slowly put his fingers inside me and I felt like I was getting stabbed to death. My mouth silently screamed. It hurt so badly. I grabbed his wrists.

"I'm sorry."

"What the hell is wrong with your fingers?"

He started laughing against my breasts. "Nothing." He showed me his hands outside the covers.

"Why did that hurt so bad?"

"Because you're a virgin. It's okay. It's normal." He put both of his hands on my face and kissed me. I didn't forget the fact that one of his fingers was just inside me. But his kiss made everything okay. He was so reassuring—I wanted to give him more, but if that was what a finger felt like, I didn't want to know what the rest would be.

"Are you?" I asked.

"A virgin? No. Does that bother you?"

"No. At least one of us knows what we're doing."

"We don't have to do this, Portia. I just...I don't know. I'm really falling for you." It was just like the movies. The way he was staring at me. I never wanted this moment to end, but I had to hurry up before my dad woke up and finished his beer.

"Just do it...let's just get our first time over with."

"It doesn't work like that."

"If Piper could do it in twenty-six minutes, I'm pretty sure I can, too."

"How do you know she did it in twenty-six minutes?"

"She had to be home in twenty-six minutes. I was outside in the car waiting for her and she said hold on, she hadn't done it yet. I thought I was going to be waiting there for an hour."

"And she was out in twenty-six minutes?" He laughed and I did, too.

"She wasn't about to get in trouble again for the fourth time that month."

"Let's beat her record."

After it happened, he had to go home. I lay in my bed and cried for hours. I wanted Piper right next to me. I needed her. When Piper had lost her virginity, she said she felt like a slut and didn't want to be alone. She slept with me that night and cried. I laid next to her.

I didn't feel any of that with Ethan.

He was great. My first time was perfect. I felt comfortable, but guilty as hell.

I wished Piper had felt like this her first time.

I wished she hadn't died.

I wished I had gone to the play, because if I had, I would have taken her to the after party.

No one had to die that night.

It was all my fault.

Chapter 9

After weeks of Ethan and me getting closer and closer, Dad finally started warming up to him. I understood why Ethan wanted us to get help. I didn't like it at first, but he just wanted the best for me. I couldn't get mad at that. Honestly, it made me *more* attracted to him.

Tonight, my dad and I were both going over to Ethan's and we were going to have a session with his father.

"Why are you making me do this again?" Dad asked.

"Was there anything Mom wanted you to do that you didn't want to do, but you did it anyway because you loved her?"

"You love that guy?"

"I didn't say that, Dad." I blushed.

"You love me, right?" he asked while pounding his beer.

"You love me, right?" I repeated.

"Let's get this shit over with."

I was just as nervous as he was. My dad was very unpredictable when it came to things like this. Mom never took him to any business functions or dinners because nine out of ten times he would embarrass her. Dad was a lot like me when it came to being quiet. I wouldn't say it was anxiety, but it wasn't his personality to talk with strangers about the weather or his kids. So, he would drink, and then he wouldn't *stop* talking. Mom learned her lesson after the fifth time.

I loved it because he got to stay home with me.

"Can you walk any faster?" I asked as we crossed the street.

"Nope," he said, and walked even slower.

I rolled my eyes and waited for him at Ethan's front door. I rang the doorbell and then the rest was out of my hands.

Mr. Torke opened the door. "Hi, Portia, Come on in." I looked back at my dad and then looked back at Mr. Torke.

"Hi, how are you? This is my father, Richard."

Dad looked so awkward shaking his hand. It was hard to watch. We walked into the living room.

"Coffee? Tea?" Mr. Torke offered.

"No, thank you." Dad said.

"Beer?" Ethan asked.

"Yes." Dad held out his hand.

"Dad..."

"It's okay, I had a feeling," Ethan gave him the beer he was holding. "You want one, babe?"

"No, thank you." I didn't know much about relationships, but I did know it was inappropriate to day drink in front of your boyfriend's parents. My dad didn't care, whatever made him comfortable.

"First...Portia, I want to talk to you, and your father can just listen," Mr. Torke said.

"Great. I'm really good at that," Dad joked.

I pressed my lips together and tried to fight off laughing but it didn't really work.

"Sorry, what did you say?" Mr. Torke asked.

I looked at my dad to repeat it.

"Nothing. Nothing, go on."

I shook my head. "He just said he's a good listener. He's not much of a talker." I was incredibly nervous. My feet were firmly planted on the ground together. My hands were on my knees trying to stop them from shaking. Mr. Torke looked comfortable in his own home sipping tea. Ethan wasn't in the room. I wished he was.

"Just a drinker." He laughed. My dad was acting like a complete fool—laying back with his arm on the armrest and the beer in his hand between his legs. He looked like he was about to turn the game on.

"Dad, stop." Now he was starting to embarrass me.

"It's okay. Ethan tells me you have a social anxiety disorder." Mr. Torke turned his attention to me. I could tell he meant well, but he also thought my dad was crazy.

"Social anxiety disorder? What the hell is that?" Dad looked at me as if he'd never heard that term in his life.

"I just really don't like attention, big crowds. I've always been like that. Right, Dad?" I wanted him to say something normal for at least a second.

"Yeah…that's the problem? I thought the problem was our grieving methods." Dad didn't know the whole truth about my issues because he couldn't understand the whole truth.

"We never thought that my social issues were *issues*. They're just who I am," I said.

"I love you for who you are, always have. This is not a problem. They want to change you because he wants to…you know, take you out and do guy things…" Dad said, completely disregarding the fact that Mr. Torke was supposed to be the one talking.

"It's not like that, Dad. I can't even go to school. I can't do normal things. I just turned twenty and I'm nowhere close to being an adult, and that's why they want to help me. They want me to be more independent and not be so scared of everything."

"And then what are you gonna do? Leave me." I wasn't expecting my dad to get so defensive about this. Suddenly, his demeanor changed. He sat up straight on the couch and turned to me.

"No." I put my hand on his leg to reassure him. I couldn't even believe he was thinking this.

"Just like your mother and your sister did. You want to leave our life for *this*. This fancy house. You want *him* to be your dad?" He pointed at Mr. Torke. This wasn't fazing Mr. Torke at all. Mr. Torke was writing and sipping his tea. I guess he dealt with this all the time. I wasn't even embarrassed anymore. I was hurt that my dad could think that.

"Dad. Shut up."

"Portia. Portia. Portia." I heard Ethan's voice but I just drowned it out.

"I'm going home." Dad chugged his beer, threw it on the ground.

"Dad, I'm sorry. They're not trying to take me away from you. No one could ever do that. No one. Never. I am your daughter. But I want to be more than your daughter. I want to be *more*." I grabbed his arm and turned him around. I was crying so hard. I didn't care where we were or who was around.

"For twenty years, you didn't care about any of this. Boys, friends, outside life..." he yelled.

"I changed."

"No, you didn't. *They* changed you. I want my daughter back. Thanks for the beer." He stormed out the front door, slamming it. I melted onto the floor of their living room and cried.

"Portia, look at me. I'm right here..." It was Ethan, coming to the rescue. He put my head on his chest. With my head turned, I saw Mr. Torke, still writing.

"What do you need right now?" Ethan cupped my face with his hands.

"Can you take me on a walk?"

"Of course." He kissed my head.

We walked in silence for twenty minutes. Our hands were locked but our arms were stretched out, putting distance between us. I was locked inside my own mind.

"I'm sorry. I didn't think my dad was going to react like that," I said.

"What did he say?"

"I don't know how he could ever think I would stop being there for him and leave him like Mom and Pipes. I would never do that. He's so used to me being there twenty-four seven. He was never the man of the house, Ethan. He was never the one bringing in the income and making sure everyone was okay. Mom did all of that. Dad literally just loved us, and Piper and I never had to question that like we did with Mom. We all kind of took care of him, as fucked up as that sounds. I'm the only one now. He knows that, so he thinks…I don't know…"

"I can take care of him, too." He took a deep breath and looked over to the right side of the sky.

"What's wrong?" I asked.

"I don't know what I was thinking with my dad, you know. I guess I'm jealous. My dad and I don't have that kind of relationship."

"Well, your relationship with your father was probably like mine with my mother."

"Yeah, I guess I'm really close with my mom and it sucks being away from her."

"We should really stop being sad over things like that. We have people in our lives who we care about and who care about us. Not a lot of people get that, you know?"

He smiled and nodded. We kissed.

The next morning, I had to get up at seven because I had a test. After I was done, I felt good about it, but I still felt shitty about my father. I decided to learn how to make him a really fancy breakfast by watching YouTube videos. We had all this food in the house, but neither of us used it because we didn't know how to cook. YouTube made the recipes look so easy—but they weren't. I was making a mess. It wasn't easy *at all*. I was trying to make French toast but I didn't understand how they were making the eggs a part of the toast.

They were going too fast.

I did the best I could. That was more than enough for my dad to enjoy it. I took the tray up to his bedroom.

"Daddy?"

He was out cold. He had a mostly empty six-pack spilled all over the side of his bed.

"Huh…"

"Dad, get up, you spilled beer everywhere."

"I spilled beer? I thought I drank it all."

"I made you breakfast," I said.

He kissed my forehead. He smelled disgusting. Cleaning up his mess, I realized I was over it. I was over this life. I wanted him to put in more effort—help clean the house, not drink so much so we'd have money for real things.

I was starting to sound like my mother.

"I'm going to wash these," I said as I was forcing him out of the bed to take off the sheets.

"Let's watch a movie," he said.

"I have a lot of stuff to do today, Dad. The house is a mess. The kitchen is a mess, and then I have to go to the store."

"Okay…can we watch a movie after?"

"Sure." There was a part of me that felt guilty about changing. I didn't mean to. I didn't even understand when it had happened. I loved spending time with my dad, and maybe I wasn't doing it as often as before, but I had to take care of myself and the house. We couldn't both get away with acting like this. I could never tell him that, though.

I was complaining to Ethan via text. He made me feel good about wanting to clean up, but it still sucked having to do it every day. It was moments like this where I really missed my mother.

Ethan met me at the store later that day.

"How's it going?"

"I'm exhausted."

"You finish your homework?"

I nodded.

"You cleaned your house?"

I nodded.

"Well, I think it's time for you to have some fun," he said.

Fuck. I told my dad I would watch a movie with him later.

"You want to watch a movie with my dad and me?"

He shrugged. "Will he be okay with that?"

"Yeah, he's going to fall asleep in the middle of the movie, I promise."

He smiled, kissing my forehead.

When we walked out of the store, a man said to us, "How's it going?" nodding as he went to go inside.

"Good, how are you?" I asked, barely looking at him.

"It's a beautiful day today." he said as he walked past me.

"It is." I grabbed Ethan's hand as we started to walk home.

"Holy shit," Ethan said.

"What?"

"You just talked to him."

"Are you mad? He's just a random guy, just saying hi. He was nice."

"No, babe, you just *talked to him.* You never talk to strangers."

I hadn't even noticed. A few months ago, I wouldn't have even looked at this guy and kept walking.

Who am I?

Present Day

"How long are we going to be doing this?"

"Do you have somewhere to be?" she asked.

No, bitch, I thought. *I want to see my fucking Dad. I want to know why my fucking kitchen has blood on the ground. I need to get back to clean it up.*

"What do you want from me?"

"I want you to tell me what happened."

"I told you what happened five years ago. I don't remember what happened five minutes ago. I just want to see my dad." I started crying again.

"Portia, I need you to understand that if you walk me through what happened five years ago, then I can help you remember what happened five minutes ago, or more importantly, last night."

"Am I in trouble?"

"Yes, you are, but I'm trying to help you get out of it. I can't help you get out of this if you keep repressing memories."

"I don't know what that means."

"How did you get your dad home from the hospital?"

What did that mean? If I were in trouble, that meant I did something bad. I didn't even talk to people or get involved in anyone else's life. How could I be in trouble? This was Ethan's fault. I didn't know what he did, but he was the one who should be getting interrogated, not me.

"Where is Ethan?"

"With his father at the hospital…"

"Great, *he* can be with *his* father, but I can't be with mine."

Wait? With his father at the hospital?

The baby, the blood, Ethan.

He was there. Daddy was, too.

"Ethan is hurt," I mumbled to myself. "What happened? Where's my dad? Oh my God, I need my dad." My heart was pounding again. I ran over to the window and my hands slapped against it. I just wanted it to break and escape from here. My hands quickly turned into fists. I kept punching and punching. It wasn't breaking, but my hands started bleeding. My bloody hands started my memories flowing.

I didn't want to think about any of this. I turned around.

"How *did* my dad get home from the hospital?"

The memories were hurting. I couldn't take it anymore. I screamed.

Everything was so confusing.

Two security guards and two nurses came in with a first-aid kit.

"You want to know…" She stood up.

I calmed down and glared at Elizabeth.

The security guards went to ask her something. She nodded. The nurses were fixing my hands. "We're fine. I got this." She was determined. She wanted information. She wasn't going to let me see my dad until she got it.

I still didn't understand.

Five Years Ago

I wish I could remember the week after I ran away from Susan's. I don't. I only remember crying, sleeping in Piper's room, sleeping in my parents' room. I remember not touching a thing. I remember writing the letters. I wrote my mom dozens of letters, wrote Piper dozens of letters. They're all in boxes in my room. I haven't looked at them since.

It was Sunday the twelfth, the best day of my life followed by the worst week of my life. I heard the door screech open. For a second, I thought they were all back. Piper screaming, telling me about the play. Mom fighting with Dad. Instead, it was Grandma with a bunch of suitcases and Dad right behind her.

"Daddy." I ran up to him and I really didn't think I would ever let go.

"Relax. Relax. I'm staying here or you're coming with me," my grandma said.

"What?" No. I just got my dad back and she was trying to take either him or me away. "I want to stay *here*."

Ingrid, our neighbor, was walking past the front of our house, looked over at us and kept walking. I was surprised she didn't come to hug dad or at least say hello.

"You can't, Portia. Look at me." Grandma looked out of it. She usually had her hair done up with curls and makeup. Instead she had a wrap around her hair, and it looked like she was wearing her pajamas with barely any makeup. I could tell she hadn't been able to stop crying. She kept looking at me like I was supposed to do something or was doing something wrong. Dad hated being around Grandma. She never let him be himself, always nagging. She was worse than Mom. I had to make a decision for my dad—not just me.

We had lost our family. He was barely standing.

I had to do what I had to do.

"Grandma. Go home. I'm going to take care of Dad by myself. We need this time alone. We need to deal with this alone."

"Since when do you talk?" she asked.

Was she really doing this right now?

"Since my fucking family just died in a fucking car accident. If you want to check on Daddy here and there, that's fine, but leave us *alone*." He'd had already settled in on the couch. I ran up to him. He was so weak and broken. I could tell he didn't want to be alive. I could see the guilt in his eyes.

For months, I cried in his arms. For months, I took care of him.

One day, when I was sleeping, I heard him say, "I can walk… Portia…I can walk."

I thought it was in my dream. I turned over. "Dad. What's happening? Are you okay?" I woke up scared.

"I'm great, baby. I feel fine." I looked at him and there was color in his face again. It was like nothing had happened. He looked happy. It was strange, but I didn't want to question it.

"Oh my God, I thought you were never going to be able to stand ever again!" He danced around. "Stop. You still have to be careful."

"Want me to make you breakfast?"

I nodded as I stared at him as he legitimately hopped his way to the kitchen. I laughed, not being able to believe my eyes.

"It's time for me to start taking care of *you*," he said.

Everything went back to normal, except Mom and Pipes never came home.

We adjusted.

REMEMBER

Three Years Ago

Ethan and I were kissing on my bed. When he kissed me, every-thing in the world felt like it was right where it was supposed to be. The sun was in the sky. The grass was green, the trash in the trash can. Piper was in the other room, Dad and Mom were sleeping. We were here. Just us, in the moment. I climbed on top of him.

"Whoa, whoa, you always do this."

"Always do what?" I got up to take a breath.

"Making out is cool and all, and I love kissing, but sometimes you make it hard for me."

"It's hard for you to kiss me?"

"It's hard for me to stop myself from wanting you…" He grabbed my butt and pushed me further into him and kissed my chest over and over again. I didn't know what he wanted, so I con-tinued kissing his neck.

"You have to stop. I want you so bad, Portia Willows."

"I don't understand. You have me. Aren't we girlfriend and boyfriend?"

"You want to have sex again?" He pressed his lips together.

"Okay…" I grabbed his chin and kissed him with my eyes open.

"Yeah?"

I nodded and he kissed me while lifting me up and flipping me over. My heart was beating hard. I didn't know what to do; I was a little scared. It had hurt the first time. I didn't know what the second time would be like.

"Relax. Okay? This will only work if you relax."

"If I want you to stop, will you?"

"Of course, babe. Who do you think I am?" He giggled as he slowly took off my underwear. It didn't occur to me that we didn't wear condoms. I didn't have any anyway. I didn't really care.

Why did I not care?

He didn't leave right away this time. I lit a cigarette outside while he got us beers.

"What took you so long?"

"I had to pee," he said as he handed me one.

"Was I better?"

"You were great the first time. You were great the second time. You will be great the third time," he said.

"How often do couples have sex?"

"As often as they want to."

"How much do *you* want to?"

He shrugged while chugging his beer. "Whenever you feel like it, will you tell me?"

"A guy thinks about sex every seven seconds," he said.

My jaw dropped. He started laughing. The first thing I thought about was that my dad was thinking about sex every seven seconds.

"I'm going to be sick."

"Babe. I'm not asking to have sex with you every seven seconds. I don't even think that I can do that."

"My dad…" I started gagging.

"Oh. Are you okay?"

"Yeah."

"Older males think about it every seven years," he said, and this time *I* giggled.

"That makes sense. Mom died two years ago. They were definitely not having sex."

"How do you feel?" He rubbed my forehead.

"About what?"

"You know...everything...life. School? Finals? Christmas?" I shrugged. "I'm hungry...that's how I feel."

"Do you want to go out to eat?"

"You know what, I do. As long as I bring home food for my dad."

"Yes. Yes! I'll go get ready and I'm buying." He was excited. I'd definitely caught him by surprise. He jumped up like a little kid who was just told he was going to Disneyland. He kissed me on the cheek and ran across the street. "Love you," he called out.

Wait. Did he just say he loved me?

I went inside and sat on the couch. I couldn't believe it. I just sat there. Ethan Torke just said he loved me. Someone *loved me*. I did it. I was living a normal life. How did I do this without Piper? I looked up. *Did you hear that?* I tried to keep myself from smiling. I had to tell Dad. He was going to be so happy for me. Or at least I thought he would be.

"Dad? Dad?" My dad wasn't in the house. It was the strangest thing. Both televisions were on, the one in the living room and the one in his room. I hated when he did that. I looked everywhere for him. My heart began to skip a beat. I paused. Something was off. I put my hand to my chest. A sudden rush of fear ran through my body.

"Dad!" I screamed at the top of my lungs.

"Out back," I heard him call.

I took a deep breath. That was weird.

He was in the backyard staring at the trees.

"Dad?" I walked up behind him.

"Come here…"

I stood next to him and he put his arm on my shoulder. He was just literally staring at the trees. I stared up at them as well and then stared back at him.

"What are you doing?"

"When your mother and I first bought this house and we realized we were going to raise you and Piper here, we were standing right here. Looking at the trees. Twenty-five years and those trees are exactly the same."

I looked harder at the trees, then looked over to the right to see if there was still a pink teddy bear dangling from the phone line.

"Oh my God." It was there. The phone line was lower than I remembered. I swear the teddy bear was on a different line than when I was a kid.

"Huh?"

"Is that the same teddy bear from my fifth-grade graduation?"

Dad slowly shook his head like he had no idea what I was talking about.

"No…remember? I cried for hours. I don't remember why exactly, probably because some girls were being mean to me, but I do remember looking up over there and only seeing this pink teddy bear. It was perfect. That teddy bear made me stop crying."

"These trees made me stop crying."

"We should hang out here more often, then."

"Want to go camping again?"

"Sure…but first, Ethan is taking me out to dinner. He's buying, so I'll bring you home a bunch of food."

"What time are you going to be home?"

"I don't know. I've never done this before. I'm trying something new."

"Be careful, Portia," he said as he walked inside, rolling his eyes.

"Dad, don't be like that. I'm happy. He loves me."

"I love you, too."

"That's why I'm bringing you home food and we can eat in the backyard tonight with the pink teddy bear and the trees," I said, and kissed him on the forehead.

"I love you," I said.

He didn't say anything. Lately, it felt like every conversation we had ended in a fight or me acting like my mother.

Ethan took me to this pizza café. He promised it wasn't going to be busy. He held my hand tight as we were about to walk into the restaurant. I kept anticipating the worst and took deep, steady breaths.

I knew I *could* do this. I just really didn't want to.

Before he opened the door, he looked at me and I nodded. I had this.

The hostess was really short. She smiled at both of us and said, "Two?"

I smiled and nodded.

Ethan was right behind me. "Yes," he said.

I looked at every table in the restaurant. Everyone was in their own conversation. We passed by five tables. Two were families and three were couples. No one really looked up at us except for the children. As soon as I sat down in the chair, I felt a sense of relief.

"I think I can order my own food but I would just prefer if you did."

"I got you, babe."

"Can we talk about something?"

"What?"

You said you loved me about an hour ago.

Ethan kept looking at the menu. Was that what I was supposed to be doing? I grabbed the menu and tried to fit in with the crowd. He laughed.

"What?"

"What did you want to talk about?"

Oh, yeah.

"I'm fucking starving." I gasped. "I just cussed out loud."

"No one heard you. No one can hear anything we're saying. What did you want to talk about?"

People were on their phones, laughing, touching, or scarfing down their food. The staff was moving fast—some with food, some with plates. I couldn't hear anyone's conversations, just noise and some music, but mainly just noise. It was the strangest thing. I thought public life was exactly like high school, but this wasn't high school. This was adult high school that only had lunch period.

"I'm sorry. I just got anxious all of a sudden."

"Are you still hungry?"

The waiter came over. I nodded and Ethan started to order. I couldn't help but stare at him in awe. Why couldn't this man have entered my life four years ago? Piper would have loved him. Mom would have invited him over for dinner. Dad would have just dealt with it, and he wouldn't be so obsessed with it.

I wanted to continue hanging out with Ethan tonight. I knew I'd promised my dad, but there was something about Ethan that made me want to be around him all the time. What did that even mean? Did I love Ethan more than I loved my dad? I knew that couldn't be, but it seemed like it in my head.

We never ended up talking about the fact that he said he loved me.

Chapter 10

Five Years Ago

"Describe your perfect man."

It was one in the morning. Piper had convinced me to stay up late with her to wait for this guy to text her back. We were in my room since Mom never checked my room late at night. We used my laptop as light and had our schoolbooks on the bed so just in case we got caught we could say we were studying. Piper had a lot of silly plans I didn't understand. She always talked too fast and whenever I asked her to explain, I always regretted it. I decided to just wait up with her—no questions asked.

"Why?"

"Because I'm falling asleep and I need you to keep me up."

"Piper. Go to sleep. He's most likely ninety-nine percent sleeping, too. I have to wake up at six."

"It's Saturday. What the hell are you doing tomorrow at six in the morning?"

"A study session with some AP kids from school."

"That makes no sense."

"Does to me and them. Most of those kids have a really strict schedule. Six in the morning is the only time all ten of us can study together…and yes, the libraries are open."

"Okay, hold on, you can hang out with AP kids?"

"It took some getting used to, but at six in the morning everything is calm enough so my anxiety levels out a little bit. But that's the only time I see them. We aren't friends or anything."

"Okay, whatever. Just tell me your dream man."

"Fine. Mysterious. Southern. I don't know. I want him to be quiet like me but not as bad as me, so he's able to talk for me. On dates and stuff, you know. Understanding, open-minded, smart, or at least tries really hard to be."

"Boring."

"He doesn't *have* to be boring."

"No. I mean what does he look like—white, black, Hispanic, short, tall, small, or big, you know, smooth, sexy lips or hard, thin lips."

"I don't know. I don't care about that stuff. I care about their personality. You should too, Piper. This guy is a dick. He told you he was going to text you tonight but he didn't." I knew that boy wasn't going to text her tonight. It was one in the morning and they were fourteen years old. I was sixteen, and *I* would be sleeping if I didn't have an obsessive little sister. I had upset her. She looked down at her phone and sighed.

"I'm sorry. You don't need him." I put my hand on her shoulder.

"I do. He's my dream man."

"Jesus. Piper. You're way too young for that."

"I wish I was more like you and didn't care about this stuff." If she only knew how many nights I stayed up until one in the morning thinking about how I wished I was more like her.

When I got back from my study session the next morning, Dad was making breakfast. I wondered if Piper had ever gotten the text.

Her silence at the table seemed to answer.

"So, what's everyone doing today?" Dad asked, kissing us both on the heads as he served us pancakes. "Wheat for you," he said as he gave me mine.

"Thanks, Dad."

"Since when the hell did you start eating wheat pancakes? You don't even eat wheat bread," Mom snapped. She wasn't staying for breakfast.

I shrugged.

Dad sat in between us with his coffee.

"Are you joining us?" Dad looked up at Mom.

"Someone in this house has to be productive," she retorted. Mom never worked on Saturdays but she was always busy doing who knows what.

"Someone in this house has to spend quality time with us before we all turn to shit," Piper said as she shoved pancakes in her mouth.

"Excuse me? You're going to let your daughter talk to her mother like that?" Mom glared at Dad.

"She wasn't talking to *you*," I said while I looked at Dad, whose nose was buried in his coffee, eyes drifting to find a distraction.

"*Now* she talks, disrespecting her own mother," Mom said getting in my face.

"Mom, give it a break. We all love you. Go do whatever it is you have to do."

"Yeah, Carol, just go. I'll take them wherever they need to go today...like I always do."

She was shocked. She loudly gathered all of her stuff together and then stormed out of the house, slamming the door behind her. The three of us exchanged glances.

"Okay...your mother acts like this every day. What's going on with you two? Piper, I expect this out of you, but you, Portia?"

"I didn't go to sleep until four in the morning," Piper said, throwing her head down on the table.

"I fell asleep at two."

"Where the hell were you both last night?"

"Portia's room." I looked at her. "Did he text you after I fell asleep?"

"Right after you fell asleep. We talked till four in the morning," she said dreamily. She got so ahead of herself she forgot that Dad was right there. She looked at Dad and her excitement turned to fear. I sat still in shock.

"You are grounded. Phone. Now."

"Are you serious, Dad? He's the most popular boy in school, but not, like, a jock. He's in the drama department and he invited me to the mall today," she whined. This boy was the reason she had joined the drama department, not knowing she was going to fall in love with acting. I was totally on Dad's side with this one. Who had conversations at two in the morning? I didn't care who he was in high school.

"You're never talking to this guy ever again in your life."

"Dad. No." Piper freaked out and shot up.

"Sit back down. You better delete his number from your phone and all the text messages before I learn his full name."

Piper sat back and immediately started crying. As much as I hated seeing Piper cry, Dad was right.

"Portia, you're her older sister. You were with her. You knew better than to let her do this." He glared at me.

I shook my head. "You're right, Dad. I should have known better." I glared at Piper.

"Shut up, Portia!" Piper yelled. She felt betrayed. She stormed off to her room.

Three Years Ago

I had to figure out a way to spend enough time with both my dad and Ethan. I had two people in my life now, and I was struggling. How the hell did normal people have friends, coworkers, family, *and* Facebook friends? I couldn't believe I was saying this, but I wanted to talk to my mom. Juggling people was her thing. I knew I loved Ethan. I didn't want to tell him yet, though, or mention him slipping it out the other day. I was only allowing myself to love one person, but I knew it didn't have to be like that.

"Hey, kid."

I was studying for finals. I couldn't wait to be done with school.

"What do you want for Christmas?"

"What do you mean what do I want for Christmas?" I frowned.

Dad sat across from the table with a beer and slid me one across the table. "What do you want?" he repeated.

"You never ever got us gifts. Mom just wrote your name next to hers at Christmas. You haven't gotten me anything these past couple years, so why now?"

"I want to get you something this year. We actually have something to celebrate."

"What? Piper and Mom aren't back."

"No, but you have someone in your life. You made a friend. You didn't let him fuck up your schoolwork. This year has been a good one, don't you think?"

"I don't want to celebrate Christmas."

"Come on…we have to get back to normal."

"*Oh my God, now* who's acting weird."

"We still have some time. Also remember, Ethan is definitely getting you something for Christmas, so be prepared to celebrate it anyway."

I looked down. I didn't even think about that. I'd never had to get a guy something for Christmas before, especially one I liked. What did Ethan even want?

Ethan and I were in the living room, legs intertwined. He was going off on some rant. I couldn't pay attention because all I kept thinking about was what I was going to get him for Christmas. I'd also been feeling differently lately. I wished I could explain it better. I wished I could talk about how my head felt funny. I wished I could understand why I had so much energy. It was like I was happy, but I definitely wasn't, because there was no way I could be happy without Piper. I did miss my mom, but I could definitely be happy without her. It wasn't because of Christmas, either.

"How are you feeling?" Ethan asked.

"Why do you keep asking me that?"

"I just asked you right now."

"You ask me every time you see me."

"Well, I got over saying 'how are you' because I know how you are, but I never know how you're feeling," he explained.

"You should. You're my boyfriend." I'd never get used to saying that. I kissed him. I'd never get used to doing that, either.

"What did you and your dad do for Christmas last year?"

"What we do every day. Christmas was always Mom and Piper's thing. Dad and I always just…participated."

"I hope I don't offend you, but it seems like you and your dad are more alike and Piper and your mother were more alike."

"We were all pretty different. Piper was close with Dad just as much as I am. Mom liked Piper better than me for sure, though."

"So, no Christmas, really? You guys don't get anything for each other?"

"Does beer count?"

"It does," he said, and I smiled. "Only if you put a bow on it." I shook my head.

"You guys are more than welcome to come over to my house. My mom is coming down."

"That's awesome. I know how much you miss her. I'm so excited for you," I said. I was legitimately happy for him.

"So, is that a yes? I would love for you to meet her."

"I would love to meet her, too, but not on Christmas." I kissed him. "Please try to understand."

He nodded and kissed my cheek.

A big part of me wished I could be that girlfriend who came over for Christmas, met the entire family, and talked about school, the future.

I wasn't there yet.

It wasn't fair. I could meet his mom and sister and he would never get to meet mine.

My dad and I were up pretty late the night before watching Christmas movies, so we were both sleeping in, especially since this was the only day where everyone thought was okay to sleep in for as long as you wanted. But someone was banging on the front door.

"Portia. Portia. What the hell?" my dad yelled. I had run into his room out of habit—I was scared.

"Daddy. Someone's at the door."

"Then open it."

"Ethan never bangs on the door like that, he always calls first. Can you open it?"

The banging continued. Dad struggled getting out of bed.

"Look out the window, yell up who it is, and I'll tell you if it's okay to open it or not," he said.

"Okay."

"I'll get dressed."

Waking up like that, I'd completely forgotten that it was Christmas. I opened the window blinds and saw Grandma with gifts in her hands.

"It's Grandma." She was knocking again. It felt so early in the morning, but it was already noon.

"Don't open it." Dad yelled down. I opened the door anyway.

"Hi, Grandma," I said, surprised.

"Merry Christmas, munchkin," she said, and threw herself at me.

I closed the door, walking into the dining room to put all the gifts down. She looked around the house. It was a mess. I could have sworn I'd just cleaned.

"I missed you so much," she said, and hugged me tighter.

"We missed you, too."

"We?"

"Yeah...Dad's upstairs. We just woke up."

"It's noon, baby. I heard you got a boyfriend."

"From who?"

"You know, around. Where is he?"

"With his family across the street."

"You're not over there?"

"Nope. What'd you get us?" I went over to the gifts, hoping one of them would work for Ethan. She started looking in the kitchen to see if we were stocked up on food. We were.

"Are you still in school?"

I nodded as I started opening the gifts. One of the bags had three books in there. I picked them up and read the titles aloud.

"*I Wasn't Ready to Say Goodbye?*"

"You'll love that book. We just read it in our book club," she said.

"Cool. What's this one? *Living When a Loved One Has Died.*" I didn't even read the title of the third book. "Grandma. It's been over two years. think we're fine, but I appreciate it. I'll read them anyway."

"Good. Sweetie, I'm so proud of you for staying in school, taking care of yourself, making friends. I never thought it would work out this long, but here you are…"

"I told you…what is this?" I held up another package.

"Just homemade cookies, tea, organic, healthy stuff," she said, and looked around. It was really awkward.

"Do you want me to get Dad?"

"No…"

"Well, I'm going to open up the rest with him…like a real Christmas."

"I wish I could have seen you last year. I wasn't feeling too well." She sat down on the couch. Was it bad that we hadn't even noticed that Grandma hadn't come by? She used to come over every Christmas when we were kids. Her voice was more somber than usual.

"Are you dying, Grandma?" I honestly was joking.

"No, honey, I'm not going anywhere."

I sat down next to her and she put her hand on my thigh.

"Good."

"I was thinking I could stay here for a few days."

Fuck no.

Hell no. There was no way. Dad would never allow it. I texted Ethan to call me whenever he had a chance. I doubted he would, though. He was probably having the time of his life with his mother.

I didn't say anything to her but I did get up to make her a cup of tea.

Grandma made us dinner. It was nice to have a home-cooked meal—a real home-cooked meal that wasn't chili.

"Thanks, Mom. This was great." Dad was done with his plate before Grandma took one bite.

"Yeah, it was. You should come over more often," I said. Grandma didn't respond to dad.

"Have you ever thought about getting a job?" she asked me.

"I'm going into my junior year at UCLA. I don't know how I'd be able to manage a job and school," I said as I finished my plate.

There was a knock at the door.

"Now *that's* Ethan." I smiled at Dad.

"Probably with a Christmas gift. Maybe you could give him one of these books," he chuckled.

I opened the door and I wanted to jump in his arms, but his arms were already around another woman. My mouth dropped. She was beautiful. She didn't look like how I expected her to at all.

"Portia, this is—"

"Hi!" I couldn't help myself. I just stuck my hand out. She shook it. They both had bags full of stuff. There were a dozen roses in Ethan's hand. I didn't even register that. I was still staring at his mom.

"Wow, you're the girl I've been hearing about for all these months. In the flesh," she said. She didn't look like any other mother I ever seen, more like a hot teacher. Makeup was great but not too much. They had the same icy blue eyes. Her hair was dark brown and down to her shoulders. She was wearing a Christmas sweater and Ethan was wearing a red flannel. My smile was so big. I didn't think it was possible to be this happy meeting someone else's mother.

"It's so nice to meet you," I said. I helped them with the bags.

"Here, Merry Christmas." He smiled.

I grabbed them and tears filled in my eyes. I took a deep breath.

"Portia, don't be rude. Invite them in," Grandma said, but the house was a mess.

"Sorry." I moved out of the way and guided them in.

"I don't usually have…uh…" I didn't know what to say.

"Ethan has told me all about you," she said.

"You must be the boyfriend." Grandma went over to Ethan.

I could puke right now.

"This is my Grandma," I said, and Ethan hugged her. He had the hugest smile.

"Merry Christmas, you guys." Ethan told all of us and looked over at my dad. My dad nodded to him. The four us were chatting while my dad just sat at the kitchen table drinking. There was a lot of chatting and laughing. I couldn't believe any of this. I felt weird after five minutes.

We all went to sit in the living room. I gestured at my dad to join us, but I could tell he didn't want to.

"One minute," I told them. I ran over to him.

"What's wrong?" I whispered.

"I'm going upstairs. The game's about to start."

"Ethan's mom is here. Don't you want to meet her?" I looked over at them. Ethan's mom looked at me in confusion and then looked at Ethan. Ethan put his hand on her shoulder and looked down. I turned back to Dad.

"This is all too weird for me, buddy. I guess I need to read one of those books Grandma got you, because I'm not ready for all this. Christmas. Not without my other daughter and my wife." He was broken to the core. I felt so bad for moving on. I knew he was going to try to drink fast enough before the pain started. I hugged him. My eyes were watery. Half of me wanted to disappear with him and the other half wanted to join them in the living room.

"I'm going to get them out of here. Grandma won't stay, okay?"

"I don't think you can control it. I know that woman. She's my mother," he said.

"I love you."

"I love you," he said. He hugged me and kissed me on the forehead as he headed up the stairs, waving to Ethan as he went.

"And hey, Dad?"

"What?"

"Merry Christmas." I put a big smile on my face and traced it with my fingers.

He just shook his head.

Later that night, Ethan and his mom left. Grandma decided to walk them over, which didn't make any sense, but I didn't care. It got her out of the house—hopefully for good. I went upstairs to check on Dad.

He was out cold. I plopped down on the bed next to him. I was upset he fell asleep so early, but not even five minutes later I was out as well. Talking and socializing was definitely exhausting.

"Sweetie...sweetie."

I woke up to Grandma calling me. I was still in Dad's room. I turned over to see if he was still next to me, but he was gone.

"Grandma..."

"I made you breakfast," she said.

"I thought you left."

"No. Ethan is downstairs. We want to talk to you." I was so tired.

"Grandma. It's eight in the morning. Where's Dad?"

"Um..." She looked flustered "I made him take a shower like he's seven years old," she said.

"I don't even remember the last time he showered."

"Get yourself together and let's go downstairs."

I went downstairs. Not only was Ethan there, but so was his dad. I should have listened to Grandma and made myself look presentable.

"What's going on?"

"We think it's a good idea for you to move in with me across town," Grandma said.

I giggled. I stopped and then giggled again, and then I giggled again waiting for someone else to fucking giggle. Who was "we"? And what made anyone think I cared?

"You're serious?"

"Babe, hear me out. Your grandmother tells me that this family can thrive on selling this house. If we get it together, you move in with her. I'll still see you every day. You can afford to graduate from UCLA."

"UCLA is not cheap, and neither is this house," she said.

I couldn't say anything at all except laugh.

"Portia, this is *your* life." Grandma stepped closer to me.

"Exactly. This is *my* life. What do *they* have anything to do with my life?"

"We're willing to help. I know a lot of realtors for this area," Mr. Torke told me.

"Susan wants to help you as well."

"Grandma. Excuse my French, but fuck off. All of you."

Her eyes widened as she stepped back.

"Dad. Dad?" I ran up the stairs.

"What's going on?" He came out of his room.

"They want us to sell the house. Is it really that bad? Are we really falling behind? I'm not living with Grandma or Susan and I'm damn sure not selling this house." As I realized everything they were saying, I started to panic.

"Stop. Stop. I'm going to fix this. Right now. Stay up here." He grabbed me. Looking into my dad's eyes always calmed me down. I took deep breaths and leaned against the wall and screamed in my head. How could they take this house away from me? I knew there were adult decisions that needed to be made, but why now? Why on

Christmas?

"Everyone out of my fucking house right now. How fucking dare any of you come in here on Christmas and act like you care about my daughter with these gifts and sulky looks. Ethan, you should know better. You know my baby better than any of them. Get out of my house. Now," Dad yelled.

That wasn't how I'd imagined he would handle it. He came back upstairs. His nostrils were flaring and he was breathing heavily. I'd only ever seen him get this mad at Piper. I looked up at him, wide-eyed.

"Did they leave?" I whispered.

"Give them an hour." He sat down against the wall next to me.

"So, we're just going to sit here and wait?"

He nodded.

"We're hiding in our own house," I said.

"At least it's still our house." He kissed my shoulder and got up. "Go do your schoolwork."

Chapter 11

Present Day

"When did you start getting sick?"

"Which time?"

"After the accident." Elizabeth was flipping through her files. How did she have so much paperwork on me?

"Like a cold? Or really sick?"

"When did you realize there was a serious problem?"

"It wasn't until after Christmas," I said.

"What did you think it was?"

"I had no idea. Ethan blamed my lifestyle. It felt like he was trying to convince me to change for years and me getting sick was a big fat 'I told you so.' Speaking of, can I have a cigarette?" I was cold. I was scared. I just wanted to see my dad.

"Sure. While I get you one, can you try to remember something else around that time? Any small details?"

I nodded. I tapped my foot. Honestly, I didn't really remember me being sick. I mean, yeah, I got sick all the time. I drank a lot. I threw up. I did remember there being a time I was throwing up a lot. I didn't think it was important. It was none of her business how much I drank. She came back in and handed me a pack of Marlboro Gold. *Ugh.* Whatever.

"So, you were really sick and…?"

I shook my head. "I don't remember. Nope." I threw my hands up.

"Okay. So far, you're living on your own with your dad still in your house. How did you afford to live?"

"UCLA and the house were getting paid for by Susan, who replaced my mom at the advertising company."

"Did she pay the bills or did she give you the money?"

"She and Gary took care of all of that. Why does any of this matter?" I understood that she wanted me to remember what happened last night, but why did we have to go back *years*?

Three Years Ago

I woke up vomiting. I couldn't remember the last time I had even felt queasy. Hopefully, something wasn't severely wrong with me. It could have been from drinking, but I'd been drinking beer like water for years now and I had never thrown up.

"You okay?" Dad asked.

"Yeah...I think I may have the flu."

"You talk to Ethan?"

"No, Dad. I told you. I don't want anything to do with him."

"He's been by the house every day. He's begging for you to just talk to him. He's sorry. I mean, sweetie, if I can forgive, you should, too."

"I should never have started seeing him in the first place."

"Well then, break up with him. Don't just ignore him. You're a grown-ass woman. Grow some lady balls and tell him how you felt attacked by his dad and him. Who gave him the right? Now you've got me getting mad again."

"I don't know yet. Right now, I just feel sick to my stomach."

"Okay...well, get cleaned up. He's downstairs."

"What?"

"I told him you agreed to talk to him."

"Ugh." I shoved him out of my way.

After brushing my teeth and washing my face, I walked downstairs and saw him sitting on the couch in the living room. I didn't realize how much I'd missed him until that moment. He had two cups of coffee sitting on the coffee table.

"Hi…" Jesus. I just wanted to kiss him. I couldn't lie about that. I sat next to him. I wanted to touch him. I was shaking so badly because I didn't really know how to feel.

"You okay?" he asked.

"Yep, I think I'm coming down with something."

"Have some coffee," he said.

The coffee felt good against my throat even though it tasted off. No one could make coffee as good as my father.

"How are you feeling?" he asked.

I just stared at him.

"Sorry. I just missed you so much. I don't really know what to say. I know it's only been a week, but it's been the longest week of my life."

"I missed you, too."

"I just wanted to say I'm here for you. Just me. I don't care what you do or what you don't do. I want to make you happy. I just thought…I don't know. I'm stupid. I hate seeing you upset," he said.

I put my head on his shoulder, but I was still distant. "You're not stupid. You aced your chemistry final."

"Thanks to you."

"Can I ask you something?"

"Huh?"

"Do you love me?"

He put his head down and took a sip of his coffee. I took a sip of mine. I still felt weird and not myself. I just wanted to go to sleep. This past week I'd been so upset—I had just slept. I felt sick. I felt gross. I assumed it was stress. I assumed everything would be better if I saw him, but I felt worse.

"I do." He stared deeply into my eyes.

I didn't want to blink. He put his hand on my knee and caressed it. Tears pooled. I inched in closer to him and kissed him.

"I love you too," I said, and we kissed again. As soon as he put his tongue down my throat, I felt bile coming up. I pushed him away from me. I threw up—all over the coffee table, the couch, and it splattered all over him. I was mortified.

"I'm so sorry," I sputtered, but I wasn't done. I ran into the bathroom. He came in after me. "I should have said I loved you sooner." I threw up again. One of his hands was rubbing my back and he held my hair back with the other.

"Did you?" he asked.

"Did I what?" I mumbled, but it echoed from the toilet bowl.

"Love me sooner?"

I took a deep breath and threw up again. What did I eat? Vomiting was so painful it moved my entire body. Ethan was doing his best holding me up and holding my hair back.

"Because I loved you the first day I saw you outside the door," he whispered in my ear, and I tossed my head back into his chest. This was so romantic. "You good?" He grabbed my hair softly, just petting my forehead.

"I don't know what's wrong with me. I've been sick all week."

"Should we go to the emergency room?"

"No. My dad has been doing a great job taking care of me," I said.

He kissed me on the cheek.

"Gross." I went upstairs to brush my teeth.

I never got better. My dad was so sure he could take care of me and that it was nothing. I'd taken care of him, after all.

"I think you should go to the doctor," Ethan told me.

"Doctors cost money. Your father already thinks our house is going into foreclosure."

"You still have health insurance, don't you?" Ethan asked.

I shrugged as I grabbed three beers from the fridge. I didn't feel sick. I wasn't coughing. I just felt drained and dehydrated.

"Maybe you should drink water instead of beer," Ethan said.

"He's right." Dad grabbed my beer and slid it closer to him.

"You guys do everything together. If you need to stop drinking, your dad needs to stop drinking. Maybe it's the smoking. You getting sick doesn't surprise me whatsoever," Ethan said.

"I've been drinking beer ever since my family died. This is the first time I've gotten sick..."

"Ooh, she's saying it's your fault," Dad joked.

"Well then, let me take you to the doctor," Ethan said.

"If I'm still sick in a month, take me to the doctor, okay?"

"Compromise?"

"Is that *not* a compromise?" I looked at Ethan and Dad.

"For a month, no beer and no cigarettes. If you get better, no doctor, you got a break, you can go back to this. If not, let's go to the doctor."

"He's joking, right? You know how long a month is?" Dad said.

"Just no smoking," I said.

"Fine. Deal?"

I nodded.

"Sealed with a kiss," he said, and puckered his lips at me.

I glanced at Dad, he put his head down.

I kissed Ethan quickly.

It was so sweet how Ethan was helping me get through this month without smoking. Signing up for classes was stressful—I had to actually go to school again.

"This reminds me of when we first met," he said, looking over at me.

"Yeah. Let's hurry this shit up. Just the bookstore. I don't need this other crap."

"You think I can get into UCLA?"

"Of course you can," I said. We were holding hands. I wasn't even looking at anyone else. I just focused on our conversation. I loved it.

"Don't flatter me. This school is just so beautiful. It's just crazy that you pass this up for your living room."

"Every day."

"I guess the drive would get annoying," he said as he was looking around.

"You should apply. There's a program at SMC that guarantees you into UCLA."

"I couldn't afford it, regardless."

"That's what scholarships are for," I said. "My stomach is killing me. And I haven't even had anything to drink."

"I know, you've been drinking water. I've been proud of you. I just didn't want to say anything in case you'd stop."

"I think I should still go to the doctor just to see what's going on," I said.

He let go of my hand. I wouldn't have noticed if there weren't so many people around us. I stopped walking. I felt imbalanced as soon as he let go. It felt like all the people around us were closing in on me. Ethan hadn't noticed that I wasn't right next to him. My pulse began to skyrocket. He kept walking into the crowd.

And just like that, he was gone.

I stood there twirling around, struggling to breathe. I closed my eyes with my hands on my heart. My heart was constricting.

"Watch where you're going."

I bumped into someone.

I started to panic. I looked around to find a spot or a tree just to sprint to and die. I hurried in the opposite direction, and someone grabbed me from behind. I immediately started screaming. Everyone stopped and stared at me—my worst nightmare.

"It's me. It's me. Shh. Calm down." Ethan guided me over to a tree.

My lungs. Not working.

"Take…ttta…take…me…home…"

"Deep breaths."

I shook my head.

"Breathe, Portia, it's me. I'm so sorry I let go of you. It was just for a second. I got side-tracked by this kid…ugh…this isn't help-ing."

I still couldn't. I just wanted to sit and die. I still wanted to die.

"Can you make it to the parking lot?"

I wanted to get out of there. I nodded even though I didn't feel like I could move. He put his arm around my waist and helped me walk to the car.

Once we got to the parking lot, he picked me up and put me in his passenger seat.

"Try and breathe for me, baby."

"I'm tr—I'm trying!" Fuck. I couldn't get my shit together. We weren't even in the crowd anymore. He sped off so fast I threw up in the car, and immediately rolled down the window.

I started to calm down even though I was still covered in puke and still felt dehydrated.

"Where are we going?" We weren't going toward home. I tossed my head back. This was what my death was going to look like.

"To the hospital. It's right here." He was driving so fast.

"Are you fucking kidding me? I'm covered in puke."

"You just had a panic attack."

"So?"

"You couldn't breathe for more than five minutes."

"More like two, Ethan. I'm fine now. Take me home."

"We don't live near a nice hospital. We're already on this side of town, so we might as well. At least to make an appointment. Jesus, Portia. Listen to me." He punched the steering wheel and sped up.

"Ethan."

"End of discussion. We have it your way all the time, Portia. You know I could never say no to you, but this—I'm standing my ground."

I'd never seen this side of him. He always did what I said—so passive. I liked that about him. He was quiet and just there. I knew him and I saw him for him, but not like this. I loved this even better. It reminded me of my dad. He was passive-aggressive except for when it came to the people he loved. In that moment, I knew Ethan really loved me—puke and all.

Chapter 12

Present Day, Twelve Hours Ago

"Let's go!" Dad screamed.

I couldn't move. My hands were shaking. Dad was tugging on me while I knelt on the living room floor, blood all over my hands. I looked up, there was blood splattered on the walls.

I heard a baby screaming.

Susan was holding a baby but it wasn't hers.

Dad's hands were covered in blood, too. He threw me over his shoulders, and ran outside. I couldn't stop crying. I couldn't stop trying to figure out what just happened. He threw me in the backseat of the car and we drove off. I kept looking back. We weren't going to clean up our mess? We couldn't just leave our house looking like that. Dad was speeding, making sharp turns.

"You okay?"

I nodded as my forehead rested against the window. When I moved, there was blood where my head had been.

"We need to get cleaned up somewhere."

"Where? Dad, we should go back."

"We cannot go back or we are going to jail, Portia. Do you get that?"

"I think the police will understand—"

"No, Portia. No. We need to both relax and calm down. Everything is going to be okay if you just listen."

I had blocked out what had happened. I was pretty sure my dad and I talked about everything on the way to the woods—camping, hiding out. We probably had a plan, but I didn't remember it. I just knew we were dirty and bloody. Dad was super calm, like this wasn't his first rodeo. I didn't know where Ethan was, nor did I care. It took forever for us to set up our tent. We went camping in the backyard all the time, but this felt different. I couldn't remember why we were doing this. Why were we in such a hurry? Why wasn't my dad telling me what was going on?

Dad was asleep when I woke up to the lights shining through the tent fabric. Car lights. I tried waking him up. He didn't wake up. The lights turned red and blue. It was the police. How did they find us? My dad was right. We were going to jail.

"Portia Willows?" a deep male voice said my name.

I walked out of the tent with my hands in the air. There were dozens of them. Guns drawn. All I heard was my deep breaths and my hands were shaking so much, it was like I was doing a chicken dance.

"Dad. Wake up. The police are here," I said.

I had no idea why.

"You are under arrest for attempted murder—" One put away his gun and gripped my arms.

I cut him off.

"What? No. Daddy. Daddy. Daddy. Wake up." They charged at my dad. I did not think my lungs were capable of screeching as loud as I did when I saw them put handcuffs on him.

"No! Just arrest me. Please, no. Not my dad."

"You have the right to remain silent. Anything you say can and will be held against you in a court of law." They put handcuffs on me. The policeman put his hand on my head roughly and threw me in the backseat with my dad.

"Daddy. Daddy." I clung onto him, not ever planning to let go.

"It's all right, sweetie, just don't say anything."

"Why is this happening?"

"You didn't do anything wrong, okay? It's only because you were with me." I just kept crying. Dad's eyes teared up. I knew he didn't want to see me like this.

"You have the right to speak to an attorney. If you cannot afford a lawyer, one will be provided for you…"

My whole life shattered around me.

My heart was pounding. My eyes were twitching. My throat was constricting.

They were going to take him away from me.

"Just don't say anything at all. Susan will help us get out of this."

"What happened? What did we do?" I asked him.

"You didn't do anything."

"I obviously did *something*, Dad. They're *arresting* us. This is real. There's blood on our hands. I can't remember!" I shrieked.

The two police officers in the front seat kept looking back at us. Then at each other. I wondered what they were thinking. They couldn't really take me to jail. They couldn't take my dad. This couldn't really be happening.

"Where's Ethan?" I asked Dad.

"Ethan Torke?" the police officer in the passenger seat asked me.

"You know him? Did he call you guys? Where is he? He's going to be our one phone call and he'll figure all this out."

They just looked at each other again.

What did that even mean? Why weren't they talking to me? I still couldn't stop crying.

"Thank you for letting my dad in the same car as me. I know you guys don't usually do that," I said, changing my tone.

"Portia. Shut up," Dad snapped.

"Okay. Okay. I won't say anything, but they're going to ask me questions."

"Not a word."

When we got to the police station, the phones were ringing off the hook. There were a lot of people waiting. I overheard so many different conversations.

"I wasn't there. You can't name me as a witness if I wasn't there."

"Are you guys doing anything to find my daughter?"

"He needs a real lawyer."

I didn't belong here.

"Sit down here," an officer said.

I sat in the chair at one of the desks. I looked around. They had taken my dad somewhere else.

"Where did they take my dad?" I asked the lady who was at the desk. She had my ID in her hand, and was typing away at the computer.

"Your dad?"

"Yes. The man I was brought in with."

"I didn't see anybody."

"He had to have gone somewhere."

"He probably went into booking."

I couldn't say anything, anything at all. I was shaking my legs and scratching myself. I bet it looked like I was on drugs. I'd never been in a police station before, not even when Piper and Mom died. Dad was still in the same building as me, though, so I would be okay.

It felt like it was hours and hours before anyone acknowledged me.

"Portia Willows," another officer said as he walked up to me.

"Yeah?" I immediately stood. The cuffs were really starting to hurt.

"Come with me," he said.

I tried to make my hands more comfortable. The policeman stopped.

"What are you doing?"

"Nothing, sir, they're just really digging into my skin," I said.

He looked at my cuffs. "Who put these on you?"

I shrugged. I didn't remember them going on—let alone the guy's name.

He took them off and paused. I felt his eyes on my neck.

"Am I allowed to stretch before you put them back on?"

"Go ahead." I thought he was going to back up a little bit but I guess not. I put my hands back behind my back. He put them on again. They felt different this time.

"Better?"

"Much, thank you," I said. We walked into a room. I'd seen this type of room in the movies and on television shows. It was an interrogation room.

No windows.

Bright. Small. Tight.

Plastic table against a concrete wall with a fold-up chair on each side. A camera in the top right corner. It was really cold. I was shaking. I had no idea what was going to happen to me. I just hoped my dad was okay.

"Your lawyer is going to speak with you first—"

"I don't have one," I said.

A woman with a medium skin tone walked in. She would burn up in this cold room with what she was wearing. A button-up, a blazer, a skirt, stockings, and boots. Jesus.

"Who are you?" I asked.

"Susan's attorney, and now yours—I'm Rose Harper."

"I'm Portia Willows."

"I know who you are. I need you to not say anything to the police, Portia."

"That's fine, but where is my dad?"

"I'm going to be the attorney for both of you. I will help you both get out of this situation."

"Okay…"

"How did you end up here, Portia?" She looked up. "Actually, don't tell me. The less I know, the better."

Well, that was great, because I didn't know anything. Stupid question after stupid question, Rose Harper left. I ended up waiting a whole other hour.

I cried out for my dad. I kicked the door. I banged my head against the wall. I was so bored. I didn't know what to do. I just wanted to see Ethan and my dad. At this point, I even wanted to see my grandma, Susan, any of those damn kids.

I just wanted something to happen.

Then she opened the door—the woman who would get me out of there.

"Portia Willows?" I backed into the corner, squeezing my legs together, trying not to piss my pants, and then I slid down into the fetal position.

"I'm Elizabeth Smith, LAPD's forensic psychiatrist." She showed me her badge. I didn't care. She came over to me, bent over, and wiped away one of my tears.

"I am going to take care of you."

"And my dad?" I cried.

"Let's go."

I remember I looked at her like she was sent from heaven. She was so pretty, the way her bright blonde hair swayed across her face. Her eyes were strong and fierce. I trusted her immediately. I followed her out, looking for my dad in every window. I got in the back of a police car, handcuffed, she was in the front seat.

"Wait…wait…if you're taking me home, we have to wait for my

dad," I said.

The driver was about to speak, but Elizabeth stopped him, "Unfortunately, Portia, you can't go home. You're still under arrest, but I'm going to take you somewhere you need to be."

"Home?" I asked.

She chuckled, as if I'd made a joke. I was serious.

"It's a hospital, okay? Your dad will meet us there. He already knows."

"Okay. I don't care where you take me as long as my dad knows. I'm okay."

It felt good to be out of jail.

"When do I get my phone call?"

"When you get booked."

"What does that mean?"

"You aren't booked because you haven't been charged with anything yet," she said.

"Is my dad booked?"

"I have no idea."

"My attorney, Susan's friend, is probably with him. I hope he gets his phone call. One of us needs to call Ethan," I said.

"What makes you think he'll call Ethan?"

"Ethan lives across the street and I'm with him all the time. We've been together for three years."

"That's nice! So, you think Ethan will know what happened since you don't remember?"

"Exactly. He always knows what to do."

I fell asleep. Don't ask how I could in the back of a police car with handcuffs on and my dad not being by my side, but I did. I was exhausted.

I didn't just fall asleep. I had horrible visions—nightmares— whatever. I kept seeing my mom's dead face. I tried to shake it off, but then I would see Piper's face in her coffin at the funeral. Then I would see my dad's face, as if he had died, too. I screamed to wake myself up.

"Portia. Portia. It's just a dream."

I woke up, but not to Elizabeth, all I saw was blood and a baby crying. It was freaking me out. Someone was trying to wake me up and I was trying to wake up, but I felt trapped in this nightmare.

"Portia. We're here. Wake up."

A woman was shaking me.

My hands were cuffed. I started screaming, trying to shake the handcuffs off.

What's happening? Where am I?

I started rocking. She grabbed both of my arms and pinned me down to the back of the car.

Holy shit. I was in a police car.

The policeman jumped out and drew his gun.

"Stand down. I've got this. Portia, look at me. Look at me," she tried to out-scream me. "We made it. We're here. You are okay." She was really close to my face, looking into my eyes. I couldn't look at her or anything else. She smiled and held up keys to unlock my handcuffs.

I shook with pure fear.

"Who are you?"

Now, here we were, still sitting in the same room I had been brought into.

"It was great that you just remembered all of that. It helped out a lot," Elizabeth said.

"Well, obviously not that much since I still don't know what happened. This baby keeps popping up in my head." She looked up at me from her paper.

"Do you remember when you first went to the hospital?"

"Yeah, when I was six. Piper—"

"No. Since your family died."

"Oh. I haven't."

"You don't remember Ethan taking you to UCLA?"

"The school? He took me all the time. He started going there. I got more comfortable at the campus. We even took a class together. I couldn't believe it."

"What class was it?"

"Some childhood development class? I don't know."

"So you don't remember going to the hospital at all within the last three years? You never went to the hospital because you were sick?"

"Nope." I shook my head. I knew she wanted me to remember something, but I couldn't help it. I didn't.

"Let's go for a walk," she said.

"You mean, leave this room? Yes, please." I jumped up.

"I want you to tell me about the first time Ethan took you to the hospital."

I laughed. "Ethan never took me to the hospital."

"He did. He took you to the hospital more than fifteen times over the past few years."

"What? Why?" I was taken back.

"You can remember. I know you can. We just need something to help you," she said. We walked down the hospital hallways. It wasn't the same hospital my dad was in after the accident. It wasn't like the hospitals on TV either. The rooms seemed more…permanent. There wasn't much staff running around in the hallways. There was nothing about this place that looked familiar to me. It was definitely not going to bring up memories.

"Are you saying Ethan brought me *here* before?"

"No, this is a mental institution. Once we're done, you will be staying here until your trial."

This is a psych ward?

I was here because I was crazy.

"Trial?" What? I thought this was my punishment. There was a possibility I could really go to jail. What could they possibly be charging me for?

"I need you to remember something super important," she said.

"For my trial?"

"Yes." She had a recorder in her hand as we were walking, like I was supposed to say the magic words to get me free.

I wished she would just tell me what she wanted me to say.

We went into the waiting room and there was a lady with a badge standing to my right with a toddler. It was the baby from my visions, but a little older. There were a couple paramedics at the reception area, too. I only noticed the toddler because Elizabeth looked over there first.

"Why did you bring me to this hospital? What's going on?" My heart stared to constrict. Fear was slowly rushing in.

"Because this hospital will play a pivotal role in your trial. You are not well," she said.

"Mama..." I heard her from beside me.

Oh my God.

I immediately turned around and ran to the voice.

Her voice. So small. So pure. So innocent.

Pypes.

The lady let her go and she ran to me. I picked her up and squeezed the life out of her. All the memories came rushing back. I cried so hard into Pypes's little shoulders as I swung her around.

"I had a daughter."

I looked over at Elizabeth.

She smiled at me.

Two and a Half Years Ago

The emergency room had to take the cake on the most uncomfortable public place in world history, especially when I was feeling fine.

"You've never been to the emergency room before?" Ethan asked me, like it was normal for someone to be sent here.

"I never went out, so I didn't get hurt," I said.

"You never got hurt in your house or at school?"

"Nope. Never even broken a bone."

While we were waiting, we talked.

"What's your favorite color?" he asked, but I was too distracted looking at all these people that were apparently here for a real emergency. They all looked fine to me. There was a little girl curled up in her mom's lap. That made me shiver.

"Babe?"

"What?"

"Your favorite color? Is it black?"

"Mmhmm."

"Knew it."

"Yours?" I wasn't in the mood for making conversation, but his voice helped me relax. My eyes still wandered to everything that was going on around me—like the receptionist being a bitch to people demanding information.

"Green. What are you looking at?"

"Are you sure we're in the emergency room?" I whispered to him. He turned my head to the big red sign that read *Emergency Room*.

"I don't think anyone here has an emergency."

"Shh…" He put his hand on my knee. I never thought I would ever get shushed. Ever. I was the one who usually shushed people. It didn't sit right with me. I nudged my knee away from him and scooted an inch away from him.

"I want to go home."

"We already filled out all the paperwork. What's wrong?"

"I don't want to be here," I said.

"You were fine five minutes ago."

"And now I'm not, Ethan." My tone rose to a higher pitch. I looked around and saw a couple people were staring at me. I looked down and started shaking.

"Portia Willows," I heard someone say. Thank God. I walked quickly over to the nurse and we went to a room with a scale and a bed inside.

"May 1, 1992?" she asked.

I nodded.

"Have a seat."

I sat down. She shined a light in my eyes. She was moving so fast. Ethan hadn't even told her what was wrong with me yet. While she was measuring my heart rate she asked, "What brings you in today?"

"She passed out earlier," Ethan said.

No, I didn't.

"When's the last time you ate?"

"This morning."

"How much water do you drink?"

"She has a social anxiety problem. It's not unusual for her to have panic attacks in public places. This was…scarier. I was just worried if there was something going on that was making it worse for her. She's been getting better," Ethan told her. I stared at Ethan while he stuttered, explaining. The lady just stared blankly. No expression at all.

"Are you on any medication?" she asked me.

I shook my head.

"Pee in this cup, but it's most likely just the disorder. We have brochures for mental health at reception," she said.

I nodded as I took the cup into the bathroom. How was I supposed to pee in this cup? I didn't have to pee. Ethan kept talking to her. I couldn't make out what he was saying—something about my dad? I couldn't hear her. Maybe she wasn't talking back? I put my ear against the door.

"Like I said, referrals are at the front desk. We only deal with emergencies here," the lady said back to him.

"Okay, thanks," he said, and they stopped talking.
That was when I felt the pressure—I got a little out. Hopefully, it would be enough. I opened the door and handed her the cup.

"I'm also going to run a mandatory pregnancy test, okay?"
I nodded, and she left.

"What were you guys talking about?"

"Just asking if there was anything else she could do," he said.

"What do you expect? Dying people are coming here to be saved. I'm not dying. I don't need to be saved." I kissed him on the cheek.

"Well…sorry…this was a big waste of our time."

"At least I'm okay."

"Yeah…" he said, and put his arm around my neck and kissed my head. We were both smiling when she came back in with a piece of paper in her hand.

"Did you know you were pregnant?"

I didn't understand what she'd said until I felt Ethan's hand leave my shoulder. I froze. Nothing came out.

"Are you sure?" Ethan grabbed the paper.

"I wish I could sit here and talk about your options but there are a lot of people waiting…congratulations."

Ethan slowly walked out of the room ahead of me. He couldn't keep his eyes off the paper. He wouldn't even look at me. At the time, I didn't really believe it. Doctors made mistakes like this all the time.

There was no possible way. Was there?

"You didn't say anything the whole way home," I said as we pulled up in front of my house. I was still in denial. I would have laughed if it weren't for Ethan's face. He looked so confused. What did he expect? He didn't wrap it up. I couldn't tell what he was thinking. I hated that feeling more than anything.

"This can't be happening."

"I was so careful. I was so fucking careful." Ethan's tone was so harsh I jumped in my own seat. I guess this was real. Ethan never cussed.

"No, you weren't."

"I always pulled out." He sounded so defensive.

"We only did it like five times," I said.

It was slowly starting to hit me. I needed to make sense of it. I thought back to every time we'd had sex.

How did this happen?

"All right…um…" He took a deep breath.

Neither of us wanted to leave the car.

"I can't believe this is happening." My chest started closing in. I couldn't hold it in. I broke down crying. "Oh God. Oh God. I'm…I'm…what the fuck."

I felt like throwing up.

"I need a cigarette," I choked out.

"Tell me about it." Ethan grabbed the cigarettes, put one in his mouth, and then handed one to me. I moved my hand to grab it but he pulled it away from me.

"What?" I asked.

"Shit."

He looked down at the cigarette.

"Fuck," he said.

I closed my eyes and tears started to stroll down my face. I got out of the car and slammed the door. I heard him follow me.

"Hey, look at me."

I didn't want to. I didn't even want to look at myself. I turned around and dried my tears.

"Get some sleep tonight. We're going to talk about this tomorrow, okay?"

I nodded.

He hugged me. I didn't let go. A part of me was happy because he was hugging me.

But he was going to walk away after this.

In the movies, the guys never come back.

"Can we tell our parents together?"

He nodded.

"They do that in the afterschool specials," I said.

"This isn't an afterschool special. This is real life," he told me as he wiped my tears away.

"Do you still love me?" My voice choked up as tears rolled right over his fingers.

"Of course, baby. We're going to figure this out. I'm not going anywhere," he said, and we kissed. I trusted him as he walked across the street, but I was still more scared than I'd ever been in my life.

I didn't want to check on my dad. I didn't want to talk to him. I didn't even want to see him. I had a lot of homework to do, but all I wanted to do was sleep, wake up, and pretend that tonight didn't happen.

The next morning, I got up early. For the first five minutes, I forgot about yesterday, but as I was walking down the hallway to wake up my dad, it hit me. I stopped dead in my tracks. I put my hand on my stomach and shook my head. I felt tears start to form, but I had to shake them off.

"Hey, Dad." He was already up in his room getting dressed. I just stared at him.

I should tell him. I should tell him right now.

"Hey, buddy," he said. "You okay?" He noticed.

"Yeah, is there coffee?"

"Yup."

I went down into the living room and sat next to him. I kept glancing at him while I did my homework. I really wanted to say it—just blurt it out—but I was terrified. I kept thinking about what Piper would say. Mom would kill me in a heartbeat. Piper would tell me exactly what to do. I had always thought that if I got pregnant too young, I would get an abortion. There would be no way I would "just figure it out" like so many girls did on *Sixteen and Pregnant*. Now that it was really happening, though, I didn't have my mother or my sister. Things were so different, I didn't know what to think. When I tried to wrap my head around this, I gave myself a headache.

"You sure you're okay, hon?" He scooted closer to me.

I quickly closed the tab I'd been looking at—the Planned Parenthood website.

"Yeah, why?"

"You seem different. Are you still feeling sick?"

"Nope. I feel a lot better."

"Good. You're not going to smoke a cigarette with your coffee?" he asked.

I shook my head. "I had one earlier."

"Hmm…" Dad knew me way too well. I always had a cigarette with my coffee, like clockwork. I had to tell him soon or else he was going to think something worse. I hated lying to him. Whenever I lied to him, he always found out. I wasn't good at lying like Piper always was. Ethan needed to come over, quick.

I decided to go upstairs and write Piper a letter, something I hadn't done in a very, very long time.

Dear Piper,

I miss you so much I can't even look at someone else's face without wishing it's yours. I just found out I'm pregnant. Ethan is being really nice about it. I don't think I'm going to keep it. I can't, right? I really need you right now. I really need you to tell me what to do. What if Ethan breaks up with me? What if Dad hates me and kicks me out? I don't even have a job. Oh, Piper. I wish you were the one pregnant. I feel like you would definitely want to get an abortion. I would tell you no just because I'm your big sister, and I wouldn't want you to go through that. If you were dead set on having one, I would be by your side, holding your hand, the whole time. I can't deal with this. I can't deal with having a baby without you. I love you.

Always thinking of you.

Your big sis,

Portia

There was a knock at the door. I stopped writing.

"It's me," Ethan called.

"Come in," I said.

He came in with his laptop and books. Like he was coming over to do homework—just this time the homework wasn't for school.

"Hi," he mumbled, kissing my forehead and then sitting across from me. I smiled. "What are you doing?"

"Nothing," I said. I stashed the letter in the box with the others and put it away in my closet. "So…" I started.

"I've been doing research," Ethan said as he opened his computer.

"Me, too. Planned Parenthood has horrible reviews. We can't go to a free clinic, but I can ask Susan for some money…"

"Wait, wait, wait. Slow down. You don't want to have it?"

"Ethan, we can't!" I was taken aback.

"I did research on how we can make this work," he said. I couldn't believe it. We were way too young for this. But he wasn't joking. He legitimately wanted me to keep this baby.

"I already have a father I have to take care of. I still have college I need to get through…how *exactly* do you think we're going to make this work?"

"We have to tell Susan, and your grandma. I have to tell my family. We'll have help."

"I can't ask them for that," I said.

"We can both get jobs."

"Me? Get a job?" I always knew one day I was going to have to get a job. I was just hoping I was going to graduate first and I would work in an office or from home. I was never going to get a part-time job. That wasn't me. I still had panic attacks. There were so many reasons why I couldn't have this baby.

I really had no idea where Ethan was coming from.

"Portia. My mom had an abortion before she had me. Sarah and I were supposed to have an older brother. I always felt like I took his place. He never got a chance at life."

I couldn't believe I was hearing this right now. I empathized and wanted to comfort him, but couldn't deal with it.

"Oh my God," I groaned.

"You have to get help with your issues. Our lives are about to change. It's going to take a lot of work, but if we are by each other's side the entire time, we can make it through," he said earnestly. I usually loved when Ethan talked like this. It warmed my heart. But this time, I just felt like throwing up.

"I don't think…I don't know…we have nine months," I said,

panicked.

He grabbed my arms and gripped my wrists.

"Look at me," he demanded. I didn't want to.

"Portia," he said.

I looked at him, but not like I usually did. I felt like I was completely alone in this. I wanted this baby out of me. Not an inch of me thought this would ever work out, no matter what we did. Susan could give us each one million dollars and I still wouldn't be able to be a mother.

"Let's go tell your dad." He grabbed my hand and stood up.

"Can we tell yours first?" Anything to delay telling my dad I was killing this baby and I needed his help.

"Sure…" he said.

I'd never walked more slowly in my entire life.

"Come on. We got this." He pushed me gently to make me walk faster and then massaged my shoulders.

My heart was beating so fast, I felt like it was going to explode, and I wouldn't care because the baby would die and I would die, too. I wouldn't have to be here.

Portia Willows did not deal with issues like this.

Portia Willows kept to herself and didn't talk to anyone. She stayed out of drama.

This was why Portia didn't let anyone into her life.

I wished I could say I regretted meeting Ethan, but I didn't. I was still in love with him, just not in love with his baby.

"Dad, Portia's here." Ethan called when we walked into his house. We sat in the living room.

"Oh. Great. I'll be right in," he answered.

"Can you get us some water?" Ethan yelled. I thought it was strange because Ethan never asked his father to do things. He would normally have just left me in the living room and gotten the water himself. It was sweet he didn't want to leave me alone.

"Deep breaths," he whispered to me.

"I'm fine." *I was fine*. I was nervous at first, but as soon as I sat down on that couch, I realized that just because we were telling his father didn't mean I had to have this baby.

"How are you? It's nice to see you." He gave me a hug and placed a glass of water on the coffee table.

"It's been a while. Hasn't it?"

"Yeah, I guess," I mumbled. I looked at Ethan.

"Dad, we have to tell you something."

"Okay…" He sat back in his chair. I drank the water.

"Portia, uh, wasn't…feeling too well yesterday, so I took her to the emergency room," Ethan said.

Mr. Torke immediately contorted his face to a worried look

Oh, just you save that.

Ethan was sweating bullets. I couldn't help but wipe his face with my bare hands and then wipe my hand off on his jeans. He had been so confident two minutes ago.

"What's going on, boy?" Mr. Torke's face was stone cold and hard. The way he was staring at Ethan reminded me of how my mom looked at Piper and me when we were acting out.

"She ended up being fine, just a panic attack, but when we were there…"

"I can't take this. I'm pregnant," I burst out. "You were taking way too long," I said, looking at Ethan.

Mr. Torke slammed his fist down onto the coffee table. "Dammit, Ethan. What the hell were you thinking?" He screamed in Ethan's face. Ethan just stayed sitting with his head down.

Maybe we should have told my dad first.

"Did your mother never fucking teach you to fucking put on a condom?" Mr. Torke's face got bright red.

"Dad. We did. I was careful. It just happened," he said. Ethan was scared.

"No. It didn't 'just happen.' You guys were irresponsible. What the fuck are you going to do now? You don't have jobs. You're in community college, Ethan. She's sick. She needs help, and now you went and got her pregnant." He threw his water against the wall. He wanted to punch Ethan, I knew he did. Ethan's hands were shaking. I felt so terrible.

"I'm not keeping it." I stood up. I couldn't let this fight go on anymore.

"Yes, we are." Ethan stood up and looked his dad in his face with regained courage.

"Figure it out, but know this, I am *not* helping you. I helped you enough with this one," Mr. Torke said calmly, pointing at me.

"Dad, she's right here. Have some respect."

"Clean this up." Mr. Torke stared at Ethan with disappointment.

"I'm going to go…" I turned around and ran.

I burst through my front door crying.

"Daddy! Daddy!" I ran around the house looking for him. He came running down the stairs.

"Portia? What's wrong?"

I ran over to him and he picked me up like he used to when I was five. I cried so hard into his arms. He walked us over to the couch.

"Are you okay? Are you hurt? Talk to me."

I sat down. I started hyperventilating.

"Relax, honey. What's going on? Do I need to call 9-1-1?"
I shook my head. "No. I need your help."

"Anything," he said, and put his arm around me. "What's going on?"

"I'm pregnant. I need you to come with me to get an abortion. Ethan wants to keep it. Mr. Torke is pissed and everything is falling apart, Daddy."

He didn't say a word, just hugged me and rocked me. I felt like a little girl again in his arms.

I wanted to be that little girl again.

"It's going to be okay. You're going to be okay."

"Since I'm getting an abortion, you think it's okay to have a cigarette?"

He nodded and got up.

"Better yet, relax," he said. He came back with a beer *and* a cigarette.

I instantly felt better.

Ethan came over later after my dad went to sleep. I was lying down.

"Portia…"

"What?"

"Can I lie down with you?"

"You already got me pregnant. Nothing worse can happen," I said.

He lay down next to me and I turned to face him. "I really don't want this kid, Ethan."

"I made an appointment for us at a women's clinic. They specialize in helping make a decision," he said.

"So, you're not making me keep it?" I got up.

"Of course not. It's your decision. It's not just *my* life." He was sad. He looked down at my stomach, and I could tell he was holding back tears. I knew because of how much he was blinking.

"I'm sorry. Since you're compromising for me, I'll compromise for you—I'll listen to what they have to say about keeping it," I said.

"I love you." His voice cracked as he kissed my forehead.

"I love you, too. Should we have sex or is that inappropriate?"

He laughed and grabbed my face, pulling me into him.

Chapter 13

We were at a clinic on the west side. It was on the second floor of an outdoor plaza. It was a small office, or at least it looked small from the waiting room. There were huge pictures of families every-where. Brochures galore. Ethan grabbed all of them. There was only one other girl in the room. She seemed young. She had long black hair. I felt bad that she was alone—she was too pretty to be pregnant and alone.

I'd been out in public twice this week. Ethan thought I was doing so much better. He appreciated me going out more for him. But I hated it. I always would. I would never be able to take my kid on walks or to the park. Oh my God. I wondered if I would get over that. I'd never even asked myself if I wanted kids. I'd never even thought about it. Dreaming about the future had been Piper's forte.

"Can you just fill this out for me, please? It's stressing me out," I said, handing him the clipboard. I noticed that he didn't ask me how to answer any of the questions on there. He knew everything there was to know about me.

We got called in twenty minutes later. There were baby pictures everywhere.

"Hi. I'm Ashley." A short girl with short brown hair, green eyes, and the hugest smile in the entire world practically screamed at me.

"I'm Ethan, and this is my girlfriend, Portia"

"Nice to meet you both. Let's have a seat in our secret room," she said. She was talking to us like we were little kids, but she was extremely nice. Way too nice for pregnant me. We sat on the couch and Ethan put his arm around me.

"First off, why don't you guys tell me a little about yourselves?"

"We're both students. Portia is a junior at UCLA and I'm in my second year at SMC."

"UCLA. Wow. You must be really smart."

I didn't know why everyone thought that. There were a lot of dumb students in my online classes. Ashley smiled with her big mouth. I shrugged.

"So, have you guys thought about what you want to do?"

"I don't want it. He does," I said.

"I don't feel like we're ready right now, but I feel like if we start now, we could be ready in nine months."

"Let me tell you, no one is *ever* prepared to have a baby. Not even aspiring parents who have been trying for years. You have no idea what it's going to be like until you actually experience it. Every baby is different. We offer classes for first-time parents, young parents, and low-income parents. We can definitely help you on this journey," she said. It must have been music to Ethan's ears.

"Do you guys help with the other options?" I asked.

"Of course. Our referrals are the best. If you want to put the baby up for adoption, we have hundreds of potential families," she said.

I hadn't thought about adoption.

We spent an hour talking about all the possibilities. Ashley was definitely gearing us up to want to keep it. It was like Ethan had given her a heads-up or something. At the end of the meeting, I really didn't know what to think anymore. There was a lot to take in. It was extremely overwhelming.

"Would you guys like to know the sex today?"

I could have sworn she asked if we wanted to have sex today.

"Yes." Ethan didn't even hesitate.

I looked at him like I wasn't sure. Ethan looked back at me and nodded.

I nodded back. Here goes nothing.

"It may be too soon to tell, but Nurse Lily will take great of you."

I timidly took off my clothes in the bathroom. I just looked down the entire time. All of sudden, I had this huge rush of fear. I was trying to keep it together before walking into the room where I would see it. I quickly slipped on the gown and opened the door. Ethan was standing right there. I jumped.

"Jesus, you scared me." I rolled my eyes.

"I wanted to make sure you knew what room to go in. It's this one." He pointed to the door on the right.

I took baby steps. No pun intended.

"Hey, look at me real quick. They're obviously pro-life here. Ultimately, it's your decision. We don't have to know the sex if you really don't want to." He placed his hand on my back and I suddenly realized why I was scared to know the sex—because if I knew the sex, I would want it. I would start to imagine our lives with a baby girl or a baby boy. I walked into the room and sat down on the chair covered in white paper.

"I hope it's not too soon. Too bad she didn't tell us how long you've been pregnant."

"Well...Ashley was super nice."

"Yeah. She definitely made me feel a lot better." He smiled at me as he grabbed my knee and shook it. *God, who knew this would be happening to us?*

"This is way too much for me right now. I don't want to talk about this anymore today. Ashley talked enough," I said. Nurse Lily came in.

"Portia Willows?" I nodded. "Birthday May 1, 1992?"

"Yes."

"Awesome. Have you ever had an ultrasound before?"

"No. I've never been pregnant before."

"They're not just used for pregnancies. Just lay back and relax," she said.

Ethan stood up and grabbed my hand.

"It's going to be a tad bit cold at first, okay?" she said.

I nodded and just looked at Ethan. I didn't want to see the screen. I tensed up when the gel spread beneath my belly button.

"Relax, babe."

"So it looks like you're four weeks along. You can see it...right there..."

I wasn't going to look.

"I don't see anything," Ethan said.

I took deep breaths. I wanted this to be over so badly.

"Right there," Nurse Lily said.

"Oh my God. The jelly bean-looking thing?" he asked.

"Mmhmm."

"So is it a boy or a girl?" he asked.

"We can't tell yet. Right now, it's a jelly bean," she said.

I heaved a sigh of relief and decided to look.

"I like jelly beans," I mumbled, and turned my head.

She pointed to it again.

"That's a baby?" I asked, surprised.

"Yep, that's your growing baby."

"Wow." For a second, I kind of cared.

"Is there anything she should be doing now as far as making sure...?" Ethan started.

"Well, prenatals, healthy diet, light working out, getting an ultrasound each trimester. We have a booklet you guys are going to take home that has all the information in there you need. Obviously,

no drinking and no smoking."
Fuck. My. Life.

Present Day

"I remember…" I whispered. All these vague memories came rushing through my head like a tidal wave. I looked back at Elizabeth. I couldn't understand.

Ethan feeding her.

Us napping with her.

Her in my lap as I rocked her in a rocking chair.

"You remember Pyper?" she asked me.

"With a y," I said, looking back at how beautiful she was. I couldn't stop staring at her. I didn't remember her being able to talk. I didn't remember her being so big. It was like seeing her for the first time all over again. I couldn't help but get emotional.

Pypes had so much hair. It was curly. A pink headband held the golden curls out of her wide blue eyes. She held out her arms to me. I touched her. She was so soft. She was wearing a white sweater with a little blue dress that had pink flowers on it. It matched her headband. She touched my cheek with her tiny hand. My heart sunk and I almost melted to the floor. I couldn't help but cry.

How could I forget her?

Forget having her?

Forget she even existed?

"Hi, baby." I kissed her between her nose and forehead. I probably got tears all over her face.

She looked *exactly* like Ethan. The structured jawline. The narrow nose. The indent above her lips.

Oh my God, Ethan.

"Don't cry, Mama." she put both of her hands on my cheek. Instead, I cried harder and hugged her tight. I didn't want to let her go.

"I love you. I love you. Baby girl." I kissed her all over. I couldn't hold it together.

"Where's Ethan? Why isn't she with her father? Who are you?" I immediately got aggressive toward the lady who had been carrying her. I had no idea what was going on here. I just knew I had my baby in my arms and I want to take her home.

I wasn't going to let her go again.

"She's safe until we get everything situated," Elizabeth assured me.

"She needs to be with family. My dad can take her. Where is he? You brought my daughter but not my father," I said.

The lady who was holding Pypes looked at Elizabeth, confused. "She doesn't know?"

"Know what?" I backed away from her with Pyper. I could tell I was scaring her.

"Everything's okay, baby. Mommy's here now." I kissed her forehead.

She nodded and played with my hair. "Okay, Mommy." She smiled and placed her head down on my shoulder. Poor baby was tired.

"Nothing. We still have a lot of work to do. We should get back. I wanted you to remember her on your own and you did, but there are still a lot of memories we need to work on," Elizabeth said.

"How could I forget her? How could I ever forget this face?" I cried. "What kind of mother am I?" I held her so tight. I rubbed Pyper's back because I remembered that made her fall asleep faster. She laid her head on my shoulder.

"Post-partum depression is common…but we need to go now." She kept stepping closer to me and I kept stepping back. Elizabeth had a worried look on her face. I hadn't seen this look from Elizabeth before.

"Does she have her pink bunny?" I asked.

"I do, Mommy." She lifted her head up and looked at me.

Her eyes were so big.

How could I let her go?

"She does. You need to give her back to me," the woman said.

A wave of emotions came rushing through me. I couldn't believe I forgot her, and the second I remembered her, they were taking her away from me.

No.

Never again.

I would never forget again.

I couldn't.

"No," I cried. I started backing up.

"Portia…" Elizabeth came closer to me.

I kept backing up. I would run away with Pyper right now if either one of them came any closer to me.

"No. This is *your* fault. How could you do this to me? Where's my father? Where's Ethan? I want my family. Now." I cried. Pyper started crying, too.

"I'm sorry. I'm so sorry. I just don't want to leave you ever again," I told her, wiping her tears.

Nurses started to circle in around me.

"Portia. Listen to me. If you want to ever see that little girl again, you need to give her back to Rachel. Right now." Elizabeth stated with force.

"Fuck you. You don't even know her. Say bye, Pyper."

Pyper slowly waved.

I was ready to run with her. Elizabeth could tell because by the time I turned around. She had run over to me and grabbed both my arms, locking Pyper in between us. For a split second, I thought Elizabeth was on my side, but then Rachel grabbed Pyper's arm from behind me a second after.

Pyper let out a huge scream.

I turned around and saw my life flash before my eyes.

"No. No." I kept trying to push Elizabeth away from me but she wouldn't let go. As Rachel left through the doors with my baby, everyone was staring at me. I fell to the floor and screamed.

"Pyper. Pyper. No. No. Why are you ruining my life? What did I do? What did I *do*?" I pushed her off of me.

"You killed Ethan, Portia." Elizabeth glared at me and grabbed my shoulders tightly. I could feel her nails piercing into my skin.

I stopped screaming.

I stopped crying.

"Or rather, you tried to. He's barely hanging on in the hospital right now." There were tears in her eyes. She was sad for me.

What did I do? How? Why? No. What?

"No. That doesn't make any sense. Ethan is the father of my child, I love him." My eyes shifted left and right and I shook my head. "Where is he? Is he okay? I need to see him. I don't know what you are talking about, but if he's hurt, I want to see him." My voice choked. I broke down. "Is he okay?"

"Tell me everything you remember about Pyper," she said as she calmly rubbed my arm.

I took deep breaths and sat down on the floor. I was exhausted. I just wanted to see him.

I just wanted to know what was happening to me.

"I'm going to give you a cigarette in the room. I want you to relax, take your time. This is not going to be the last time you see Pyper. As your psychiatrist, I'm going to do everything I can to make sure you don't have to face a single day in jail."

"If I help you help me, will I be able to have my family back?"

"Yes. Unfortunately, not your whole family, but your new family, hopefully, yes." She helped me get up. She put her arm around me as we walked back into the room. The entire hospital was staring at me. That used to be my worst nightmare, but watching Pyper leave was so much worse.

Two Years Ago

Ethan and I decided we were going to keep it.

I hated not smoking and not drinking. The change in lifestyle was something I wasn't sure I could get used to. The only real pregnancy symptom I noticed was being hungry all the time. My dad made me everything. For once, I was into his weird food combinations.

"Spaghetti and chili, hot dog on sandwich bread...you wanna know what your mother ate when she was pregnant with you?"

"What?"

"Pickles and feta cheese."

"Do we even have feta cheese?"

"No, we never really had it, but she made me go to the store to get her some when the cravings were really bad."

"I'm not that hungry for once," I said.

"It's because you're stressed."

"I guess. I feel like we're in over our heads."

"Can you feel it?" My dad sat next to me and looked at my stomach.

"Not at all. I was looking online and they said parents should start to feel a connection with their unborn baby after three months. It's been over three months, I don't feel shit," I said.

He laughed.

There was a knock at the door. Of course, it was Ethan. Every time he came over, he brought boxes and boxes full of crap. He loved this baby. It was sweet. Ish.

"Looks like you don't need me to fix you anything. I'll be upstairs," Dad said as he walked up the stairs. I rolled my eyes at him.

"My mom sent over so many things. She wants to plan the baby shower," Ethan said.

"Baby shower?" I asked.

"Please tell me you know what that is," Ethan said, exasperated.

"I do…I just…I don't know…thank you." I sounded stressed. I was barely wrapping my head around this as it is and now his mom was involved.

"I know you need time, but babe, it's been three months," he said. He lifted my chin and kissed me. I didn't know if it was just because I kept thinking that this father side of him was sexy, but I was getting more comfortable being sexual with him. I hated talking about our plans, I hated talking about getting a job and preparing for the baby. I just wanted to have sex with him every second. It felt even better being pregnant. I started kissing his neck.

"I am so loving you like this." He lifted me up and took me upstairs.

"Be careful of my dad."

"It's fine. I don't see him." He looked around and then kissed my neck.

Everyone was so happy for us. Susan offered to help us financially. Everything seemed to be working out. Dad was ecstatic. Mr. Torke was still struggling with it, but he wasn't infuriated anymore.

I, on the other hand, couldn't get there.

I had seen the ultrasounds.

We had been to the doctor more than once.

I couldn't feel anything.

I didn't understand how people could expect me to be a mother when I didn't have mine. I didn't have my sister. I couldn't just bring in another life when I couldn't get over losing two other lives that were so crucial in moments like this. I needed my mother. I needed Piper. I cried every time I thought about it. God, what they would say. Piper would be so happy. I could just see how big her smile was. Mom, Oh my God, I could just see her disappointed look.

Actually, if Mom were here, I was pretty sure she would have *made* me have an abortion. Who knows? They're dead now. I had to figure this out myself. I was just not ready to face a baby shower that my mother and my sister should be at. I didn't *want* to move on. I knew they would want me to. I knew they would be happy for me. I tried to tell myself that all the time but I needed the real them to tell me that it was okay.

I wanted Mom to tell me that she was excited to be a grandma.

I wanted *them* to plan my baby shower, not Ethan's mother.

I couldn't tell Ethan. Everyone was so happy for me and I didn't want to let anyone down. I wanted people to think I was getting better. I wanted people to think I was healthy and capable of being a mother. I knew I could be.

I just needed time—and it felt like I was running out of it.

Ethan and I were lying in bed and I was tired. I was getting ready to take a nap but he could tell something was up. Ethan looked at me with his worrisome eyes.

"I love you. I love this baby. I want us to start a family. I want you to give a shit about us, about her, about yourself."

"Her?" I asked. We never found out the gender. I didn't want to know. I still wouldn't look at the ultrasound. I still didn't want this to be real. But I knew it was happening. I just couldn't process it.

"Shit..."

"You knew?" I asked, sitting up.

"Yeah...I know *you* didn't want to know yet. You didn't even get to see her, but I did. The nurse gave me the ultrasound pictures. They're in my room—right next to a picture of you," he said, and sat up next to me.

I couldn't respond to that.

"I'm sorry. I didn't mean to slip," he said as he rubbed my legs.

"Stop. Stop being so perfect. You're allowed to be worried, to be scared. We don't have to have everything figured out when this baby comes," I said, slightly annoyed.

"When *she* comes." Ethan smiled and got closer to me.
I backed away.

"Give me time. In the next six months, I'll be the best mother ever. I promise. I care, Ethan. I love you more than anything. I want this. I want this with you. Bear with me, please."

I think.

I wanted to think that.

I knew he needed to hear it. He was being so good. He deserved to know that everything was okay even though it wasn't. I kissed his cheek.

He nodded.

Chapter 14

A couple weeks later, I was feeling more comfortable with the fact that I was going to have a baby. Ethan and I were in a really good place. I was up to take a walk because Ethan had read this book that said it was beneficial for pregnant women to get light exercise. Ingrid was watering her grass. I haven't seen her since I started showing and it wasn't like I talked to her. She stopped watering and looking at my stomach. Her hand went to her mouth and then she smiled.

"Oh my. Congratulations, Portia. So happy for you."

I smiled. "Thanks, Ingrid, have a good day." I kept walking and looked over at Ethan, smiling at both of us.

"Susan and your grandma want to take us out to lunch," Ethan said.

"When did you guys exchange numbers?"

"When we first met. Speaking of Susan, she offered me a job at your mom's advertising company. I didn't say yes or no. I told her I would have to talk to you first," he said.

I stopped walking. I didn't know why I felt off about it. That company was the reason we still had a house and why I got to continue studying at UCLA. It just felt weird for Ethan to be working there. It made me think, *Should I be working?* This was legitimately the first step to our adulthood. I knew it was coming but it felt really soon.

"You can do that and keep going to school at Santa Monica College?" I asked.

"I'll be getting my AA this semester. I was thinking maybe you and I could take a class at UCLA. An early childhood development class. It'll help us in more way than one."

No. No. He was absolutely insane.

There was no fucking way.

"Yeah, sure," I said. I hated not being able to express my feelings.

I *wanted* to be able to tell Ethan that I wasn't a hundred percent happy with having our baby because of my dead mother and sister.

I *wanted* to be able to tell him that everything was happening so fast and I didn't know how to deal with it.

"What do you want me to do, Ethan?"

"What do you mean?" he asked.

"I need you to tell me what you think I should do. Do I need to find an office job or something? Do I need to completely change everything about me?"

Because it sure fucking sounds like it.

"No. You're destined for greatness. You're smart. You need to graduate and get a real job—a career. Relationships are all about sacrifices, Portia," he said.

"Okay, so what's the plan? I continue going to UCLA online. We take that class together. I get a part-time office job. You have the agency job. How do we take care of our baby?"

"I'm going to talk to Susan. You may not need to get a job, you'll be taking care of her twenty-four seven."

Ethan had this all planned out. He was beginning to make me think we could actually do it. I just didn't think I could actually *be* a mother, especially without my mother and sister helping. How was I supposed to raise my child to be the greatest when I couldn't even take her out in public? There was still a lot I needed to work on before I took on someone else.

"We need to figure out my social issues first," I said.

"What do you mean?"

"I need to get over my fear of going to public places."

"You are. I can't believe you haven't noticed. Look around, you're outside. You said hi to Ingrid for God's sake. When I first met you, you would have never agreed to this," he said.

"Yeah, when I'm with *you*. But I still can't actually go to UCLA. I can't make any new friends. I can't order my own food at a restaurant," I said, frustrated.

"Like you said, everything can't be perfect." He stopped and turned to me.

"What?"

"Relax, babe. We got this." He rubbed my arms in reassurance. I believed him. Because he believed in me.

Susan, Grandma, Ethan, and I were having lunch at Troy's Bistro. The last time Grandma and I had been out together in public it was the funeral, and before that, it was never. Susan was on her lunch break so I knew no matter what, it wouldn't last long.

"So, Ethan, I want to bring you back with me to meet with some of the trainers. We're going to see where we can fit you in and we'll give you a tour," Susan said. *I'd* never gotten a tour of my mom's company. I heard they had a huge picture of her in the reception area. I really didn't want Ethan to leave me with Grandma, but I knew he had to do this for us. He was the one sacrificing by leaving school.

"Did you see any of those doctors I told you about in my letter?" Grandma asked me. I hadn't opened any mail in two years. I was definitely not going to start now.

"No, Grandma, I didn't get your letter."

"What kind of doctors?" Susan asked.

"Portia still has a lot of issues she needs to work out before she becomes a mother," Grandma said.

Technically, I'd needed to work out those issues a long time ago, but no one had said anything then.

I guess I should have gotten pregnant at sixteen.

"We all know that, but I mean I think those problems will work themselves out once the baby comes. You'll be forced to change. I was forced to change…five different times."

Susan was a horrible mother.

Susan also sounded exactly like *my* mother.

I could definitely mother a child if she could. I may not be the best mother but I could keep up.

"I'm talking about the dad issue," Grandma said as she looked at Ethan.

"What's my dad's issue? He's fine. Grandma, don't start, please," I said.

"He's not, baby. He's not. And you need to move on from him. You're about to have a baby. You can't take care of him anymore," Grandma continued lecturing.

"That's interesting, because while Ethan is at school, Dad is taking care of *me*. He fixes me dinner. He's really getting a lot stronger and better," I said.

Grandma glared at Ethan. Ethan looked down as he stuffed his face with pasta. I couldn't believe Ethan wasn't defending me. He was there. He saw what went on in our house more than anyone.

"Let's not talk about this anymore. Can we please talk about the baby shower?" Susan interrupted.

"Susan. I don't want one," I snapped. All of sudden, I just felt so emotional. I wanted to cry. I looked around the restaurant and it felt like everyone was watching my family attacking me.

It got really hot.

I felt my heart closing in.

I downed the water that was in front of me.

"I don't care. It's free gifts. Your mom would kill me if I didn't throw her child a baby shower," she said.

I looked at her like I had been immediately convinced because she mentioned my mother. I calmed myself down, miraculously.

Grandma nodded with her mouth full. I couldn't believe how chill everyone was being. Why was no one mad at me? Why was this a good thing, as if I hadn't been trying for years?

"Can I ask you guys something?" It was my turn to talk.

"Yeah, babe, what's up?" Ethan put his arm around me.

"Why are you guys being so chill about this? Mom would kill me. Mom would ground me forever. Mom would make me get an abortion. Piper wouldn't want me to keep it either. Dad doesn't care what I do as long as I'm okay. But you guys..."

"Portia, you're not a teenager anymore. You're an adult. This happens to adults. I had a child in high school. I made it work. Gary and I weren't even together then. You're going to one of the best schools in the state, you have a boyfriend, and you have a home. You're twenty years old," Susan said.

Grandma started crying.

"You need this baby because you lost everyone. You deserve this." I'd never seen Grandma this vulnerable before. But I completely understood what she meant. I'd had four people in my family—but now I only had my dad. With Ethan and this baby, it was four again and the baby would be Piper's niece, Mom's grandchild.

"This is horrible timing. I'm so sorry, but my break is over," Susan said.

I panicked for a minute because I wasn't going to have Ethan by my side to walk out of the restaurant but I had to be able to do this.

"It's okay," I told her.

Ethan got his stuff and kissed me. "You sure?" he asked.

I nodded.

He kissed my forehead and whispered, "So proud of you. You're doing great."

"Thanks. Do you need me to pick you up?" I asked him.

"No. I barely like you driving home alone."

"I'm fine. I'm going to be a mother. If I can't take care of myself…" We kissed. He left with Susan.

"Are you ready, sweetheart? Susan already got the check," Grandma said.

"Okay," I said.

Grandma got up. I looked around the restaurant and then looked at Grandma wobbling out and I followed her outside.

"I love you, honey. I don't mean to get on you, I just want you to be the best you can be," she said.

"It's fine, Grandma. I understand. I have six months to get better. If you want me to see someone, I will, but only for six months." Her face brightened. She hugged me so tight I got embarrassed.

"You and I should go out more often," she said.

"Maybe…with the baby," I said.

"I'll take it," she giggled.

Five Years Ago

"Portia, sweetie, you okay?" Grandma came up the stairs. I was staring at myself in the mirror wearing black jeans, a black t-shirt, and a black baseball cap.

"Yeah," I mumbled.

"You're wearing that?"

"Dad's not ready yet," I told her.

"We need to leave in five minutes. We're already running late."

"Don't blame me. Dad's still getting used to moving around," I said.

"Car. Both of you, five minutes."

My dad was tying his tie in the mirror. I hopped on the bed and looked at him.

"You really don't have a black dress?" he asked.

"Nope. I wish someone would say something else to me. It's my sister and my mother in those caskets and you're really going to tell me to put on a dress?"

He laughed.

"Dad, you shouldn't laugh. Our family is dead."

"You're right. Beer me?"

179

"You already had, like, three and it's only one p.m."

"Our family is dead, Portia."

Touché.

Dad was sitting in the backseat of Grandma's car when we saw what seemed like the whole world waiting at the church. I'd never seen so many people in one place in my entire life. I looked at Dad in the rearview mirror.

"You think we would get the same turnout if you and I had died?"

Dad met my eyes. He was drunk. He didn't want to deal with this and neither did I, especially since there were so many people here and all the attention was going to be on us.

"Dad, if you leave me, I will kill you and put you in a casket right next to them," I hissed.

Grandma looked over at me. Dad grabbed my shoulder and squeezed it. I didn't know what I would have done without him. What if he *had* died? Dad knew me best. He was just like me. All my personality traits, I got from him. What if it was Piper and him and I was stuck with just Mom? I loved Mom, but we always fought. Dad and I never fought. It sounded so fucked up, but right now, I just knew that I lost people I loved and I had to mourn them in front of a hundred people. My hands wouldn't stop shaking. I didn't want to be here. I didn't want "here" to even exist.

"Just look down," he said.

I did. I had sunglasses on. He had sunglasses on. We both just looked down and walked. We followed Grandma. I felt everyone's eyes on us. I could feel the tension and the pity. Some of my dad's friends were there, too—it was strange.

"Dad, do you know those guys?" I asked as we sat in the re-served seats in the first row. Every now and then I looked around to see who had come. Basically, the whole high school was here. I saw a lot of my teachers. It was the most surreal funeral ever.

"We'll have to talk to them later."

"You don't have to talk to anyone, just talk to me. I won't leave your side."

"Shh. We don't want to give people more to talk about," Grandma said.

What? Are you fucking kidding me?

I looked at my dad, I was about to punch his mother in the face. He grabbed onto me tightly and I put my head down on his chest. I just wanted to be buried. People kept going up and talking about Mom like she was a fucking saint.

The thing was, she was a saint. Not at home, though. She did a lot of charity work. She wasn't a mean boss. She was strong, detail-oriented, badass, and strict. She wasn't abusive, unfair, or insane. She was like the perfect parent, just not the perfect parent to a fucked-up child like me.

Listening to everyone talk about Piper was heartbreaking. Everyone loved her. They told stories with inside jokes that I didn't get, but I remembered hearing about them in my bed, in my room, on my floor, in the bathroom. She used to tell me everything that happened to her. It was like I was being reminded of how great she was. I kept crying, but couldn't stop smiling. It was so hard. I wanted to go home and keep writing letters. I wanted to be in her room. I wanted to dress up in Mom's clothes. I wanted to pretend they were both still here. The hundred people standing here telling me how sorry they were made it real.

They were dead.

They were gone.

They weren't coming back.

181

Susan held the wake at my house. I hadn't touched anything, so it was like they could come in any minute. Maddie was eating a brownie Aunt Dora made.

I didn't say anything, just looked her up and down.

"I was wondering if I could see her room. She always told me if she ever died, I could have her pink skirt. She told me that in middle school. She loved that skirt. I don't plan on ever wearing it. I just want to have it," she said.

"Come on…" I took her up to Piper's room. When I opened the door, she immediately broke down crying. Maddie was Piper's best friend. She came over to dinner a lot, but we never talked. I never talked to any of her other friends. Most of her friends thought I was weird, but *everyone* in high school thought I was weird. Maddie was the only friend who had actually tried with me. She said hi. I would say hey—that was the sum of our relationship.

"It's like…"

"I haven't touched anything. I don't plan on it," I said.

"Oh God. All her stuff. Her clothes are everywhere," Maddie said.

"She couldn't figure out what to wear to school that day. She was listening to Britney Spears. She was too busy dancing around… so this is what her room was like."

"She was so happy and excited."

"Yeah, it was definitely the earliest she ever woke up. I heard she was telling everyone in school about the play."

"She asked the teacher to make an announcement. She did it in all her classes." Maddie sat down on Piper's bed.

"Yeah…the library was the last time I saw her. Lunchtime. Twelve hours before she died. Well, maybe not exactly, but it was way too long," I said.

"Oh my God."

"And it was only for five seconds. I had no idea those were going to be the last five seconds I was ever going to have with her…" I trailed off.

Maddie came over to hug me. I backed away from her.

"Find the skirt." I nodded at Piper's closet. She began looking through it.

"Portia…" Dad was coming up the stairs.

"Yeah, Maddie just wanted to grab something Piper said she could have."

"Okay…I can't handle all that downstairs. I'm going to take a nap," he said.

"With a six-pack," I mumbled. He had a six-pack of Heineken. He probably got it from one of his friends at the funeral. He grabbed one and gave it to me.

"Here…"

"Dad…I'm only seventeen," I said.

"Our family is dead," he responded. It had become a thing between us now. I had never drank before—not even a sip, but if it could help my dad deal with it…

"I found it," I heard Maddie call, and went back into Piper's room.

Maddie asked, "What were you doing?"

"Drinking a beer," I said, holding it up.

"I'm really sorry, Portia. I'm here if you ever need someone to talk to," she said.

I nodded and took a sip. It was disgusting. I lay down on Piper's bed. I just kept asking myself why couldn't they just have come home? Why couldn't they just come home after the play? Why? We never got into car accidents. My dad was a great driver, especially with us in the car. I didn't get it. Something wasn't right. I knew death was not supposed to make sense and it happens and we're supposed to deal with it. But how the fuck was I supposed to deal with this? How the fuck was I supposed to accept that my little sixteen-year-old sister had to die on the opening night of her high school play because of a goddamn car accident. The world could not be this cruel.

The beer tasted much better now.

"Knock, knock..." Dad said.

"What?"

"Everyone is gone. It's just you and me."

"Thank God. Can I have another beer, Dad?"

"I don't know, Mom would be so disappointed and would have my ass," he said.

"She's dead." We both headed down to the kitchen and saw that a lot of people had brought food.

"Oh my God. I don't think Mom ever cooked this much."

"There are brownies, salads, pasta...everything." As we were looking at all the flowers, food, and leftover crap people brought, I saw a letter on the coffee table that said *Portia*. I froze.

"Dad. Dad." I freaked.

"What?" he said, his voice muffled with his mouth full of potato chips.

"Who left that note?"

"I don't know, I didn't see."

I picked it up. It was from Susan.

Dear Portia,

I'm so sorry about what happened. I'm taking over your mom's advertising company. I wanted to tell you before you heard from someone else. I'm not replacing your mother by any means. I loved her. She was my best friend and taught me everything I know. I'm going to make sure this company thrives in her name. She loved you more than anything. She talked about you all the time. She was worried about you. I want you to be able to go for your dreams in your mother's honor. Go to UCLA—your tuition will be paid for. Stay at

the house if you like—the mortgage will be paid for. Get an apart-
ment near school or live on campus, do whatever you want. Gary
and I are here for you. We love you. Please don't hesitate to call us
if you need anything. I won't be a stranger in your life. I will always
be there for you.

    Love,
    Susan

Chapter 15

Susan was Mom's best friend, the company *should* go to her. It was nice that she was willing to pay for everything. I was just so happy we got to keep the house. Mom and Piper were still here with me when I was in it. I didn't ever want to leave.

"It's a letter from Susan," I said.

"She was just here, why did she leave a letter?"

"I don't know. I was in Piper's room."

"So…what did she say?" he said, and plopped down on the couch.

"She's going to take over for Mom—for work and us." I read the letter over again because I was sort of in shock. I sat on the edge of the chair across from Dad and sat the letter on the table.

"What does that mean? She's not living here. I'm not sharing a bed with her."

"Dad! No, she's just going to pay for our house because I know *you* didn't pay for the house. She's going to send me to UCLA. Remember when I got in? Everyone was so happy for me."

"Yeah…I'm glad that it could still work out. And who told you I didn't pay for the house?" He got defensive.

"Piper overheard you and Mom fighting about it in your room. She was scared that you guys were going to get divorced, and she woke me up so I could listen."

"Damn it! So my baby girl knew, too."

"Dad, it doesn't matter. Mom was the one with the job."

"I had a lot of jobs, you know. I wanted to be the working one. Her job just made more money than mine did. She didn't want to hire nannies, so it was up to me."

I got up from the chair and sat closer to him on the couch.

"Dad, no one cares. Do you really think I care that you didn't pay for the house because you're the *dad*?"

"I wanted to make sure you guys grew up knowing I was the provider," he said.

I laughed. "Wow. So you were going to raise us to be sexist. It's 2010. So what?"

"Thanks, sweetie. What do you have to do for UCLA?"

"I don't even know right now. I have a couple months to figure it out."

"Until then, we mourn." He pulled a pack of cigarettes out of nowhere.

My mouth dropped. "Where did you get those?"

"My secret hiding spot...under the cushions. Since when did you ever see Mom relax on this couch?" He smiled as he pulled a cigarette out with his mouth.

"Never. I never really saw mom relax at *all* now that I think about it."

I knew he smoked, but he did a really good job hiding it from Mom and Piper. I caught him once freshman year. He told me he was quitting and I never cared if he actually did or not.

"You're going to smoke in the house now?"

"Yup, want one?" What the hell was going on? First, he gave me a beer. Now, he was giving me a cigarette? He must really be hurting. I felt so bad.

"I don't know how to help you, Dad," I said.

"I don't know how to help *you*. I just know this helps me," he said.

I grabbed it from him. "What do I do?" I asked.

"Put it in your mouth like this," he said as he grabbed another cigarette and put it between his lips. I did the same. I put it way too far into my mouth at first. He grabbed it and fixed it.

"Just lips. Just press it with your lips." He lit it. "Slowly suck and inhale," he instructed.

I didn't *slowly* suck. I coughed. It was so disgusting. I had to spit.

"You didn't do it slow enough," he said.

"I'm good, Dad." I laughed and passed it back to him. I didn't know what to think. I couldn't really tell dad not to drink and not to smoke. That's what mom would say and I didn't want to be like her. Or should I tell him not to because that's what mom would do? I wanted my dad to feel better—physically and mentally.

For now, if this was it—so be it.

Two Years Ago

Ethan was still in school while he worked an entry-level job at my mom's company. He described it like being everybody's assistant. We were taking the child development class at UCLA. We sat in the back. Ethan took notes like a maniac. Whenever I looked over at him, I couldn't help but giggle. This class was one of the only times we got to see each other. He was always so tired from work. He never wanted to go anywhere—which was awesome—but he definitely wasn't himself, so I knew something was really wrong.

"Hey, you okay?" I asked one day as we were walking out of class. There were thousands of students staring at me because I was visibly pregnant. I wasn't scared or panicked. You couldn't say I was cured, but I was definitely capable.

"Yeah, I just can't wait to be done with school. I'm going to be up until three in the morning doing homework and then I have to up at seven thirty for work," he said.

"Do you want to come over? I can help you with homework," I offered. I always helped him with homework. I was surprised he hadn't already asked me to.

"I don't want to keep you up. Plus, my dad wants to make sure I'm doing everything I'm supposed to be doing." He sighed.

"What's that supposed to mean?" Since when did he care so much about what his dad thought? I didn't like this new dad Ethan.

This adult Ethan. Ethan was so good at taking care of me. I didn't know how to take care of him when he was feeling like this. Now, I was anxious.

When we got back home, he didn't come inside.

"Let's talk tomorrow. I love you." He sounded stressed.

I just stared at him as he crossed the street.

This wouldn't be happening if I'd decided to have an abortion.

When I walked inside, I saw Dad was eating at the dining room table.

"I made you a plate." he said.

I didn't know what he made but the smell made me instantly want to throw up, so I ran straight to the bathroom. Dad came running after me.

"You okay, sweetie?" He peeked his head into the bathroom.

"I fucking hate being pregnant." I took a deep breath and relaxed on the floor.

My dad plopped down next to me and chuckled. "Ha, you sound just like your mother." He shook his head. "She hated being pregnant so much."

I smiled. Hearing about things that my mom and I had in common warmed my heart— especially now that she wasn't here. I didn't feel so bad about not being her perfect daughter.

"I had no idea it was going to be so rough. Not just physically, but mentally. Everything Ethan is going through just to be a father."

"Yeah...a baby changes things. You changed our lives. Not gonna lie, it wasn't easy, but once we settled into the lifestyle, I never wanted to change it."

It got me thinking. Maybe we just needed to settle in.

"Dad..." I really did miss seeing Ethan all the time. I didn't want my dad to have to take care of me so much. That wasn't his job. It was Ethan's. I was starting to think Ethan should move in.

"What?"

"So, I'm having Ethan's baby, right?"

"Hope so."

"I think he should move in. He could help around the house. His dad has been really pushing him since I got pregnant."

"What does he think?"

"Before I even mentioned it to him, I wanted to make sure you would be okay with it," I said, stumbling to get off the bathroom floor. "You're still my dad, Dad." I hadn't really thought much about it myself. I just thought it would be kind of a good idea. Ethan was already at the house a lot anyway. Ever since he met me, he'd done so much for us. Now I was having his baby, so the least I could do was offer my house. Right?

"Why not? I like him. I can be myself with him. It's not like Susan, with all those kids, or Grandma."

"Dad. Ew. Never…"

"Yeah, make the offer. Let's see what he says."

I was shocked. I thought for sure my dad wouldn't be okay with it. Now, this could potentially be happening. I felt like throwing up again. I shouldn't be scared of change.

Change was happening whether I was ready or not, so I might as well start the motions.

"Are you serious?" Ethan asked while he was cleaning my kitchen. It was perfect timing, actually.

"Yeah, I mean, I'm not going to do your homework for you every night, but I would love to wake up to you every morning," I said.

He came over and kissed me. "You lost me at not doing my homework," he said.

I smiled.

"Okay, fine, don't move in," I joked.

He sat next to me and put his hand on my stomach. "I want

more than anything for all of us to be under one roof."

I kissed him on his cheek. "Now…how do you think your dad is going to feel about it?" I raised my eyebrows.

"I don't think he'll be too keen on the idea."

"He hasn't looked at me in the last four months. This baby is going to be his first grandchild. Does he get that?"

"Yeah, he's more upset with me in general for…other things," Ethan said.

"Like what? I didn't know you guys were still having problems."

"I didn't want to stress you out."

` "You already are. What the hell is going on?"

He was hiding something.

Early one morning, a few weeks after Ethan moved in, there was a knock at the door.

"Who's that?" I shook Ethan awake as he lay next to me. He had to be up in an hour for work, I knew he was going to be upset with me for waking him earlier.

"What time is it?" he mumbled.

"Fucking six in the morning and someone is knocking," I complained.

"No…you're hearing things…go *back* to sleep." He rolled back over.

As tired as I was, I could have gone back to sleep, and I wanted to, but the knocking got louder and louder.

We both hopped up.

"It's my dad." Ethan rolled out of bed, struggling to put clothes on. I knew *my* dad was going to be pissed.

"Portia…what the hell is going on? You know what time it is?" Dad asked, getting out of bed.

I rushed over to him. "It's Mr. Torke. Something's wrong," I said, worried.

"I don't care. No one knocks on my door like they're the police at six in the morning," Dad said. As he was getting dressed, I went to the top of the stairs, trying to listen to what Ethan and his dad were fighting about, but they were whispering. I didn't like that at all. What could they possibly be whispering about?

Dad came over and we hovered at the top of the stairs.

"This is ridiculous. Why am I sneaking around in my own damn house?" he said.

"Just wait. I want to hear what they are saying." I couldn't hear them to save my life.

"Babe? Is everything okay?" I tiptoed down the stairs.

Dad nodded at me to just go down. My dad was all talk, no play my entire life. He would always say, "Do as I say, not as I do." He told Piper and me what he wanted of us but never did what we wanted of him. But at the end of the day, no one cared.

"Portia," Mr. Torke greeted me, "I was just leaving." He left, slamming the front door.

"What was that about?"

"He wants me to come home," Ethan said. He walked over to the kitchen to start the coffee, but he was irritated and so aggressive with the coffee maker it wasn't working. "Did we upset you too much? How do you feel? You think you're going to be sick? What do you feel like eating?"

Ethan was talking so fast.

"I'm fine. Not everything is about me and my pregnancy. What's going on?"

He went from mad to sulking in two seconds. Ethan never let himself look defeated in front of me. He was really good at always having his shit together even when he didn't. He felt like he had to look like it. He sat down on the living room couch. He grabbed the remote and just started flipping through channels.

Ethan hated watching TV.

"Babe?" I sat down next to him.

"What do you have planned for today? Shit. Is it your doctor's appointment?" he asked. He was scaring me. He was so agitated but didn't want to talk about it.

"Stop." I put my hand on his back and my other hand on his knee.

"What? I'm fine. My dad is just being a dad. I can deal." He threw the remote down. His face got red.

"No, you can't. You have to talk about it."

"Like you talk about *your* problems?" he yelled, getting up . There was sweat coming from every body part—head, nose, neck. Who was in front of me right now?

"I do," I screamed. Now, I was fucking irritated.

"No, you don't. You expect me to just know how you feel. I know you, but I don't know what you're thinking constantly. We're never on the same page, or I never *feel* like we're the same page."

I didn't know what the hell Ethan was going on about. I'd never seen him like this. I thought we were fine. I felt like we were happy. He'd moved in. We'd been reading these stupid books. We were getting ready to build our little family.

"What the hell did your father say? And what the fuck else is going on between you two?" I said calmly. I didn't want us screaming at each other anymore.

"Nothing," he stated sternly, sitting back down. "He wants me to move back home. He made some really good points. I'm an adult at twenty-one. I'm giving up my college years to have a family and work at an office. I'm doing things I'm supposed to be doing ten years from now."

He had to say that at six in the morning.

"Fuck you. I am the one pregnant. I am giving up a lot here too, you know. You told me we could do this. I believed you. I trusted you. After everything I've been through, are you fucking kidding me, Ethan?" I broke down crying. I couldn't believe this argument was happening. Not now.

"Please don't cry." He stepped closer to me as he suddenly felt bad for everything he'd said.

"You know what? Fine." I backed up and stared directly into those icy blue eyes.

"Fine what?"

"Leave. Move back in with your dad. Go to college. Go back to fucking Florida for all I care. My dad and I got this," I snapped.

"You and your dad will kill this baby and you know it. It won't last a day," he yelled.

"It?" He was calling the baby *it*. "Now I feel sick. Get the hell out of my house." I stood up and he didn't fight back. He left and slammed the door just as hard as his father did earlier. I really did start to feel sick. I bent over—I was going to throw up, but didn't. I just needed to lie down.

"We don't need 'em," Dad said as he came hopping down the stairs to grab a beer.

"Where were you ten minutes ago?"

"Letting you guys handle it." He shrugged.

"Well. It's handled," I said.

"Can I tell you a story, sweetie?"

"Can I lie down first?"

He lifted my head, sat next to me on the couch, and placed my head on his legs. He played with my hair while he told me his story.

"Seventeen years old. Betty Byers. Beautiful. Sexy…"

"Dad, I already feel queasy, please…" I complained.

"I got her pregnant. I didn't want her to have it. Her mother, though—I wasn't getting out of it. I was going to have a kid at seventeen years old. I never played it cool. I was never okay with it. I even threatened to leave her and leave the baby. I didn't care. I wanted to be me. I was going to deny the kid was mine…"

"Really?"

"I know. I was an asshole," he said. "Point is, I never once acted how Ethan is acting. Are you kidding me? He loves you and he loves this baby. The situation sucks. You guys are way too young. Your lives are ruined, if you ask me. This little fight over what you guys are going through is nothing. I know that boy will come back tonight. I know he's going to apologize. I know he will always be there for you and this baby. You may be the one carrying the baby, but he has to go through the emotional upheaval of becoming a father—something I wouldn't even consider at his age."

"How did you react when mom was pregnant with me?"

"I was really happy it was your mother instead of Betty Byers," he said.

"Really?"

"Oh yeah. You wouldn't want Betty as your mother anyway. I only wanted her because she was the most popular girl in school."

"I don't know what to do. I accepted the fact that we're having a family. I asked him to move in. I've done everything to make this easy for him," I said.

"There's nothing you can do. This is all in his head. He needs time alone. He needs to think. He needs time to accept the entire situation."

"I thought he did that already," I said.

"You guys just switched—"

"You think he switched to the point where we can still have the abortion?"

"Portia, it's way too late in the game for you to be saying things like that," he said.

I *did* feel some type of bond with this child inside me. It sounded terrible, but my dad was right—our lives were changing and neither of us wanted this, but here we were. I swore if Ethan and I got through this, we could get through anything.

"Hey, Dad?"

"Yeah?"

"What happened to Betty Byers' baby?"
"Oh, she had a miscarriage."

Chapter 16

Susan's kids were over and they were giving me a headache. She was smoking a cigarette and talking on the phone while I played with the little ones in the living room. Every other time I'd played with them, it was easy. I played dolls and cars and then they went home.

This time, I noticed things I wouldn't have before. I asked Susan if they needed to be changed, when was the last time they ate, could I give them a piece of candy? I wondered if my baby was going to be as cute as hers.

It was different. Not going to lie, I didn't like it.

"Portia, give me all your friends' phone numbers," Susan yelled over at me.

I didn't respond. She should know that I didn't have any friends.

I missed Ethan. What if my dad was wrong? What if he didn't come back? He told me he was staying at his dad's tonight and he would be back tomorrow. I had been expecting to wake up to breakfast with him or something. Nope, just a bunch of kids in my living room. I waddled over to the dining room table where she was sitting. She hung up the phone but immediately started texting.

"What are you doing?" I sat down at the table. Sitting down had never felt as amazing as it did every time I did it now.

"Planning everything. The shower, your doctor. Your mom

wouldn't want her grandchild to be brought into this world by any hoo-haw," she said.

"How long until you started smoking again after you had your babies?" I asked.

"You miss it, don't you?"

"My dad said I wouldn't miss it after a week. It's been six months..."

Susan laughed. "Where is that guy?" She stopped looking at her phone and stared deeply into my eyes. I thought it was strange that she didn't look around for him. Was I supposed to know something?

"Sleeping."

She was being so weird.

"Oh, okay." She snapped out of whatever it was. "You want to know a secret?" she asked.

I nodded.

"I smoked *while* I was pregnant." She handed me a cigarette. I looked into the living room and saw Stefan banging on my DVD player because it wasn't working. The twins still had food from this morning all over their clothes. They were a mess.

"I'm good," I said, pushing it away. I went to pick up the twins. I had to clean them up. I had never been worried about this stuff before. I had never realized how fucked Susan was as a mother.

"Portia, honey?"

"Yes..."

"What would you rather do? Not go to UCLA for your last year and build your family in this house, or attend UCLA and get a part-time job while struggling to raise your child?"

Where did that come from?

"Huh? Is it really that tight?"

"I have five kids myself, Portia. I know how expensive they are. I know how important UCLA is to you. You and Ethan really need to sit down, plan this out, and think about what each of you want to do," she said.

"All I ever wanted was to be happy. Ever. I never wanted friends, a boyfriend, or a great job. I didn't care about any of that superficial shit. I just wanted to be happy. Ethan and my dad are the only two things that make me happy. Fuck UCLA. I want to build my family in this house with Ethan and my dad and our little girl," I said.

She looked up at me and smiled, brushing my cheek with her hand.

"If only life was that much of a dream," she said.

Ethan came bursting through the door. He looked awful, but I didn't care. I was just so happy to see that he was in my house and wanted to see me. I ran to him like I hadn't seen him in years.

"I missed you so much." I hugged him so tight.

He hugged me back and kissed my forehead, then pulled away from me. "I told you I was coming today." His tone was lower than usual. I knew him so well. I could tell there were still issues we needed to sort out but right now, I didn't care.

"Is everything okay?" Susan asked.

"Yeah, I hope so." I didn't want to let go of Ethan.

"I'm sorry for scaring you. I love you," he said, and kissed me.

"Hey, so I'm throwing a baby shower. Would your sister or any girls in your family want to come?" Susan asked Ethan.

"Uh, let me think about it, but definitely not my sister."

I thought this whole baby shower thing was hilarious. We didn't know anyone. *I* didn't know anyone. All Susan had so far was every coworker who worked for my mother, her kids, a couple of Piper's friends, and their mothers.

"We're having it here. I need this place spotless, you guys. *Spotless*. You know everyone is talking about you guys? Wondering how you guys are doing living in this house? Make everyone shut the fuck up. Your dad *cannot* be at the baby shower. He has to go somewhere," she said.

"He'll just stay upstairs. We already talked about it. I'm going to get him all set up so he doesn't have to come downstairs."

"And no going to check on him…" Ethan put his arm around me. I really had a lot to talk about with him. I wanted Susan and her children out of my house, now.

"So when is this going down?" I asked.

"In a couple weeks. You have time, but not that much. Get this house together," she said as she pulled out another cigarette. Thank God, that meant she was leaving.

We were lying in my bed later that afternoon when I decided to tell Ethan about UCLA.

"I'm taking a break from UCLA after this semester and our class."

"Well, when the baby is born…" he started.

"I meant before." I didn't know how he'd react so I just waited.

"Like when? What do you mean before?"

"We can't afford it all," I said.

"But we talked about it…if I stopped going to SMC and I got this job. I don't get it," he said, sitting up.

"I don't either, Ethan, but, I mean, she's paying for it. It's her money, so, like, I can't really argue. I'd rather keep this house more than anything."

"I'd rather you graduate from UCLA more than anything. You have one more fucking year. We can get an apartment, babe. You can get a job," he said as he looked at me in confusion.

"Yeah, yeah…no."

"You need to grow up, Portia, really fucking think about what you're deciding to do." Ethan sounded different, maybe not to anyone else, but to me, he was different.

"I *did* think about it when I wanted to have an abortion. Because I knew we were going to be faced with decisions that I didn't want to have to fucking deal with, but here we are," I snapped.

"We really need to figure this out. You're going to have this baby in three months. I think we should see a professional," he said.

"Was that an idea from your father?" I asked suspiciously.

"No, it wasn't. I've just been thinking…"

"About what?" I hated fighting with Ethan—but it kept happening.

"Us. You. This family. It's a lot…" he trailed off. There was something Ethan wasn't talking about. I had been honest with him, but there was something Ethan couldn't talk about with me.

Ethan and I fought every single day leading up to the baby shower. I didn't have the energy to clean the house, so Ethan did it—yet another thing we fought about. I felt so bad for my dad having to hear it all the time. He stayed in his room to avoid our fights. It was like he was scared to come out.

"Daddy?" I brought him breakfast while Ethan was at work. It was the day before the shower and I was two seconds away from breaking up with Ethan.

"Hi, buddy." His room was a mess. Well, the house was so clean, this room looked especially messy.

"Ethan is at work."

"The house looks really clean. He did a good job," Dad said.

"Yeah, I helped…a little," I said.

"You're pregnant, baby. You don't have to help. Sit down."

"I miss it just being us two. I love Ethan. I really do. I just wish we could go back to how it used to be," I said.

"I feel like we're always wishing that for ourselves instead of appreciating what we have," he said, and pulled me into his chest. I started crying. I was just so overwhelmed. At that moment, I didn't want this baby. I didn't even want Ethan. I wanted all of this to go away. Tomorrow, our house would be full of people. I'd never dreaded anything more in my life. I'd grown so much with my social issues, but I could feel all of them coming back. I didn't want to speak to anyone. I didn't even want to *look* at anyone.

I slept all day and woke up at eight p.m. I couldn't understand how that happened. I opened the door and peeked out into the hall.

"Ethan?" I called. Dad wasn't around. No one was.

"Dad?" Nausea came rushing in hard. I ran straight to the bathroom. I was still so tired. I fell asleep on the toilet seat.

"Babe? Babe?" I woke up to someone shaking me. I was so confused.

"Oh my God. You're okay. She's fine. I'm so sorry. She woke up. She's six months pregnant and I just found her passed out on the toilet but she woke up." Ethan was on the phone with someone.

"Who are you talking to?" I asked.

"How do you feel?"

"Fine. I just fell asleep."

"Okay...okay, thank you so much." Ethan hung up the phone. "That was 9-1-1. I thought something happened to you," he said.

"Where were you?"

"I was working and then I went to have dinner at my dad's," he said.

"Ethan. It's just been one of those days. I don't want to fight. I want to go to sleep."

"I thought you were going to decorate the house today so you had less to do tomorrow," he said.

Shit. I'd forgotten. No, I didn't forget. I'd fallen asleep. I didn't want to tell Ethan I slept all day because he was going to think that I was drinking or smoking. I didn't want to lie to him either, so I just didn't say anything. I went straight to bed.

"Are you drunk?" Ethan asked suspiciously.

Jesus fucking Christ.

"No, Ethan. Can we have one fucking night of us not fighting? I'm stressed the fuck out. I'm about to have a million and one people in this house tomorrow. I want to sleep," I said.

"I'm just wondering what you did all day."

"I can't do this anymore, Ethan. I really fucking can't. I really can't deal with you anymore," I snapped.

"Oh, really?" he said sarcastically.

"Tomorrow night, we're reevaluating this fucking relationship. You can sleep on the couch or go back to your dad's tonight."

He slept on the couch. I cried all night long. I couldn't go to sleep after that. It sucked. I hated everything about my life. I missed Piper more than anything. I just knew she would be able to snap Ethan out of this funk. Whenever Mom and Dad fought in front of us and it became this huge family fight, Piper was the one who snapped everyone out of it by making everything about her, but it always worked.

I woke up to Ethan putting up decorations. I started helping him but didn't say anything.

"You hungry?" he mumbled.

I shook my head.

"Okay."

All these decorations looked disgusting. Pink pompoms everywhere. Pink tablecloths. Balloons and banners that said *Welcome Baby Girl.*

Today was supposed to be a happy day.

"What are you going to do today?" I asked, looking at the decorations. Ethan and I could barely look at each other. He was so focused on getting the decorations perfect when he knew I could care less how they looked.

"Uh...I don't know. Set this up. Hang out with some dudes from school." He shrugged, still not looking at me."

I'm not dropping out of UCLA," I said. I didn't know for a fact if that was the underlying reason for all of our fights, but I did feel like it would help.

"What about Susan?" he asked.

"What about her?" I went closer to him and took the pompom out of his hand, forcing him to look at me. "This is *our* family. We'll figure it out. Just you and me. But UCLA is something that I can't just let go of," I said.

"That's really smart of you," he said, and snatched the pompom out of my hands. Nope, that wasn't it. He still had this look on his face like he hated me. I really didn't want him to leave me with all these people, but I also didn't want to be around this version of Ethan.

"I just want to make you happy," I said.

"I am." He looked up at me after he hung up the last pompom. "Susan is bringing over the rest. I'll see you later." He started walking toward the front door.

"Ethan?" He couldn't leave me like this. I hated all of this.

"What?" He shook his head at me.

I started bawling. I sunk to the ground and covered my face. He walked slowly to me and kneeled.

"I'm sorry. I'm sorry." I cried, not having any idea what I was apologizing for. I covered my face as I broke down but he grabbed my hands and wiped my tears. He looked me in my eyes but was silent. He was literally torturing me. He pushed my head into his chest and held me. I could feel his heart beating. It was racing.

"Everything is going to be okay." He took a deep breath. I really wished I could believe him.

"What's going on with you and your dad?" I asked.

"What?"

"Tell me the real reason your father doesn't want you to be with me and have the baby."

He stood up.

"Ethan. Do not lie to me."

"He doesn't think you are mentally healthy enough to be a mother, and he doesn't think I am mature enough to deal with you and be a father."

Well, duh.

"I didn't tell you because it doesn't matter. It is what it is. He doesn't get that but he will. Until then, I am going to be stressed. You are going to be hormonal. We are going to fight. We are going to hate each other at some point, but I love you, Portia Willows." He grabbed my face and looked me in my eyes.

"I love you, too."

"And I *am* happy. I am happy with you. I want all of this and I am willing to struggle as long as I need to just to make this work."

I was so emotionally exhausted I needed to sit down.

"Can you stop crying and enjoy this day...*please*?" He sat next to me and grabbed my knee.

I nodded, wiping my tears.

"I'm going to go now before people start coming. Just remember everyone coming loves you and they are your family, they're not strangers. If you can't handle it at any point, your dad is upstairs and you can call me."

I nodded and sniffed.

He kissed my forehead and then my lips. I instantly felt calmer and better about everything.

Within an hour, my house was crowded. I felt sick. An anxiety attack was coming on and I didn't know what to do. All of my mom's friends were touching my stomach, smiling at me. Ethan's mom couldn't make it down from Florida. Of course, I wasn't going to invite Sarah. I couldn't talk to anyone. My voice felt locked. I couldn't stand their high-pitched chit-chatting bullshit. I was stuck. I couldn't leave. I was the center of attention. I couldn't even keep track of all the questions they were asking.

"Do you have a name picked out yet?"

"What cravings are you having?"

"Has she kicked yet?"

"When are you due?"

"How often are you sick?"

"Are you guys staying in?"

"How's UCLA?"

"Are you getting a job?"

"You're so lucky to have Susan."

"Piper would have loved to have planned this."

"Your mom would be so proud of you."

"You look just like your mother when she was pregnant."

My hands got clammy. A migraine was coming on. My breathing started to get touchy. I felt like I kept skipping breaths and my vision became blurry.

"I'm going to use the bathroom," I said, and rushed out. I fell to the floor, closing the door behind me. I leaned back against it. Deep breaths. I should probably go check on my dad. He could calm me down. I took a couple more deep breaths and opened the door.

Maddie was standing there. She scared the hell out of me.

"Hi…" I said.

"Are you okay?" she asked.

"Yeah, just had to pee."

"This must really suck for you."

"Being pregnant, or this baby shower?"

"Both?" She smiled and giggled. "That's something Piper would say."

"Yeah, this seems like a party she would enjoy," I said.

"No. She didn't like your mom's friends."

I looked at her in confusion. But Maddie had said that so confidently. I never knew that. There was something about Piper that I didn't know.

"I didn't know that."

"She didn't talk about it that much."

I looked down. I didn't want to go back to the party.

"Did you have to use the bathroom?" I wondered why she was still talking to me.

"No. I was just checking on you."

"Oh. Thanks."

"You want to take a break from all this and talk?" she asked.

I didn't say anything.

"I know talking is not really your thing."

"No, no, no. I'd rather just talk to you than everyone in there."

We went out the back and sat on the steps right outside. It was such a nice day. We should have had the shower out here. Our backyard looked so deserted. Sitting there with Maddie reminded me of all the times they would play out there, or Piper and I would play out there. We had a swing set and a trampoline. We had to sell them in a yard sale years ago, but looking out at the lawn, I could still tell exactly where they were.

"Wow, dude...I don't know how I would deal with all of that. I don't even know how Piper would deal with all of that," Maddie said after I told her how I have been feeling about this pregnancy and the fighting with Ethan.

"I just can't believe I got myself into this position in the first place," I said.

"Love. Love has this effect on people. It cures a lot, but it also causes a lot."

"I just want my old Ethan back."

"You'll get him back. This is just a battle you guys have to get through—and you will, because you love each other." She sounded like a fucking Hallmark card. She didn't remind me of Piper because Piper would have given me real advice instead of something I could have read on the internet, but being around her energy made me feel like a normal twenty-year-old.

Chapter 17

The next morning, the house was a mess. What was the point of cleaning the house just to make it messy again? Some decorations had fallen. Cups and plates were strewn all over the place. The dining room table was filled with gifts. Ethan was making a fresh cup of tea. I didn't even know where to start.

"Do you work today?" I asked as I plopped down at the table. I started looking through all the gifts.

"Nope, it's Sunday." Ethan sat down at the dining room table.

"You want to help me open these gifts? It could be fun," I asked.

He nodded.

"Can you give me a kiss?" I wanted to see if we were still good. He took a sip of his tea and scooted his chair towards mine. He grabbed my chin and kissed me. I sighed, tilting my head back.

"What?" he asked.

"I was really scared it was going to feel different," I said. I took a sip of my tea, not taking my eyes off of him.

"Why would it feel different?" He moved my bangs behind my ear and kissed near my cartilage. I put my hands in his hair and rubbed my thumb across his cheekbone.

"Because you've been on edge and distant. I feel like I've been losing you. I miss you. I love you. I just want you back." I grabbed his face and he kissed me back. "I guess this is what a real-life relationship is like, huh?"

"I didn't realize you felt that way. I didn't know how much it bothered you. Arguing sometimes is healthy."

"Not *every* day," I said.

"It wasn't just you. I've been so stressed at work, babe. I actually have a lot of responsibilities."

"I believe you. I want to help. I'm here for you. This is what girlfriends do. Just because I don't do your homework for you anymore doesn't mean I can't help you with real life."

"Thank you, babe, that means a lot." He kissed my cheek.

"Let's open these gifts…"

Ethan and I got our groove back while we were laying out all the baby clothes and toys. Opening the gifts made me realize this was happening.

This was really happening.

I was actually having a baby.

"You know normal pregnant girls open these gifts *at* the baby shower," he said.

"And apparently people play games at baby showers," I said.

"You didn't do that either?"

"Nope. Everyone just talked and talked and talked…but I had a good, long conversation with Maddie."

"Really?" He was more shocked than I would have thought.

"Yup."

"What did you guys talk about?"

"She told me something about Piper I never knew before. She didn't really get along with my mom's friends. Overall, I was fine by the end of it."

"I knew you could do it." He smiled.

"So, I've been thinking, we need to think of a name."

"You have one picked out."

"How did you know?" I asked.

"Because I know you, and as much as you didn't want this baby, I know you think about it late at night."

"I was thinking Pyper, but with a Y instead of an I. We could call her Pypes for short?"

He was silent.

My heart stopped. I tried to tell myself it wouldn't be a big deal if he didn't like it.

"I think it's beautiful…just like you," he said, and kissed me again. It was a lot of kissing for how we'd been these last couple weeks. I straddled him and started kissing him more and more. He picked me up and I laughed.

"Stop it. You can't carry me—I'm so fat." I hopped out of his arms, then grabbed his hand and guided him upstairs. He slapped my ass.

"I missed you," he said.

I turned around. He grabbed my waist and ran to my bedroom, closing the door and throwing me onto the bed.

Present Day

"Do you remember delivering Pyper?" Elizabeth asked.

My face was swollen and my eyes were clogged with dried tears. It felt like I wasn't real. Like I wasn't there at all.

But I had to be there to find out what the hell was going on with me. It felt like my baby was being taken from me all over again. I couldn't put my head around why. I didn't remember her being taken from me the first time, so how was it possible to know what that felt like?

"This isn't about what I did or what my dad did. Is this about me and my sanity?" I whispered. I didn't have the energy to talk any louder.

"Portia, I really need you think back to when you had Pypes," she said.

"I remember a little. I remember my dad not being there. I remember Susan yelling at doctors. I just don't remember *her*...I remember everything up to it," I said. I thought back to that day. I was scared. I didn't want it to hurt. I kept thinking that.

Did it hurt? I didn't remember if it hurt.

"It's okay. With your past anxieties, this is completely normal. Post-partum depression is something a lot of women deal with," she said.

"So, let me get this straight. I did something to Ethan but I don't remember what and now he's hurt. And just like how I don't remember what happened with Ethan, I can't remember that I had a baby…"

"Exactly, and there's more. About the night of the play when your family died," she explained.

"No. No. No. I remember everything about that night like it was yesterday. Running back to my house, the letters, waiting for them. I remember *everything*. That was the worst night of my life—I could never forget it," I said.

That knock on my door.

I almost didn't answer it because I knew Dad and Mom had a key and I was in the middle of eating pizza.

I remembered everything from that day.

"Close your eyes."

I looked at her and she nodded in assurance.

Whatever. I closed my eyes.

"Susan is yelling at the doctors. Can you picture it?"

I nodded.

"How did it smell?"

"I was sweaty. I just feel sweaty. I don't know how it smelled."

"Good job, keep your eyes closed…"

Two Years Ago

I'd never been in so much pain in my life.

"Deep breaths, baby. You're going to be okay." Ethan was squeezing my hand so tight. It was like he was in more pain than I was.

"No, I'm not. I'm going to die. I *am* dying," I cried.

He laughed.

The doctor wasn't the one Susan had chosen to deliver my baby. I didn't really care. My body was going to be in this much pain regardless of who was staring at my vagina.

"How come none of the books talked about how excruciating this was going to be?"

"Imagine if you were doing it without the epidural," the doctor mumbled.

Don't fucking talk to me, just get this baby out of me.

"Babe, look at me," Ethan said.

I looked at his face. Sweat was dripping from his forehead and his face was bright red. Are you fucking kidding me? I was the one going through this. Why did *he* look a mess?

"Now look over to the other side, and imagine your mom and Piper holding your other hand."

I looked to my other side and lifted my hand up. I felt Mom's soft hands that I rarely felt when she was alive. I only remembered feeling them when she would pull me somewhere I didn't want to go. I imagined Piper sitting on the edge of the bed, commenting on every little thing. She would be looking underneath the sheet and telling me exactly what it looked like. No, she probably would be recording it.

All I knew was that they weren't really there. My dad wasn't here either. He didn't want to ever set foot in a hospital again no matter the circumstances, and I completely understood. I did want him here, though, and I missed him, but Ethan was doing a better job than I expected.

"Two more big pushes and Pyper is here," the doctor told me.

One long push. I didn't know if I was supposed to do that or take a breath between two.

"You got this. Keep going. Just like that." The more I pushed, the harder Ethan squeezed my hand. I looked at him and his sweating got worse.

He was drenched. I was drenched.

"Here she is…" the doctor said, and that was when I heard it—the screaming, the crying. I blacked out. That was the last thing I remembered. I didn't hold her. I didn't see her. I didn't do any of that.

I woke up a couple hours later in a hospital room in a lot of pain and annoyed. There was no one around and it was dark. I wanted to get up and get out of here. I wanted to see my dad. I wanted to go home. I didn't know why I was in the hospital. I pressed all the buttons and unhooked my IV.

What the fuck was going on? Where was all my stuff?

Ethan came rushing in. "Portia?"

"What the hell? Why am I here?" I asked him, struggling to get out of the bed.

"Because you blacked out. How do you feel?" He shoved my wet hair out of my face and sat next to me on the bed.

"I feel fine. What happened?" I backed away from him. Some nurses came in with a wheelchair.

"I bet you've been wanting to see your little one," one of the nurses said.

What the fuck? What was she talking about? I looked at Ethan in horror.

"Come on...I'll roll you over," he said.

"Over *where*? I can walk...I think." I got up but I felt strange, so I sat down in the wheelchair.

"She's beautiful, babe," Ethan said.

"Who?" I looked up as Ethan rolled me out the door.

The nurses looked at him.

"Pyper," Ethan bent over and whispered to me.

I dropped my legs on the floor and stopped the chair. I needed an explanation before I rolled anywhere.

"Babe. What the hell is going on? Why are you showing me Piper's body? She's not even here anymore."

The nurses looked concerned.

"Do you want me to get the doctor?" One of the nurses said as she looked at Ethan.

"No..." Ethan lifted up my feet and rolled me super-fast to the corner where no one else was around. He got down on his knees in front of me.

"Do you know why you're here?"

"No. Tell me. Did I get too drunk or something?"

"Portia, you haven't had a drink in nine months. You're here because you just had our baby that you named Pyper with a fucking Y. What the hell is wrong with you?" I'd never seen him so angry.

"Oh yeah...wait. I just had her."

I looked down at my stomach.

I put my hand on my stomach.

How did this happen? I instantly started to feel sore. I remembered being pregnant. But I didn't remember delivering the baby at all. I didn't even remember coming to the hospital.

"Oh yeah?" he said sarcastically. I could understand why he would be so angry. This was supposed to be a special moment and I'd just completely blacked out.

"Let's go," he said.

"Home? I want to see my dad."

"No, to see Pyper, our baby. And when we leave to go home, we're taking this baby with us."

"Okay, stop it. Ethan, I'm not stupid, I'm just exhausted. I want to see her…" As Ethan was rolling me to the maternity ward, I looked around. I saw other mothers holding their babies in their wheelchairs. I couldn't describe the feeling I felt, but it felt wrong. Pyper was not my first priority. I wasn't upset that I couldn't remember the delivery. I knew I should be. I knew I should be happier than I was. He stopped pushing me. I looked at him and he looked right. I turned and looked through the windows. I couldn't really see. I struggled to stand up. Ethan grabbed my arm and my back to help.

There were so many babies. Was I supposed to automatically know which one was ours? Ethan pointed and said, "Fourth row down…three babies in. That's Pyper."

I counted.

Holy shit, she was small.

They were *all* small but Pyper looked like a doll.

"Can we?" I looked up at Ethan. He glanced around the room.

"I think so…I mean, why not? She's our baby." He walked into the room and spoke to a nurse. She walked us over. The nurse picked her up.

I was scared. I didn't want to drop her.

I didn't want to hold her too tightly or too lightly.

Ethan grabbed her.

"Be careful, babe," I said.

"She's so soft," Ethan said as he ran his finger down her cheek.

I could have cried but I didn't. I looked at Ethan. He was crying. It made me cry, too. My arms were shaking as I reached for her. Ethan never took his eyes off her as he placed her in my arms and I melted. I started bawling my eyes out. She had blue eyes just like Ethan. She had curly hair like mine and a really tiny face. I couldn't stop looking at her. She was mine and Ethan's—both of us put together. I saw more in her than I saw of my parents in me.

She was so beautiful.

"She looks just like us," I sobbed.

Ethan put his arm around my shoulder and rested his other hand on her head. "Make sure you hold her head up," he said.

"Okay..." I placed my hand under his hand.

"Can you believe it?"

"We have to. She's here." I heard someone knocking on the window. It was Grandma, Gary, and Susan. I waved for them to come in.

"Only the parents are allowed," the nurse who was watching the babies said.

It was crazy. There were hundreds of babies in this room, but I could only look at little Pypes. We brought her up to the window. Susan was taking pictures of us through the glass. Grandma was crying. It was a beautiful moment, except we were missing my dad. I couldn't wait for him to see Pyper.

It took a couple days before we could bring her home. I could already tell Pypes loved car rides. I was in the passenger seat, but I couldn't stop looking back at her. Her blinks were so slow. Her eyes wouldn't fully open. She looked so comfortable. I didn't want to move her.

"Shh, try not to wake her…" I said as Ethan pulled into our driveway. He was just so excited to get Pyper home.

Susan didn't want to leave us. She was walking around the house making sure everything was baby-proofed.

"There's no beer and there's no cigarettes. We're good." I was pretty sure those weren't the only two things that meant a house was baby-proofed, but we wanted to be alone with Pypes.

We took her to my room, where the crib was. We lay in bed with her in the middle. She didn't really move much. The first thing I noticed was how much hair she had for being a few days old. I swear, as the minutes went by, her eyes got bigger and bigger. She had Ethan's eyelashes. Long and full.

"I'm going to get my dad real quick…okay?" I whispered. Ethan nodded while tickling her stomach.

I knocked on my dad's room door. "Daddy? Daddy?" Nothing. Strange. I was surprised he wasn't at the door when we first came in. I opened it all the way and walked in. His room looked clean, well clean for him.

"Dad?" I said as I stood there. He wasn't there.

Are you fucking kidding me? Where could he be? I looked everywhere.

"Hey, babe? I have no idea where my dad is," I called to Ethan as I ran down the stairs. There were no empty beer cans. I didn't see a carton of cigarettes, so he could have easily gone to the store, but he would have told me if he'd gone out. Why would he leave the day I was going into labor? I called his cell phone. No answer, but he never answered his phone. Whatever. He'd be back. There just wasn't anywhere he could have gone for long.

I came back into the room to lie down on the bed next to them.

"Hi, baby." I said.

"You find him?" Ethan asked.

"No…I think he may have gone to the store. The house is cleared of booze and cigs, even in his room," I said.

"Weird," he said, and stared at me. I was staring at Pypes but I could still feel his eyes on me. I looked up at him.

"What?" I asked.

"Nothing, just watching you. I love this and I love you," he said, smiling.

"I love you too," I said, and kissed him.

She started crying.

"And now it starts…"

"We had a good five minutes," Ethan joked while he picked her up.

"What do we do?" I asked.

"She's either hungry, or we need to change her," he said.

"Or both…" I laughed, taking her from Ethan.

"Maybe she just needs to be walked around," I said. I put her on my chest and walked around the room.

Pyper demanded our attention twenty-four seven. I had to breastfeed her every two hours, and when I wasn't breastfeeding, I was pumping. There was always something to do. I was getting really overwhelmed. I wanted to walk outside. I wanted a break, but I'd only had her for a day—there was no break time.

"Why won't she go back to sleep?" I complained.

"I don't think babies know what sleep is at this age," Ethan said. He put her in a rocking carriage someone got us at the baby shower. Thank God we'd had that shower. We were using each and every one of those gifts. In the back of my mind, I kept thinking of my father. I was getting stressed out that it was the middle of the night and he still hadn't come home. I took advantage of not having Pyper in my hands to call him, but still no answer.

"Babe, I really don't know where he is. You think I should call my grandma or Susan?"

"It's three in the morning. Let's wait until tomorrow," he said.

We kept passing Pyper back and forth.

It was five in the morning when we were finally able to sleep. It was the best sleep of my life. I woke up and it was three the next day. I heard Pyper screaming her lungs out downstairs. I couldn't believe I'd slept so long. I rushed downstairs. The kitchen was a mess. There were baby things everywhere.

"Why didn't you wake me up? I would have helped." I grabbed Pyper from him.

"You looked so pretty sleeping, and I know you really needed it. I mean, you just gave birth," he said.

"Come here, baby." I cradled Pyper and looked into her beautiful blue eyes. I sat down on my dad's chair, still thinking about him, but I had my own child in my hands. I couldn't get my mind wrapped around that yet. I created this body that was in my hands. She was going to grow up into a person just like me—well, hopefully not *just* like me. I hoped she wouldn't have to go through trauma like I had to. I hoped she just stayed this innocent and beautiful. I got teary-eyed looking at her.

"I used the rest of the bottles you pumped."

I took off my shirt so she could breastfeed. I sighed, looking around the house.

"What's wrong?" Ethan sat next to me, putting his arm around my shoulder and kissing my forehead.

"I just still can't believe it," I said. Ethan looked at her, too. "I really want my dad to see her. What if something happened to him?"

"Why don't you give your grandmother a call?"

"Okay…pass me my phone."

Ethan went to go find it.

"How's my beautiful baby girl?" Grandma sounded so excited for me over the phone.

"Me or Pyper?" I giggled.

"Both, honey."

"Pyper is a beautiful mess. We're tired but she's worth every second of it."

"That's so sweet. Well, you know, if you need any help or you need a break, I'm just a phone call away."

"Thanks, Grandma, but I was calling because I can't find Dad. He never leaves the house, and the day he does leave the house is the same day I go into labor?"

"Huh, interesting."

Huh, interesting?

Really? Even Grandma should know this was fucking strange.

"What did Ethan say?"

"To call you."

"I don't think you should worry about it. You have a newborn baby, Portia."

"Dad hasn't even seen her yet. He was so excited for us and he's just gone. I don't get it."

"I don't know what to tell you."

I was shocked. I knew Grandma and dad had their issues but this was sort of a big deal.

"Grandma, we need to find Dad. Can you help?"

"Sure." She hung up.

Okay. Well, that was weird.

Then Pyper started crying again and I forgot about it.

Present Day

"How long was your dad missing?" Elizabeth asked.

"A while. I don't even think it was a full week. It was just a few days, but they were intense and scary," I said.

"What made it so scary?" she asked.

"Just…I don't know…I don't want to talk about it. He came back and he's fine. That's the end of it."

"We do need to talk about it, though," she said.

"Why?" I asked.

"What did they tell you?"

"Who are 'they'?"

"What made you freak out?" she asked.

"For some stupid reason, Grandma told me that he died. That he'd *been dead*." I furrowed my brows and huffed. "But she never liked him. To her and a lot of people, he may as well have been dead. They think if someone isn't going out and mowing the lawn every morning at eight a.m., they're dead. He was just grieving. I was, too."

"Why would your grandmother tell you something like that if it wasn't true?"

"I lived with him for the past five years. He's definitely not dead," I said.

"*Did* you live with him the last five years, Portia?"

"What the hell are you talking about?" I rolled my eyes. This was getting ridiculous.

"You're almost there, Portia. I just need you to say it."

"I need to see my dad. Now." She was starting to scare me. I stood up and moved towards the door. Elizabeth stood in front of me.

"Why do you need to see your dad so badly?" she asked.

"I don't know. Please. Just let me see him. You let me see my daughter but you won't let me see my father. Oh my God." Something occurred to me. I hopped up and ran over to the window. "He's in jail, isn't he?"

"Why would he be in jail, Portia? Sit back down."

"I don't know, but I see what you're doing, You're trying to get me to say something that could be used in court against him. Whatever he did, he didn't mean to. I know that sounds really childish, but I am not going to testify against my father no matter how fucked up my mind is right now."

Elizabeth sighed and sat back into her chair and just stared at me.

"What? Did I say something you didn't want to hear?"

"No. Not at all. Your dad is not in jail. Your dad did not do anything. Your dad is not here."

"Okay. Where is he, then?"

Two Years Ago

My dad had officially been missing for almost a week. No one cared and it was pissing me off. Pyper distracted me at first, but now it was time to get down to business. Where the hell was he? I decided to call the police. They didn't come until five in the afternoon, though I'd been up stressing since eight.

"Hi. I'm Portia Willows—Ethan. They're here," I called. He was upstairs with Pyper.

"We have a newborn," I explained.

"Congratulations. I'm Detective Riley and this is Detective Jones," he said. They weren't in uniform, which was interesting.

"Thank you so much for coming. My grandmother is on her way. She didn't want me to call you guys, but it's been a week."

"Your father is Richard Willows?" he said.

I nodded as Detective Riley squinted at his phone and looked back up at me.

"According to my records, Richard Willows is deceased. Died in 2010." He showed me the phone. I didn't look at it. I didn't need to. It was obviously a mistake.

I chuckled. "Definitely wrong, Detective Riley."

Riley looked at Detective Jones and started talking.

"So, your father didn't die in a car accident with his wife and sixteen-year-old daughter?"

"No. No. Now you're getting confused. My *mother and sister* died in a car accident in 2010. My father was hurt, he was hospitalized for a week, and then he came home. He never really fully recovered, that's why it's so important that we find him." I heard Ethan coming down the stairs behind me.

"I'll take it from here, Detectives. Thank you for your time." Ethan came down the stairs with the baby monitor in his hand.

They started to leave.

"No, Ethan. What the hell are you doing? They don't even have a picture of him yet to blast all over the news." I grabbed the door. "Wait. Don't leave," I ran after the detectives.

"Good luck, son," Detective Riley said to Ethan.

"What the fuck?" I started punching him. I was so angry.

"Sweetheart, you need to sit down. You see, they're right. I should have told you the first time I met you…"

"They're right about *what*?" I yelled.

He walked across the room and picked up my computer.

"Babe…you're scaring me. You know where my dad is?"

"I do," he said, and started clicking away at the computer.

"*Where*?" I asked.

"The same place you sister and mom are," he said.

"Then let's go fucking get him," I screamed.

He stood up and grabbed my arms and pushed me down on the chair in front of the computer screen.

"No, honey, try to understand, he's *dead*. Just like them. He died *with* them almost five years ago. Look…"

I looked. It was all of their obituaries. I saw my dad's face right next to Mom's and Piper's.

It didn't make any sense.

I didn't like it.

I threw the computer down.

"How fucking dare you," I screamed at Ethan.

"Portia. Listen, you have a baby now. You have to start living your real life. It's just us now. Your dad was never here. I never met him."

I paced the room and Ethan was circling me. "Stop talking." I snapped.

"The reason my dad wanted to help you wasn't for social anxiety issues but so you can stop hallucinating that your father—"

"Hallucinating? Fuck you."

I did *not* hallucinate a human being for the last five years.

"My dad and I have been fighting because I haven't told you. No one knew how to start…"

My mouth and eyes widened in shock. I didn't know what to think or say.

How could the father of my child do this to me?

"I'm going to give you some time to think this through. I'm going to take Pyper with me to my dad's. If you need me, I'll be right across the street." He hugged me.

I stood there frozen. As he was leaving, Grandma walked through the door.

"She knows," Ethan announced.

I didn't know *anything*.

I just knew my dad was still missing and everyone thought he had died.

What was wrong with them?

"I'm so sorry. We all tried telling you in the hospital. I couldn't bear to see you like that, that's why I let you live like this," she said. She gave me a big hug.

What the hell was she talking about?

"Let me make you something to eat or drink. If you want to visit his grave, I'll go with you."

"Grandma, can you just leave?" I said.

Grandma looked at Ethan.

"Actually, do you mind watching Pyper while we talk? Maybe take her upstairs," Ethan put his hand on Grandma's shoulder.

"There's nothing to talk about!" I started laughing. This was the most ridiculous thing I had ever heard.

Grandma didn't even look at me. She sulked and went upstairs to see Pyper.

"I'm really sorry, Portia." Ethan eyes were filled with water, his lips were quivering.

I stared deep into the icy blue eyes and took a deep breath.

I guess a part of me knew—had known—but at the same time, there was no way he was right.

I shook my head, grabbed my keys, and left.

"Portia, where are you going?"

I ran to the car.

He followed as far as the front door.

It was getting dark, so it was going to be harder to spot him. I remembered where he would go when Mom and he would fight—the pool hall, the bar on the 58th. I was weaving down the roads, flashing my high beams at every human being. I needed to find him and I had to find him *fast*. His disappearance had gotten everyone talking crazy.

Why would the father of my child say all those things?

Why would Grandma act so weird?

I had so many questions that only Dad could answer.

Chapter 18

Present Day

"I remember my dad hurting Ethan—but you said *I* did. My memories aren't making sense."

"It's okay. Just tell me what you see."

"I remember someone—maybe Ethan—telling me my dad was dead. That he's *been* dead. I remember Pyper crying. Blood. I remember my dad. Blood. He was there, in the flesh and everything. I don't know. *Help me*." I screamed. I was done playing this game with her.

I wanted her to *tell* me what I was supposed to know.

My mind had played tricks on me before.

I wanted her tell me what the hell was going on.

"Your father is dead. He died in the car accident with the rest of your family five years ago. I wanted *you* to remember, because if you unlocked that memory, you would unlock five years' worth of memories. Things that you thought happened…most likely did not."

"I don't get it."

"You don't remember the doctor in the hospital telling you he was gone? You were right there, lying next to him. You watched him die. You don't remember? You don't remember looking at the screen and watching his heart stop?"

Now *my* heart started to stop.

I did remember seeing that.

I *did* remember laying with him.

I remember he was holding on tight.

I remember him trying to talk to me and then everything stopped.

His arm went limp.

The beeping.

It was the worst pain in my entire life. I couldn't stop screaming. I couldn't stop begging him to wake up.

"But he woke up after that?"

"No, he didn't, Portia. Your mind tricked you into thinking he did."

"For *five years*?"

"You should have been hospitalized then and there. The nurses knew you thought he was still alive. Your grandmother and Susan, they all let you live this lie."

"Even Ethan?" I asked as she nodded.

"It's not your fault."

"I remember my grandma saying something about how she tried to tell me…"

"They probably *all* told you, but that's not how Post Traumatic Stress Disorder works. That's why I don't want you to spend a single day in jail."

"Why would I spend a day in jail if my dad was the one…"

Holy fuck.

"No. no…" I cried. "It was me."

REMEMBER

Five Years Ago

"Portia. It's time. Your grandmother wants to pull the plug. I'm sorry."

Daddy looked so peaceful, I didn't want to let go of his hand.

"Can I stay?" I mumbled at the nurse, and climbed on top of the hospital bed.

"Sure…" She went to the other side.

I put my hand on his cheeks. "His cheeks are really cold."

"He's in a lot of pain right now," she told me.

"I know." I laid my head on his chest. I knew he wouldn't feel better but I did feel his arm move on top of me.

"That's sweet." She kept talking to me while she was killing my father.

It felt wrong. I closed my eyes.

I didn't want to watch this. I felt his life leave his body. I couldn't take it.

"No. Stop. Stop! Don't hurt him. No!"

That's when other nurses came in and grabbed me.

I saw the screen. His hand dropped away. I couldn't breathe. I was hyperventilating.

"Give them a minute," the nurse who killed my father told the others. They let go of me. I rushed back to him. There's no way it happened that fast. I grabbed him and shook him to wake him up.

His shoulders were so heavy but I still lifted them over and over again.

I tried waking him up for hours. He finally did. I started crying.

"Buddy…"

Daddy!

"You made it," I cried.

"You're so beautiful."

"Daddy, I was so scared."

"Don't be. I'm here. I'm never leaving you. I promise."

Except, he had.

Grandma was here to pick me up.

Dad wasn't upstairs getting ready. I was in my dad's room by myself, not watching him get ready.

I was by my grandma's side the entire time at the funeral.

Grandma shushed me because I was talking to myself. That's what she meant when she'd said, "We didn't want to give people something else to talk about."

I was holding her hand looking at the caskets.

There were three, not two.

Dad's friends were here to pay their respects to *him*.

When we got back to my house, everyone was there. I had never been with my dad. He was gone too, just like Mom and Piper. While Maddie was in Piper's room, I went downstairs myself and grabbed a six-pack of Heineken.

Holy shit, my dad's friend had popped one open for me and said cheers. He already had his own. I took a sip, slightly smiled, and grabbed the rest of the Heineken and headed back upstairs. Everyone was staring at me, but no one said anything. Not one word.

Why would someone take everyone away from me like that? My entire family?

Of course I didn't believe it. It's unbelievable.

After everyone left, Grandma let me stay there alone.

Why?

I went into my father's room. I was alone in there all night.

I never helped my dad recover. He never started walking again. He never danced.

I'd found his cigarettes in between the cushions on my own. I showed *myself* how to smoke.

Two Years Ago

I couldn't find him anywhere.

So I checked the woods. Whenever Mom and Dad would fight, he would drive an hour to go shooting or hunting. This was his getaway, but also the only place he could have gone that doesn't have cell service.

"Dad? Dad? Where are you?" I was screaming for him, scanning the woods with my flashlight.

A computer screen going flatline kept popping up in my head.

I kept seeing my dad's face lying in the hospital bed.

They could *not* be right.

"Dad. Dad. Please come back. Please show me and them that you are not dead."

I kept screaming into the darkness.

"Is this about Pyper? My baby? Dad, come on. We'll figure it out. Just come back." I cried. My voice was giving out. I fell down and crawled over to a tree. I kept whispering to myself, "No."

The visions of that session with Mr. Torke. It was just me fighting with myself.

Me yelling at my family to "get the fuck out" when they wanted to sell the house.

I cried harder when I envisioned shaking Ethan's hand when I was introducing them.

All those times the three of us were drinking beers and smoking cigarettes.

It was just me and Ethan.

I was laughing at no one.

I never toasted dad with a beer. I was drinking *two*. I closed my eyes. I was tired.

"Wake up. Wake up, buddy." My shoulder kept getting pushed into a tree. I opened my eyes.

"Daddy?" I screeched, giving him the biggest hug in the world. "I found you. Where have you been?"

"I needed some time."

"I don't care. I'm just happy I found you."

He helped me get up. "Ready to get back home?"

"I can't wait for you to see Pypes—unless…was she was the reason you left?"

"No, I can't wait to see her." We were walking through the woods. He walked faster than me. I stopped for a second. I rubbed my eyes to make sure I wasn't hallucinating. He stopped and turned around,

"What are you doin'?"

I smiled and ran up to him and put my arm around his waist. I told him about being in labor and how for a second I completely forgot I had Pyper. "Also, Dad…Grandma and Ethan had the audacity to tell me that you *died* from the accident the night of the play and I was *hallucinating* you! *Hallucinating*, Ethan actually used that word."

He laughed.

"Well, buddy. I'm not the same fun dad I was before. A part of me *did* die."

"Well duh, a part of me died too, but even the cops were saying you died."

"Portia…" He turned to me and bent down so we were at the same eye level like he did when I was little.

"I'm never going to go anywhere. I'm never leaving you again. I love you and you are all I have left."

I hugged him.

He was back.

When we got to the house, it was empty.

Perfect.

I assumed Ethan had gone to his dad's. Grandma had probably left. Frankly, I didn't care that they were gone. I was so happy for my dad to be back. My boobs were so sore because I needed to be breastfeeding more than I was pumping. I needed Pypes.

"Guess what?"

Dad plopped onto his chair in the living room.

I went to the kitchen, grabbed a pack of smokes and two beers.

"I'm not pregnant anymore." I threw him his beer and cigarette.

"That's right. I missed this." Dad and I cheered.

"Technically, I'm not supposed to because I'm still breast-feeding, but I missed you." I smiled. I lit his cigarette for him. The cigarette tasted gross—but it just felt so good to be back to the old us again.

Dad was fixing breakfast. It smelled so good.

"I'm crazy hungry." I was so used to having to feed Pyper in the morning that not having her there felt wrong. I was wondering how Ethan was taking care of her by himself.

"Where are they?"

"He's probably at work and his dad is taking care of her."

"Go get her."

"His dad is still…fishy about me. She has to come back sometime today anyway."

"I'm sorry I left. I thought you weren't going to need me anymore. You have your own family,"

"Never, Dad. I'm always going to need you. *You* are my family. Mom and Piper will always be my family, too. I'll eventually forgive Ethan and everything will blow over. Hopefully." I didn't really believe that.

Dad and I were in the living room watching television when we heard the front door open.

"That's them." I punched my dad, he was falling asleep.

"Ethan?"

He came walking through the door with a sulking look on his face. He looked defeated.

"Hey."

"Let me take her...you look like shit." Pyper looked like the sweetheart she was. I took her over to Daddy. I was still sort of upset with him that he hadn't been at the hospital.

"Dad...this is your granddaughter, Pyper. Pyper, say hi to Grandpa."

Dad stood up and looked at her. His mouth dropped and he held out his arms.

"She needs to eat. Now." Ethan snapped.

"She looks just like you, Portia...holy crap."

"Watch her head, Dad,"

"*Now*, Portia." Ethan was angry.

"Okay. Jeez. This is the first time my dad has seen her." I glared at him. Had he forgotten? I was supposed to be mad at him. I took Pyper back and started to breastfeed.

"We need to talk..." Ethan went to go sit on the couch.

Oh my God. Those four words.

He had cheated on me, wanted to take the baby away from me, or wanted to break up with me.

"Dad, can you watch Pyper for a minute?" My heart started to beat hard.

"No, stop." Ethan seemed like it was about to have nervous breakdown.

I did. I sat down next to him.

"Not if you're breaking up with her. I don't want to hear that shit," Dad said as he started to leave, but couldn't resist grabbing that cute little face out of my hands.

"*Are* you breaking up with me?" I definitely did not know what to expect. I just knew I was terrified.

"No. This isn't about us. This is about you."

"Okay…what?"

"Portia, baby. I love you so much. I don't know how to tell you this…" He started crying.

"Just tell me. Is it really that bad?"

He grabbed my face. He put his forehead to mine. He was crying so hard. All my anger left. I was instantly worried about *him.*

"Baby…what's wrong?" I put my hand to his cheek.

He took my head and moved it in the direction of my father. I looked at my father, who was mesmerized by Pyper. He wasn't paying attention to us.

"*What?*"

"There is no one over there."

I was confused. I looked at him, but he held my head.

"Trust me, please."

He needed help.

I didn't know what was going on with him but it was heartbreaking seeing him so upset over something I couldn't even understand.

"My dad is holding Pyper, Ethan. Are you okay?" I checked his forehead. "Did you take drugs or something?"

"No, babe, you're still breastfeeding her."

I looked down and then I looked up. She was there. I'd lost a few minutes was all. I just needed sleep.

"You need help, Ethan."

"*I* need help?" He chuckled sadly. "For five years you've been seeing someone who isn't really there." Tears rained down his face.

"Fuck you. I'm not doing this with you *again*. My dad is here. Say something, Dad. He was camping in the woods, that's why he wasn't at the hospital. He's not like your father. He's lazy and he's a drunk but he's still a human being."

"The police fucking told you he was dead."

"No," I screamed.

He ran upstairs and came running back down quickly with the pamphlets from the funerals.

"Fuck you," I screamed as he forced the one of my father in my face.

"How could you?" Pyper was done and I held her up against my chest for her to burp.

"We've been together for over two years now. There have been so many times I wanted to tell you. Like the first time I met you. You said you lived with your dad. I stood there, knowing he was dead. Everyone knew, but I left. I'm sorry. I don't know what I was thinking. But now we have a baby. We can't do this anymore."

I gave Pyper to Ethan and I ran.

Again.

After roaming the streets for an hour, it was getting cold and my thinking was done. I knew what I had to do. I knew the choice I needed to make. I didn't want to believe it, but I had to. I walked in the front door, feeling broken. Ethan was sitting in the living room smoking a cigarette.

"I was so worried about you…" He hopped up.

"Where's Pyper?"

"She's sleeping upstairs. I'm listening to the monitor."

I nodded and sat next to him. I wasn't looking at him—I couldn't.

"How are you?" he said softly.

"I'm sorry,"

"It's okay. I understand what you must be feeling right now. It's all my fault." He sobbed into my legs.

"I need you to leave."

"What?" He let go of me.

"My father is the only family I have left. You are *not* going to take him away from me."

He put his hands on his face. He stood up and paced.

"This is my fault. I knew I shouldn't have let it go on this far. Susan, your grandmother, they all said you'd just get over it. That one day, you'd wake up and you'd realize he's gone. I waited and waited for that day." Everything he was saying was going in one ear and out the other.

"Believe what you want, but not in his own damn house."

"So, what? You're going to take care of Pyper all by yourself?"

"You can take her. I'll pump." I still couldn't look at him. I just kept looking at my knees that wouldn't stop shaking.

"You're just going to abandon your daughter like that? Jesus, Portia, think. Think back to everything."

"My father comes first, Ethan. I love Pyper. I really do." I looked up, crying.

"So don't tell us to go." He started to walk up the stairs. I followed.

"I'm sorry." I choked the words out.

"Oh my God, you're serious."

Tears started flowing, so I walked away. He started gathering his stuff in our room while I sat in the hallway and cried.

It took him about thirty minutes to pack up. I was sitting on the steps and my dad came to sit next to me. I collapsed in his shoulders crying—maybe I collapsed on the wall.

I didn't know anymore.

Chapter 19

The next couple weeks were hard and lonely. Ethan didn't want to even look at me, so his dad came over to get the bottles of pumped milk. It was heartbreaking, especially since Mr. Torke wouldn't say a word to me. I missed Pyper. My dad and I drank and smoked because that was what Willows did. I would look out the window and watch them.

Ethan's mom came to town. While Ethan was at work, his mom was watching Pyper.

I had no calls. I had nothing but my dad. He was worth it. He was worth all of it. Even though he would disappear here and there.

I didn't look for him anymore because a part of me *knew*.

"What are you doing?" He handed me beer.

"Ethan's mom just brought Pyper home. I wonder where they went."

"I still don't understand why exactly you guys broke up."

"I don't want to talk about it."

"Are you going to fight for custody?"

"I emailed Susan about it, she hasn't gotten back to me yet."

"Weird."

"I'm thinking he'll get over it. She'll get older and ask where her mommy is and he'll say right across the street and bam, I'm a mother again."

"And it's all my fault…"

"No, Dad. It's not, don't think that. I don't want you ever leaving me again."

"I won't, but just because I won't leave you doesn't mean you should leave your child." Dad got up so fast like he was up to something.

"Dad?" He was pacing the room.

"March over there and demand your baby back."

"It's not that easy. They think I'm crazy. They'll send me off to a psych ward or something."

"Then stop feeling bad for yourself. You're drinking and smoking way more than I am. Go back to school."

I didn't drop out of UCLA, I just hadn't signed up for any classes my last semester. There was no way I could focus on anything except for how fucked up everything was.

Present Day

"So he came back?" Elizabeth was jotting notes in her little black book while my head was still trying to process everything.

"I need to see him," I mumbled. I didn't really know what I meant by that.

Elizabeth looked behind me at the door. "I think I can swing that."

"Swing what?"

"We can go see your family...together. Except this time, maybe you'll remember everything."

"Like me hurting Ethan? You think you could make that happen?"

"Yes. Maybe. I'll try."

"Why do you care?"

"You know, you're not the only person who has asked me that."

"So? I would be in jail right now if it wasn't for you. Why me?"

"I'm called in on special cases. Plus, I don't think people like you get treated fairly in the justice system. The justice system gives innocent people the death penalty. They put mentally ill patients in solitary." She was talking from experience.

"What happened?"

Tears formed in her eyes, but she blinked them away.

"This isn't about me, Portia. I want you to remember everything you lost these past five years. What happened to you is unfair and not your fault." She got herself together and wiped her tears.

"Just because I don't remember something doesn't mean it's not my fault."

She pressed another button on the camera.

"Can you imagine yourself capable of hurting Ethan Torke physically?"

"No, never. I don't even kill cockroaches or spiders. I would say, 'Ask Piper,' but you can't."

"All right, let's go."

"We're leaving?"

"To St. Marshall's. It's time to see your family again." She got up.

I stayed seated. I didn't know if I was ready.

"It's okay…"

When I got here, I'd expected to see my dad on the other side of the door when they let me go. I didn't. Was he really gone? Had he been gone this entire time? I tiptoed out of the room. I looked around, half-expecting to see him.

"My dad's not here." I looked at Elizabeth.

She shook her head as she put her hand on my shoulder.

"I don't know if I can do this," I choked.

"You should have done this five years ago."

I was silent on the drive, but Elizabeth let me smoke in her car.

"Is there still something you're not telling me?" I asked.

She stayed looking at the road. "Like what?"

"I can take it."

"Portia, you just learned that your father is dead. Has been dead."

"So, I'm cured now."

"Unfortunately, mental illness doesn't work like that. And technically, I'm not telling you anything you didn't already know."

"Great. Another memory to un-fucking-lock."

"Do you remember the first time you saw Ethan?"

"Yeah. At the store, he was smoking a Marlboro Red."

"That's what made you look at him?"

"Yeah, why?"

"Just making conversation."

"And his eyes, his build, his hair. He was way too hot to be standing outside my liquor store."

She laughed.

Seeing the cemetery took me back to bad memories.

"I need a minute."

"Do you still have your social anxiety issues?"

I looked at her questioningly.

"I read your file."

"And you fell in love?" I joked.

"Pretty much." She grabbed her purse. "Come on."

My heart was pounding. My arms were getting numb. I guess I still had my issues. I walked slowly after her through the door and down corridors. Elizabeth flashed her badge as we walked through a second set of doors. A nice black man at the front desk escorted us to the columbarium.

I stopped at the doorway.

"You ready?"

I took a deep breath and nodded.

"The Willows are right over here. Piper Willows is at the top. Carol Willows in the middle." I watched as he pointed to each plaque in turn.

We came all the way here for me to look at their *names*?

"I know their names. That's my family."

"You okay?"

I stared at my mother's and sister's names. "My family is in a fucking wall." I crumbled. "It's not fair. She was sixteen years old. I'm still alive."

Piper would have loved the fact that she was on top, though.

Ten Years Ago

Piper was in so much pain. I thought she was dying. I was wiping away her tears.

"What's happening to me?"

"Your appendix ruptured. You're going to be okay, the ambulance is on its way."

"Where's Mom?"

"On the phone with 9-1-1."

Dad came running into the room with a warm towel and put it on her head. "My baby." He lifted her so she could lay on him.

"Dad, she doesn't have a headache. Her appendix busted." She was screaming in pain. Mom was at the door, unable to look.

"How do you know that? They're coming, baby. I promise they'll be here any minute." He was panicking.

"Because I read and pay attention, Dad."

We heard the sirens. Mom ran downstairs. Piper was holding onto my hand so tight. I cried for her, feeling her pain.

"Look at me, Piper. You're going to be scared because they are going to take you away from us and they're going to use all these medical instruments you're not used to seeing, but you will be fine and back with us before you know it."

"No. I'm so scared. Don't leave me."

"We are not leaving you. We will be right behind you."

"You're going to be at the hospital?" She knew that was the last place I would ever want to be. My little sister was in the most pain she probably ever felt, yet she was still worried about me and my stupid issues.

"Of course."

"Then I know I'll be okay." She took deep breaths.

The paramedics took over.

Seven Years Ago

I was doing homework in my room and listening to classical music when Mom knocked twice and then just came in.

"Hey, sweetie."

"What do you want?"

"Heard you had a tough day at school today." She sat on the edge of my bed.

Fucking Piper telling her my business.

"It was just an anxiety attack...wasn't my first and won't be last."

She took a deep breath. I was interested why she cared about this time.

"If you want to be homeschooled, I'll support that."

I put down my book. I was shocked. I've been asking since middle school.

"Really?"

"I didn't realize how serious your issue was. I made a call and I'm going to get you on medication that will help ease whatever you have...I think." This was mom trying to make sense out of her daughter not being able to walk the halls at high school

"Thanks, Mom, but I already talked to my counselor. I won't be able to get into UCLA on time if I switch to homeschooling...that's why I dropped the idea." She put her hand on my thigh. Her eyes were watery.

"I love you. I want you to be able to talk to me. You don't have to get your sister to tell me things."

"I don't. She just does."

She smiled and walked away.

"Hey, Mom?"

"Yeah, sweetie?"

"I love you, too."

Present Day

Underneath theirs was the name Richard Willows.

The man pointed.

I looked away.

"You accepted that your mom and sister died five years ago, Portia. Why didn't you accept your father did, too?"

"I don't know…I just couldn't see it. I couldn't imagine it."

"I need you to understand something that might be really hard. I need you to stay strong,"

"What?"

"Your father is going to stay there."

But I had seen my dad wake up from the dead before.

I nodded anyway.

I was terrified to read his name. I knew he was dead but I didn't think I was ready to accept it.

"I'm right here." Elizabeth assured me. I took a deep breath and stepped forward. I touched the plaque.

"That's not him."

Six Years Ago

Dad was yelling at Piper for some reason. Piper fought with our parents at least three times a month, but this time Dad sounded really mad, so I decided to listen.

"What the hell is wrong with you? Smoking? Drinking? I should ground you for the rest of your fucking life."

"I wasn't. I was around people who were." Piper wouldn't smoke a cigarette, but she probably did drink a little.

"That doesn't make it any better. I raised beautiful, smart children to make the right decisions. When you see someone pulling that shit, you walk away."

"But, Dad."

"But nothing. You. Walk. Away. You are not going to this dance. You are not going to any football games. You're in rehab for the next thirty days."

"Rehab for not doing anything, for saying *no*?" Piper was livid. Dad was being really harsh. I felt so bad for her.

I opened my door, they both stared at me in the hallway.

"That's unfair, Dad."

"Stay out of it, Portia."

"You're just mad that I'm not like *her*. You don't want me to have a life just like her!" Piper yelled, and stomped out.

"If it makes you feel any better, Sis, Mom is always mad I'm not more like *you*." I couldn't be mad, I knew she didn't mean it. "We're not going to be able to please both of them, ever."

"Both of you. Rooms. Now. Before I start saying shit I regret." He stomped down the stairs.

Present Day

"This is where they've been? This entire time?"
Elizabeth nodded.
I walked out.

Chapter 20

One Year Ago

For the past year, Ethan would visit with Pyper for hours at a time once a week. Maybe more, if I was lucky. I was just food to Ethan. His daughter's mother. I could tell he'd fallen out of love with me. To be honest, that hurt more than losing Pyper.

I saw him coming over through my kitchen window. She was *walking*. I rushed to the door.

"Oh my God! Look at you!" I bent down with a huge smile.

"Hi baby," I wrap my arms around her tightly. "I am so proud of you. I missed you so much." I kissed her forehead. "I love you, don't ever forget how much I love you." I picked her up.

"She needs to be fed."

"What? Still?"

"Yeah my mom says it's still a good idea."

"Your mom is in town?" I had known, but I didn't want it to seem like I was spying on them.

"Yeah, she's been helping with the baby."

"I miss you, Ethan."

He didn't say anything, just pressed his lips together and tears formed in his eyes.

"Can I take her just for one night? I can do it. I know I can."

"I have to ask my mom."

"Ethan, she is *our* child."

"I don't know if it's a good idea."

"She's my daughter, Ethan. I miss her. *Please*."

"Okay, but I stay, too."

I smiled and nodded.

"You get to stay with Mommy tonight." I kissed her forehead. I walked backed into the house. Ethan came in and looked around.

"What?"

"Nothing." He looked around again. "I see you went back to drinking and I smell you went back to smoking." He tapped his fingers on the table.

I pulled Pyper away from my boobs and pulled my shirt and bra back on.

"Wait. Don't say anything. You're going to blame it on your father." He looked over at the television. "Does your *father* mind if I change the channel? Is he sitting on the couch right now?"

I didn't recognize this Ethan. I stood up and grabbed Pyper's toy and threw it at his head.

He dodged it. "Where is he, Portia?"

"You know what, take her. I am not doing this."

"Okay. When you decide to accept the truth, let me know. Your daughter will be waiting." He grabbed her. Pyper started crying.

My heart started to constrict. I'd never felt anything like this before. This wasn't Ethan. This wasn't happening. He wasn't taking my daughter away from me. I slid down the cabinets and sobbed on the kitchen floor. My dad never came down to see if I was okay. The pain of being alone was overwhelming. The pain of everyone abandoning me was overwhelming.

Ethan was gone.

Pyper was gone.

Mom and Piper were gone.

My dad wasn't here.

Present Day

"What did you do this past year?" We were back in the room. The video camera was on. I didn't answer. I stared at the corner on the wall, wondering what I did.

"Portia?"

My heart started to beat a little faster. I stood up and walked around the room.

"I don't remember." I stopped and stared at her and the camera.

"You don't remember what you did this past year?"

I shook my head.

"Portia, this part is really important. This case is most likely going to trial. This past year plays a pivotal role in what gets you free."

"I think that's when I forgot about Pyper." I sat back down. "Ethan betrayed me. He took Pyper away from me. It broke me, and then the rest is just a blur. I think I just went back to living my life."

"You started school again?"

"Yes. I was happy. I think."

REMEMBER

Six Months Ago

"Dad! *Aerial Cities* is on again," I yelled upstairs, holding two beers and a pack of cigarettes, one already in my mouth.

"What city are they doing?"

"I don't know yet. You still have that bag of Doritos?"

"Yup. Bringing them down now. You got me a beer?"

"Of course, Dad."

He came over and plopped down next to me.

They were doing New York.

"You ever thought about going back to school?" Dad asked.

"Yeah. I have. It would give me something else to do. I feel like we've already watched every television show that ever existed." I grabbed a Dorito, "Mmm, I wonder if we still have that dip I got from Ralphs that was on sale." I got up and ran to the kitchen.

"I love that you drive places now. Speaking of, you want to take me to the hardware store tomorrow? I want to try to fix that faucet in your bathroom."

I heard what he said but my eyes were focused on the window watching Ethan get out of his car. He had gotten a new one. He pulled a little girl out of the backseat and she ran inside the house. It was like she lived there. Sarah was living there full time, too. Did Sarah have a baby? Whatever. I grabbed the dip and sat next to Dad and watched New York.

"Is that a no?"

"What? Oh, yeah, sure."

"You okay, honey?"

"Yeah. It's just weird. Mr. Torke has a full house now."

"I saw that. And I think he's having an affair with Susan."

"Ew. Wait, first of all, you mean Susan is having an affair with Mr. Torke. Second, why do you think that?"

"I've seen her over there a lot. Plus, when Ingrid came over to bring us that casserole, she mentioned it. Remember?"

"Oh yeah, that was delicious. Maybe I should go over to Ingrid's this weekend. I'm bored."

"Okay, but *after* you take me to the hardware store."

Twenty-Four Hours Ago

It was the most normal day. I was cleaning up the house, reminiscing about when I first met Ethan, like I always did. It sucked not really knowing what happened between us. I just remember one day, we looked at each other across the street and it was like we were complete strangers.

There was a knock at the door. I turned off the vacuum. It was Susan with a few papers in her hand.

"Hey." I backed up to let her in.

"You're cleaning. I'm surprised."

"Why?"

"Every other time I've seen you, you've been drunk or passed out. I'm surprised you're alive."

"Well. I am. What's up?"

"We're selling the house. We have to."

I could have sworn I physically felt my heart crack as she passed me the papers.

"I knew this was coming."

"What did you expect was going to happen? You abandon your daughter. I thought for sure you were going to be a better mother than me," Susan stated.

"What are you talking about? I don't *have* a daughter."

All of sudden, her anger softened. She backed up.

"Is that why you haven't asked about her, haven't demanded to see her?"

"Susan, I don't have time for this. I'm tired. I've been cleaning all day. How much time are you giving us?"

"Fuck." She sighed and paced around. She took out her phone.

"Get over here now. No. Ethan. Get over here. We need to tell her *now*. Bring Pyper."

Piper? What the fuck?

Tell me what?

Piper was still alive?

"I can't believe I let this happen. You should have stayed with me. I should have put you away. None of this would be happening if you were just put away!"

Dad hurried down the stairs. "What's going on, sweetie?"

I shrugged.

"Is your dad here right now?" Susan asked.

I looked up at him.

There was a knock on the door. My heart started to pound. I put down the papers before I got to look at them. My dad came over to me. I held onto him.

"They're scaring me."

Susan opened the door. Ethan Torke was in my house again. He had a full beard—he looked different. It felt like it'd been years. I took a deep breath. I put my hand to my mouth. I had missed him so much.

"Daddy?" a little girl came crawling around his leg. I backed away.

"Who *is* that?" I mumbled, and looked at my dad.

"*What?*" Ethan looked shocked and then looked at Susan.

She nodded. "Yeah. That's what's been going on over here."

"What do we do?" Ethan asked.

I grabbed my dad's hands.

"We tell her the truth and then she needs to go somewhere."

263

He nodded.

"You need to do it Ethan. You owe her this."

"Ethan?" I cried. What was going on? Was she giving my house to Ethan? Fuck no!

"Mommy doesn't look sick." the little girl whispered to Susan.

"I'm going to take her back home."

"No. I want to stay," the little girl cried.

They left.

"Can we sit?" I looked over at my dad. He walked away. Ethan and I sat next to each other on the couch.

"I missed you so much." I couldn't help myself.

"I missed you, too." He looked me in my eyes. Something was different. They were still icy blue but they weren't innocent anymore.

"Listen to me…I did something bad, like really bad."

He started to cry. "What is it?" I wiped away his tears. I don't know how I was supposed to feel about Ethan. All I remembered was that we were in love once.

"Five years ago, the night of the school play, I was here, in Los Angeles. It was important to Sarah for my mom and me to come down. She made the school play the biggest deal. I was going through a really hard time myself back in Florida. I was depressed and lonely. Mom thought it would be a good idea for me to come back to California to see if it would help me get out of my funk. Sarah's play was the perfect excuse." He choked on his words.

"Okay…"

"My mom and I got in the stupidest fight. I don't even remember what it was about. I went and got drunk, and lost track of time. Once I realized it was so late, I felt awful about missing the play. I rushed over to the school so I could see Sarah and apologize to her." He started crying even harder.

"I drove to the school drunk."

"Ethan, why would you do that? You could have killed someone." I grabbed his hands.

"I did." He broke down. He let go of my hands and buried his head in his lap.

My eyes widened.

"It was *your* family. Portia, it was my fault. Your family died because of *me*."

I froze.

"I hit them and their car flipped."

I stood up and backed away.

"I am *so* sorry. I just fled, and never took any responsibility for what I did. When I came back to live with my dad, he mentioned that the family across the street had been killed in a car accident...I knew immediately. I was going to apologize to you in person. I had to live up to what I did."

My heart stopped.

I struggled to breathe.

I looked up at dad. I could tell all he saw was red.

Present Day

"I'm very proud of you. You've made tremendous strides."

"I guess. I still don't know how I ended up *here*. One minute, Pyper was in my arms, we were making our little family, and the next, she didn't exist." I choked. "And now I'm here with you, and my whole family is dead because of Ethan."

"We're almost done. Tell me now how you feel about Ethan?"

"I loved him. He's a better parent than I could ever be. He's *everything* to me. That's why I don't understand how all that could have been his fault. Why didn't he tell me? How could I not know? No one ever told me that a drunk driver caused the accident. How could I forget the most important things that have happened to me?"

"It's not your fault you thought your dad was alive. People just didn't know how to deal with it. There was no way they were going to tell you that it wasn't just an accident."

"If they had, do you think I still would have hallucinated my dad?"

"There's no way to tell. PTSD looks different on everyone, especially with someone who already struggled with extreme social anxiety disorder."

My head started to hurt. It was excruciating. I crunched up my face and buried my head in my hands. I wanted the pain to stop.

"You okay?"

I shook my head.

"We are *so* close, Portia."

I kept shaking my head. "I can't do this anymore. I can't. I just want to go home." I cried. "Can we please stop?"

"We can today, but it's just going to happen again. We are going to trial. Rose Harper is—"

"Why? Why? Why? I hurt Ethan. I know. I did something really bad but *what*?" I stood up and started screaming, "What? What, Elizabeth? Just tell me. Stop all this. Why are you doing this to me? I was *fine*. I was doing *just fine*. Now, my whole family is dead because of the one guy I ever loved. I forgot that I had a fucking daughter. Everyone helped me live this lie and now I am going to jail." I gave up. "Just take me. I don't care. I just want this all to stop."

"Portia. Do you want to see your daughter again?"

"Yes, of course. More than anything."

"You love her, right?"

"Yes." I couldn't even see straight. My eyes were so swollen. My head was pounding.

"Then sit down and remember."

"No. I don't want to," I screamed. It was starting to come back. "Please don't make me."

"Remember."

"No," I screamed.

"Remember."

Chapter 21

Twenty-Four Hours Ago

"I offered to help with your grocery bags because I wanted to get to know you—to see for myself if you were okay. I was going to apologize right then and there, but when I realized you had no idea what had happened, I felt like I had to do *something*. I had to be there for you. I couldn't tell you the truth because it was my fault and I ended up falling in love with you..." I was just staring at him blankly. "But believe this...I really fell for you. I fell for you hard. I never loved someone so much in my entire life. I still love you. I love *all* of you. Since the moment I first saw you, which made it even harder for me to tell you the truth."

He knelt at my feet, sobbing. I backed up, still not taking it in.

Out of nowhere, my dad hit him with a baseball bat.

The one we always kept by the door.

It was a metal bat.

The one we never touched.

"You son of a bitch. You ruined my life. You took everything away from me." My dad screamed, striking him over and over again. Ethan didn't fight back, he just ran. He ran towards the kitchen. He kept trying to grab things to throw in my dad's way. Soon,

Ethan went down. My hands covered my mouth as I looked at his bruised and bloody body and for the first time realized the damaged he'd done to my family.

I wasn't even crying.

I stood there watching my dad brutally beat the love of my life.

There was blood everywhere. I finally got myself together and knew I had to stop him. I jumped on top of Dad, trying to pull him off or get the bat away from him.

I screamed at him to stop. He was so angry and so heavy. It was so hard to get him to stop. I just kept screaming. He had blood all over him. I put myself between my dad and Ethan.

"Drop it," I commanded. I was something else. Maybe some*one* else.

Dad dropped it. I ran to Ethan and lifted his head. He was coughing up blood.

Holy shit, this was bad. He was barely moving.

I looked around.

Blood all over the kitchen floor, all over me, all over Ethan.

"I'm so sorry. Ethan, please stay with me," I cried. I didn't know what to do so I screamed for help at the top of my lungs.

"I love you," Ethan mumbled, drawing what seemed like his last breath.

Mr. Torke, Susan, and that little girl came running inside the house.

The little girl slipped on the blood and fell.

"Daddy. Daddy," she was screaming and crying, trying to crawl over to him, sliding through the blood.

Ethan had a daughter?

"Oh my God! Oh my God!" Susan screamed, and went to pick up the little girl.

Mr. Torke grabbed me. "You fucking bitch." He grabbed my arm so tight and threw me to the other side of the room so hard my back hit the back of the couch, cracking it. It hurt, but if Ethan died…nothing would be more painful than that.

"It's okay, son. Susan, call 9-1-1. Now." Mr. Torke cried into Ethan's bloody body.

I just sat on the floor, stunned.

"No. No. What did you do?" I screamed at my father.

"Get the baby out of here…" Mr. Torke screamed at Susan.

"Stay with me, son. Please don't die like this. I love you so much. I am so sorry. I should have been a better father. I should have protected you." He rocked his dying son in his arms. Susan went upstairs with the little girl while she was on the phone with 911.

"We've got to go," Dad said to me.

"Dad. No. We can't. I have to make sure he's okay."

"Do you want to go to jail? Let's go *now*." He grabbed me. We ran out the door and hopped into the car as fast as we could.

"No. Susan! She's leaving. She's getting away. Get her! I don't want to leave my son." Mr. Torke screamed from inside.

I was in the car with my dad sobbing as my boyfriend was dying on my kitchen floor. I looked in my rearview mirror. Susan was chasing after us.

Chapter 22

Present Day

"How could I do something like that? I can't even *think* it. Even if my father was still alive and *he* did that, how could I leave them like that?"

"You remember everything now?"

I thought so.

I felt even more broken.

I was not a human being.

How could I live knowing the things that I'd done? Knowing I had literally no one left.

I'd fallen for the one person who took it all away from me.

"It's okay, Portia. I can't even imagine what you must be going through right now. This is the hardest part. We are almost done. I just need to ask you a couple more questions." Her voice sounded like she was underwater again.

"If your father hadn't been in your head that night, how you would have reacted to learning Ethan was responsible for the accident?"

How could I even answer that?

"I don't know. Five years ago, I probably would have wanted him arrested. But I wouldn't have hurt him, right? I don't know. I don't know."

I started rocking, crying.

"I don't know. I don't know. I don't know."

Tears started flowing. "It still doesn't make sense to me—but I would have given him the chance. He was the father of my child. I think I would. I know I would. I would have never hurt him. Maybe a slap. I probably would have slapped him. Hard."

"That's completely understandable, Portia. Do you feel remorse for what you claim your father did?"

I nodded. "Now that I think about it, I don't even think my real dad would have reacted that way."

"That's it. You're done."

"What do you mean I'm done?"

"I have to take all of this to the DA's office. I have to present your case to your attorneys. Good news is that you have Rose Harper. You are in really good hands."

No. We couldn't be done. She couldn't just lay all that on me and leave.

Where the fuck was I supposed to go?

What the fuck was I supposed to do?

"Wait...how's Ethan?" I was almost too embarrassed to ask.

"He's alive. I don't know for how much longer. It's bad. I'm not going to lie to you. I will keep you posted on his status." Elizabeth stood up to leave.

"Hey, one thing…"

"Yes?" Elizabeth tilted her head.

"My dad told me a story. He told me a lot of stories these past five years. One was super specific though, about a girl he got pregnant—Betty Byers. How could I know that if he didn't actually tell me that story?"

"How do you know that story is true?"

I should have known I was just going to be more confused.

"Everything is going to be okay, Portia Willows."

I closed my eyes and pictured everyone in my life that I had lost.

I couldn't picture my father.

"There is *no way* I lost him." I shook my head. I looked back at Elizabeth, waiting for her to tell me everything was a joke.

How was my brain capable of making up my whole life?

She hugged me tight then two security guards came in.

I already knew where this was going.

As I was being walked through the hallways with my hands behind my back, I felt defeated, exhausted, crazy, lost, and nothing—all at the same time. They took me downstairs, at least four floors. That's when it got scary. There weren't any windows, just concrete. The nurses looked like they dealt with hell.

They put me in a solitary room with white walls, a toilet, and a twin bed.

One blanket, one pillow.

I sat there shaking until a nurse came in with a tray in her hand.

"These are your pills for the day." There were six.

"Are you serious?"

"You were prescribed these."

"Six? I need to take *six?*"

She didn't answer.

Holy shit. I was fucked up.

I was seriously fucked up. I was bat shit crazy.

I tried to kill my boyfriend. I still might.

Holy fuck, I was living in my own Lifetime movie.

REMEMBER

A Few Weeks Later

If anyone tells you they got used to solitary, they're lying.
Elizabeth kept me in the loop about Ethan and Pyper. He was doing
better. I didn't hit him hard enough to break any bones but did cause
a lot of internal bleeding and he was in a light coma. Rose Harper
came to visit me to ask me the same questions over and over again.
I was originally charged with attempted murder with a deadly weapon. It might change depending on his condition.

Honestly, I *was* guilty. Call it whatever you want. I deserved
to spend the rest of my life in this room. I took pill after pill. I was
exhausted all the time. I sometimes slept for over twenty-four hours.
I had dreams that my family was still alive. They were painful.

The door opened. It was Elizabeth. I smiled and sat cross-
legged on the bed. She had a bunch of papers in her hands.

"Hi." Her pity for me was obvious. It was disgusting to look at.

"Stop."

"Stop what?" She brought in a chair and sat down.

"With that face. You feel so bad for me, but don't. I deserve
this."

"You do *not*. Stop thinking that way."

"Thinking that way makes it a lot easier."

"We're going to get you out of here. No one can't stop talking
about your case. It's on the news and everything."

"No way."

"Look." She handed me a newspaper. It was the *LA Times*: "Young Girl Hallucinates Dead Father for Five Years."

"Great. I'm going to be a laughing stock."

"This time, the media is working in your favor. No one can understand why people let you live like that for so long."

"None of that matters. I almost killed Ethan. That's a fact."

"But you *thought* your dad did it."

I looked over to the side. A moment went by.

"Hey, I wanted to ask you something, off the record."

I looked back at her.

"You ever see your dad again? In here?"

"No," I said sternly.

"Why do you think that is?"

"Because I know he's dead now. Trust me. I *want* to see him again. I tried. I call out for him. Nothing."

"It's probably the medication."

"I hate taking it. I don't feel real."

"I know. That's pretty common."

Elizabeth took a deep breath.

I knew there was something she wasn't telling me.

"You know, it's okay if you don't get me out…"

"I know. But I will. I promise."

"You can't promise me that. Rose doesn't promise me anything. None of this would be happening if I had just believed."

"Stay safe in here, okay?" She gave me that sulk again.

I shook my head. "I will. I'm fine. Go."

Elizabeth was all I had now.

"Sweetie. Sweetie." A whisper. I woke up but was still half asleep. I saw my dad's face. I backed away.

"No. No. Dad. No."

I had taken my pills. What the hell was going on?

"I'm back, honey." He smiled.

I looked at him but he looked…different. I knew he wasn't supposed to be here. I knew something was wrong. I started crying.

"Don't be scared."

"Dad, you have to go."

"Why? Haven't you missed me?"

"Yeah. I do."

"Then come here." He reached out is hands to me.

"You are *not here*." I kicked him away from me and just like that, he disappeared. I started crying.

"I'm sorry. I'm sorry. I didn't mean to do that. Come back. Come back. Please." I stood up. I twirled. Nothing.

"Dad, I'm sorry."

He came through the wall, but he was like a ghost this time. I couldn't touch him. I couldn't feel him. I barely could see him.

"Dad?"

He didn't speak.

"I'm sorry. I love you. I miss you." Then he solidified again and went to hug me. I hugged him back and cried in his arms. I held him so tight. When I left his arms, I looked him in his eyes.

"You have to go."

"I don't want to."

"Dad. You are dead. You died." I was sobbing.

"No, I didn't."

"Please, don't make this hard. I don't want to say bye either. I have to do it for Pyper."

"Then don't." He grabbed my arms.

I jerked them away.

"Dad. Stop."

He stopped.

"Go. Now. *Go*."

He stood there.

My head started pounding. The room felt like it was closing in on me. My arms went numb.

He kept staring at me.

I kept shaking my head. My knees became weak.

"Go. You are *not here.* I love you so much, Daddy!" I grabbed him. I kissed him on the cheek. He laid his head on top of mine. We stood there in silence for several minutes. I took a deep breath and then pushed him as hard as I could through the wall.

"I love you," he said right before he disappeared.

I knew I was never going to see him again.

I collapsed screaming. I punched the walls. I kicked the bed. I banged my head against the door.

Eventually, I knocked myself out.

Chapter 23

Two Months Later

"Fuck no. Not wearing that."

"You want to wear those white scrubs to court?" Elizabeth snapped. She had visited me at least once a week. Our friendship grew whether or not she would ever admit it. She wanted me to wear slacks, a blazer, and a button-up. Gross. My mom never wore clothes like this and she had to look professional at all times.

I snatched them and started changing in front of her.

"You nervous?"

"No, I'm restless. I've been waiting for this day for months."

"Yeah, we all have. It's a media frenzy at the courthouse right now. Are you prepared?"

"You mean to have a bunch of cameras in face? Of course. I do it every day." I finished buttoning up my shirt.

Elizabeth held up the blazer for me. "You look great."

I took a deep breath. "I *am* nervous to see Ethan, though."

"I bet." She squeezed my shoulders. "Come on, we don't want to be late."

"You weren't kidding." The amount of people with cameras was unreal. "There's no way they are all here for me."

"They are, Rose should be here any minute now." Elizabeth was trying to look through the crowd for her.

I took a deep breath. I couldn't get out of this car. My legs felt numb. It was coming on again.

"Elizabeth, I've been in solitary for months. This…" I gestured out the window. "I can't."

"I know, but you have to." She got out the car. I immediately started freaking.

"Back up. Give her room." I saw Rose. She opened the door.

"Come on. Let's go."

No. No.

Elizabeth grabbed my arm. Rose was on my right. Elizabeth was on my left.

"Just look down and walk." The whole world was surrounding me with their cameras and asking me questions.

"Why did you do it?"

"How did you see your dead father for over five years?"

"Who helped you?"

"Do you feel bad?"

"Do you still love Ethan?"

That one stopped me in my tracks. I looked up to see which one had asked me that.

"Don't say a word and keep walking," Rose instructed.

It felt like the steps to the courthouse were five hundred miles long.

We got through the doors and it was instant silence and relief. I took deep breath.

"First hard part over with. Now let's go kill this case." Rose smiled. She never smiled.

I looked at Elizabeth.

"I'm right here." She put her hand on my shoulder.

The courtroom was just like television except not as nice and way more people. I saw everyone I knew walking in—Susan, Gary, Stefan, Grandma, and Ingrid. What the hell was *Ingrid* doing here?

Maddie and her mother. I started to get even more nervous.

There seemed to be hundreds of people there, but the only person I saw was him. If my heart could have physically broken out of my chest and rolled down the courtroom, it would have happened then.

He looked at me like he hadn't seen me in a long time—like he missed me—then his eyes shifted away quickly. I sat on the left side of the court room at a table with four chairs. Two guys sat with Rose Harper. I'd never seen them before. I couldn't bear to look at Ethan.   He looked great for having almost been killed by me a few months prior. There was a lot of chatter going on. I closed my eyes and wished I was back in solitary.

This was awful.

"All rise."

We all rose.

This was really about to happen. I looked over at Ethan. Tears pooled in my eyes.

How did I get here? I used to be a high school student who didn't talk to anyone. Now I was in a courtroom trying not to go to jail. I couldn't hold it together. Tears kept coming down and I kept wiping them away.

I wanted to be strong.

Rose approached the jury. Everyone looked at how high her heels were. She had a remote in her hand and pressed a button. It was a family photo—we were all smiling. I couldn't look.

"This is Portia Willows. She was *seventeen* years old when her entire family died in a car accident caused by Ethan Torke. She has extreme social anxiety disorder, meaning it is paralyzing for her to be in public. She did not have any friends. She never went anywhere. The only people she ever talked to are *in that photo*." She paused. "Now they are *gone*. On top of her extreme social anxiety disorder, Portia suffers from Post-Traumatic Stress Disorder. Doctors, who are here and whose testimony you will hear in the coming days, say that it is extremely likely for someone with these characteristics to develop psychosis and a dissociative state when left untreated." She stopped and looked every juror in the eye.

"It was left untreated all right. For *five years*. Ladies and gentlemen, for *five years*," she held up her right hand, "Portia Willows was hallucinating her father because her mind couldn't fathom that her entire world was gone because of *that* man." She pointed at Ethan. "Because he decided to drive drunk. But we are not presenting *that* case. What we *are* presenting is that he had a plan to apologize and admit what he did...but he didn't. *Fine,* don't tell her that it was your fault. You guys can understand that, right? But can you understand not telling her that no one was living in the house with her? That the father she introduces to her boyfriend, no one else can see? Instead, they fall in love, *conceive a child*." She paused. "Eventually, the truth comes out. Portia strikes. Yeah, she did. She attacked Ethan Torke and it was brutal and she is extremely remorseful." She looked over at me. I was already crying because of the photo. "But what did you expect would happen? She was sick and not just Ethan, but everyone in her life took advantage of that." She nodded and walked away.

Ethan's lawyer looked exactly like his dad. Rich, white, old. His name was Richard Samson. I remember because Richard was my dad's name.

I just said "was."

"Ethan Torke made a mistake five years ago. But Ethan gave Portia a life. He may not have apologized at the time, but what he did for her was so much more than words. He did favors for her. He would clean her house..."

What? He helped me clean twice. I think.

"He took care of her. Portia was an alcoholic. She drank and smoked cigarettes every single day. She was not the innocent, shy girl the prosecution is making her out to be. Ethan took her under his wing. He saw a broken girl who was not taking care of herself and he helped her, he tried to get her help, he got her to stop drinking and smoking. He never told her the truth about the accident because he recognized her fragile state. Instead, he apologized in *actions*. Along the way, they fell in love and they did conceive a child—a child that *she* abandoned." He stopped right in front of the jury. All twelve of them looked at me like I was a monster. "They claim Portia 'forgot' she had a child. How is that even possible? Are we going to use mental illness as an excuse *again*? Just because someone doesn't see things the same way the rest of us do does not mean they get off. At the end of the day, Portia Willows took a metal bat and struck Ethan fifteen times. *Fifteen times*."

I could not stop crying. This was brutal. I wanted it to stop.

I didn't see the point. I was pleading guilty—just take me to jail.

I wanted to go back to solitary.

Why did we have to go through this?

Elizabeth said I should get visits with my daughter. Thank God they didn't let her come to court.

A police officer was taking the stand. I recognized him but couldn't remember why.

"Detective Riley, you were called to the Willows house October 9, 2015 for a missing person report."

"That's correct."

"But you didn't make the report?" Rose asked.

"No."

"Why?"

He looked down. "Because the report was for Richard Willows, who was already deceased. We told Ms. Willows, but she didn't believe us."

"How was Ms. Willows, the house? Anything out of the ordinary?"

"Portia was clearly upset. Someone she cared about was missing. I remember her boyfriend was there."

"Is he in the courtroom today?"

"Yes." When asked to identify him, he pointed at Ethan. "He seemed like this was a normal state of affairs. He told us everything was okay."

"Did he tell you that his girlfriend thought her deceased father was still alive?"

"Objection, leading," Richard Samson yelled.

"Why leave?" Rose asked.

"Excuse me?" Detective Riley looked confused.

"Portia was in distress. A young boy tells you to leave and you left. Were you sure she was safe? Did you establish Ethan was her guardian? Why would you take his word that everything was okay, and Ms. Willows was safe?"

Detective Riley coughed. "We had another call—a burglary. He seemed like he had it all handled. We left in a hurry."

"No further questions, your honor." Rose stomped back.

"What just happened?" I whispered to Rose.

"He's an unreliable witness. His testimony is trash." She threw down her pen.

Another police officer took the stand. It was the police officer who arrested Da—me. This was the police officer who arrested *me* in the woods when I fled.

"What kind of state was Portia in when you arrested her?" Rose asked.

"Complete hysterics. She kept screaming at her father. She was under the impression we were arresting him as well and that we had put him in the backseat next to her."

"Was that all that happened?"

"No."

"What else did she say?"

"She asked where Ethan Torke was."

The courtroom erupted in whispers.

"Correct me if I'm wrong, but you were arresting her because

283

she attempted to kill Ethan?"

"Yes."

"Was she aware she had just attacked someone?"

"No. She had no idea why she was getting arrested and definitely was not aware she had hurt Ethan."

"No further questions, your honor." Rose smiled and sat down. Richard stood.

"Can you please explain this photo to me, Detective?"

I gasped and put my hand over my mouth. I had never seen the crime scene photos.

I put my head down. I felt everyone's eyes on me.

Rose whispered, "Keep it up. Everyone is watching."

Was this all a game to her? I had really done all those horrible things to him.

"Oh God."

I couldn't stop crying. The jury was staring at me.

The pictures showed blood everywhere.

All over my living room, dining room, front door.

My house was a bloodbath.

Ethan wasn't in the photo. Thank God.

"When I walked in, I thought for sure I was walking into a homicide case. I was about to call the detective, but the lady told me he was on the way to the hospital. I was relieved. It was sickening though. He was one lucky guy."

"Have you seen blood like this before in your career on the force?"

"Objection. Relevance?" Rose snapped.

"I'll allow it, but get to the point," the judge stated.

"Yes, but only once before, in a murder case."

"With this amount of blood, do you think Portia Willows intended to murder Ethan Torke?"

"Objection, speculation."

"No further questions."

I didn't. I swear I didn't.

Then it was Elizabeth's turn on the stand. I took a deep breath. I wanted this to be over so badly. It was just getting started.

"Why were you called to this case, Ms. Smith?" Rose asked.

"I am a forensic psychiatrist. We get called by the LAPD to handle the assessment of a mentally disordered offender. Portia was obviously mentally ill. I wanted to find out why before we talked about what happened."

"You recorded everything, correct?"

It was me. I looked dirty, sick, not myself.

"Yes." Rose turned on a video that had been entered into evidence, it was a still frame. "This is when I first met her. She had no idea where she was, who I was, or what happened in the last five years—which is common when an additional trauma occurs with an already traumatized individual."

They played the tape.

"My name is Elizabeth Smith. I'm here to help you. I am not going to hurt you. So you don't know why you're here?"

I shook my head.

"Whenever you're ready, I want you to tell me what happened."

"Where's my dad? I need my dad."

Rose muted the tape. I kept staring at myself.

"Basically, your job, and I'll say it like this for the jury's sake, is to make sure she is not faking?"

"Correct."

"After these hours of interviews, recordings, and tests, what is your ultimate expert opinion?"

"Portia Willows has extreme social anxiety disorder. She gets a physical reaction when out in public. Ethan Torke can attest to that. It was left untreated. Loss of memory is just one symptom. What's even more common is post-partum depression. All of this combined was too much for Portia's brain to handle. So she shut it all out. When Ethan told her the accident was his fault, everything came back. The attack on Ethan was *not* done by Portia Willows. It wasn't even her deceased dad as she had claimed. It was her illness left untreated."

"Thank you." Rose shut off the video and joined me again at the table. It had been playing the whole time.

"Are we going to watch all of it? I don't want everyone to see me like that," I whispered to Rose.

"No. It's just for the jury."

"Dr. Smith, how long before this was recorded was Ms. Willows striking Ethan with a bat?" Richard asked.

"About twelve hours. Give or take."

"Did she have any recollection of what happened?"

"No."

"So she had no idea why this *toddler* is in a puddle of blood?" Richard pressed a button.

I gasped again. Who could have taken that picture? My little Pypes screaming, covered in blood.

Make it stop.

"I can't do this anymore. Please. Please." I start crying again, this time loudly and uncontrollably.

"Get it together," Rose whispered. I guess this time, I wasn't as sympathetic.

"Is everything okay, counsel?" the judge asked Rose.

"Yes. She's fine. May I ask that we take that photo down?"

"Of course." The judge nodded to Richard, who continued with Elizabeth.

"Dr. Elizabeth Smith, you have been an outstanding forensic psychiatrist for over fifteen years, but what happened in 2012?"

"Objection. Permission to approach." Rose stomped her way to the bench with Richard. Something was going on. Papers were being passed. Rose came back, not looking happy. The judge motioned for Elizabeth to answer.

"My sister got arrested for holding up a liquor store. She was schizophrenic."

Members of the jury exchanged glances.

"Did she get out?"

"No. She killed herself in jail."

The jury gasped.

Oh my God. Poor Elizabeth. No wonder she was fighting so hard.

"I'm sorry to hear that. I can't imagine how that feels. You couldn't help her. But you can help Portia Willows?"

"It wasn't the same. I am doing my job."

"Was your job to coerce Portia into acting crazier than she was?"

"No."

"You took Portia to the cemetery to visit her deceased relatives?"

"So she could remember on her own."

"It's very unusual for a patient to leave the hospital. Did you give Portia special treatment?"

"Why are they doing this to her?" I looked at Rose. She was stone cold staring at Elizabeth.

"Of course not, it was the most efficient way to treat the patient."

"Can you tell me the difference between treating and assessing?"

"I had the opportunity to do both so I took it."

"Answer the question, please."

"Treating is putting her through cognitive therapy, revisiting places so she could remember on her own and get a sense of reality back. Assessing is just asking questions and recording, writing up a report and giving it to the LAPD."

"What is in your job description to do?"

"Assess Portia Willows."

"As, per her own testimonuy, Dr. Smith was *treating* Portia Willows, and it should be obvious to the court that she was not an impartial assessor, I request these recordings be thrown out."

"Sustained."

Elizabeth gasped.

Rose sighed.

"What the fuck was that?" Rose yelled at Elizabeth in the break-room during recess.

"I did my job. This has nothing to do with my sister."

"This has *everything* to do with your sister. If I had known there *was* a sister I could have prepared for it. This case is built on you, *Elizabeth*. She is going to jail. Now, you couldn't save *two* people you care about." Rose marched off.

Elizabeth rested her head on the wall.

"I'm sorry. She's a bitch."

"She is, but a good one. Portia, I'm sorry."

"Don't be. If it wasn't for you, who knows where I would be right now."

"Whatever happens, Portia, I won't stop fighting for you." She smiled and I smiled back.

It was time to go back in.

My character witnesses took the stand next.

Maddie: "When I met her in grade school, I knew she wasn't like us. There was something extremely wrong with her. Piper never treated her differently or anything like that. But I knew she should be getting help or something. I knew that even at six years old."

Maddie's mother: "I could never tell her mother to put that girl on medication but all the parents knew she ought to be. Portia was having panic attacks once a week in school. Everyone would hear about it. She never lived a normal life. Ever."

Ingrid: "Portia is the smartest, sweetest young girl I ever met. I felt so bad for her even before the accident happened. She was the black sheep of the family. I witnessed it. I witnessed everyone go out and live their life while Portia was at home reading books. She was a lot like me in that way. When her family died, I didn't know what was going happen. Ethan was great and he gave her something really special. I loved watching their relationship evolve and seeing baby Pyper. She was so happy to be a mother. I can't imagine how she forgot, but she did love that baby and Ethan very much. They were so happy. I don't understand how this could have happened."

Grandmother: "I didn't tell her, the same reason Ethan didn't tell her. I didn't want to make things worse. She lost her mother, her sister. Let her play pretend. If that's the way she grieves, that's the way she grieves. I didn't see the big deal. She turned eighteen. Susan helped take care of the house. My grandbaby adjusted to a really bad thing that happened. Ethan should have kept his mouth shut."

Susan: "Portia's mother would complain about her all the time. 'Portia can't do this. Portia won't do this. I just don't understand. Did I mess up as a mother?' I told her no. It's just a phase. Your daughter will grow out of it. I went through a shy phase. Everyone has social anxiety when they're younger. I didn't know how bad it was. I didn't know how to deal with this situation. I take full responsibility. This is my fault. Portia didn't do this to Ethan. I did."

Chapter 24

When it was the defense's turn, Mr. Torke took the stand. Even looking at him made me anxious. His expression was the same as when Ethan and I had told him I was pregnant.

"When did Ethan tell you he'd met Portia?" Rose asked.

"He didn't tell me right away."

"Why?"

"I think he was processing the situation himself."

"If he would have told you right away, what would have said to him?"

"Leave that girl alone."

"Would you have told him to tell her that he was the one who killed her family?"

"I wouldn't have recommended it."

"Did you recommend treating her?"

"I tried a few times, but she was beyond my expertise."

"So?"

"Ethan kept on seeing her."

"No. My question is, why not call someone? Anyone? Another doctor, social services?"

"She was of age. Ethan said he had it handled."

Everyone started mumbling again.

It was as if I wasn't getting it. I was confused, missing the punch line each and every time.

"No further questions, your honor."

Rose was such a bitch. She was being mean for no reason. If Mr. Torke had called anyone, I wouldn't have allowed it. I didn't give these guys much choice. None of these people had been there. I was willing to do anything to live my life the way I wanted to live it.

Richard stood up and walked over to the stand.

"Ethan struggled with depression and alcoholism growing up, correct?"

"Yes. He took my divorce pretty hard."

"You were protective of Ethan but also trusted him?"

"What is this? Therapy?" Rose said to herself as she leaned back in her chair.

"Counselor Harper." The judge was not a fan of Rose.

"Sorry, your honor."

"Yes."

"You wanted Ethan to be happy and you offered your home and a chance at forgiveness?"

"Yes."

"You wanted to help Ethan and Portia?"

"That's all we wanted to do from the very beginning. There was never any intention to harm Portia."

Rose raised her hand. "Objection. Relevance?" She was getting frustrated.

"Sustained. Get to the point," the judge ordered.

"What did you see when you walked into the Willows house August 29th at nine fifteen p.m.?"

"I heard screaming and scuffling. Susan was at my house with the baby and she had told me that Ethan was telling Portia the truth. We knew she wasn't going to take it well, so we were already on high alert, but we never thought Portia was capable of doing something like...*that*."

"What is 'something like that'?" Richard asked.

Mr. Torke looked down.

"I thought I was going to lose him. There was so much blood. He was coughing it up. My baby boy was just lying on the ground. I went straight to him. I told him I loved him and it was my fault."

He was crying.

I was crying.

"It was the scariest moment of my life. I wasn't aware of what had happened to him physically. I just saw my boy. My boy." He cried. "My boy half beaten to the death on the ground."

"Where was Portia Willows?"

"On top of him. She wasn't hitting him though. She was consoling him, apologizing."

"What was she apologizing for? Hurting him?"

"Objection, speculation, your honor."

"Sustained."

"No further questions."

Ethan's mom and Sarah said few words. It was almost over. Ethan was going to take the stand, the jury was going to deliberate, and then my fate would be decided.

"You have to stay strong through his testimony. Okay?" I didn't think it would be that hard for me but Rose made it seem like I had no idea what I was in for.

Ethan was being sworn in. I couldn't keep my eyes off him. He struggled to look at me. I would catch him periodically glance over, but he was visibly trying not to look at me.

I *wanted* him to look at me. I wanted him to stare into my eyes. He couldn't deny what we'd had.

"Let's get straight to the point, why did you let Portia live this lie?" Rose asked.

"I don't know."

"Okay. What about Portia made you fall in love with her?"

"Objection. Irrelevant," Richard snapped.

"Overruled. I'll allow it."

He choked. "She looked at me like I was...everything. No one had looked at me like she did, ever."

"What was it like living this life with her?"

"It was hard at times, but for some reason, she had this charm about her that made everything seem okay even though things were not. She wanted to make me happy. It was the beginning of our relationship."

"Portia initially wanted an abortion because she didn't think she could raise a child because of her social anxiety, but you pressured her?"

"I really thought it would be okay. It was her choice, but of course, I wanted our child."

"You thought bringing a child into a world where the mother had daily hallucinations of her own father, the child's grandfather, would be 'okay'?"

"I thought it would stop, she was getting better."

"At that point, had you given up on the fact that you were going to tell her that you caused the accident that killed her family?"

"I had." He choked. "Honestly, in hindsight, some things are better left unsaid. Things were really good between us. I thought we could move away from the house and we could live happily ever after."

"What did you think would happen after you told her?"

"Probably a slap. A really hard one."

That's what *I'd* said. That's what I *would* have done. Ethan knew me so well.

"Do you feel like you deserved what she did to you?"

"Maybe. I guess. A little bit."

"Yes or no please?"

Rose, give Ethan a break. Fuck.

"Yes."

"Do you still love Portia? Excuse me—are you still in love with Portia?"

"Objection, relevance," Richard shouted.

Ethan looked down.

I perked up. Please say yes. But if he said yes, what would I do? Hop over this table and go run and kiss him? No. I would still end up going to jail.

Ethan didn't answer.

"Does he really have to answer this, your honor?" Richard asked.

The judge looked at Ethan.

Finally, for the first time since I'd walked into this courtroom, Ethan looked straight at me.

I couldn't help myself, I stood up and stared right back.

"Sit down," Rose snapped at me.

I sat.

The judge kept staring at both of us. The courtroom was completely silent. I felt the tension in the air. Rose was tapping her heels.

"Yes," said Ethan.

The courtroom erupted.

I smiled. The whole trial was worth that moment.

"No further questions, your honor."

I was outside smoking a cigarette. The jury was out. I couldn't focus on anything except that Ethan still loved me. Rose was talking to the press while I was in a hiding spot at the side of the building. Elizabeth came to find me.

"There you are."

"This is where they took me to smoke."

"You did great."

"I didn't do anything. *You* did great. I'm just glad you didn't make get up there, I don't think I could have done it."

"That's why I thought it best you not take the stand, as much as your mental state has improved. All this must have been really hard for you to watch."

I shrugged. "What's going to happen? Am I going to go back to that room?"

"I don't know. Ethan admitting he still loves you put what this case is really about in perspective."

"You think I have a chance now?"

"Oh yeah. You're not going to walk out without a scratch, but you probably won't have to spend a day in jail."

"Good." I smiled.

"May the foreperson please stand."

A young, bald, white guy stood up in the jurors' box.

"We, the jury, believe that the defendant is guilty of second-degree attempted murder."

I put my head down.

That was all I needed hear. I wasn't going back to my solitary room. I was going to prison.

As I lay in the cell I was going to be in for the next five years, I thought of Maya Angelou:

"I can accept the idea of my own demise, but I am unable to accept the death of anyone else.
I find it impossible to let a friend or relative go into that country of no return.
Disbelief becomes my close companion, and anger follows in its wake.

REMEMBER

I answer the heroic question 'Death, where is thy sting?' with It is here in my heart and mind and memories."

I love you, Dad.
And Piper.
And Mom.

Fourteen Years Later

Pyper was playing Thing 1 in *Suessical*, the fall musical debuting that night at Cypress High. The musical had been the only thing talked about in my house for the past three months. I was proud of Pyper. She was shy growing up, which worried me, of course. By the time she turned six, she had come out of her shell. She became popular in high school quickly—always had a bunch of friends. I couldn't wait to go watch her. It wasn't my weekend so I hadn't been able to see her beforehand. I knew I would only see her for a second after before she went to celebrate.

Pyper was the most talented, most beautiful Thing 1 I had ever seen. They had dyed her golden curls blue. It was the cutest thing in the world. I couldn't wipe the smile off my face through the whole thing.

I saw Ethan waiting at the stage door. I awkwardly walked up to be in his line of sight.

"Hey, wasn't she great?"

"Yeah, she was." We both smiled at each other. For that moment, the past was forgotten and we were both just proud parents.

"I'm glad you came."

"I wouldn't have missed it for the world."

"They should be coming out soon."

A teenage boy stuck out his fist as he walked past Ethan.

"What's up, Coach T?"

Ethan pounded him. Ethan was a really good father. He was made for this. He was Mr. PTA and the coach to the high school soccer team. It just came so easily for him.

Pyper worshipped him.

"You know my soccer team…they're really killing it this year."

I smiled.

"Dad!" Pyper came running as fast as she could toward Ethan. He hugged her and kissed her mess of hair.

"Hi, Mom." Pyper came to give me a hug.

"You were *so* good, Pypes."

"Really? Did you laugh?"

"Yes. I did. I missed you." I gave her another squeeze.

She glanced over at her friends. There was still a part of her that was embarrassed to have me as a mom. I completely understood. She backed away from me and handed Ethan her stuff.

"Okay, Dad, so we're going to the afterparty at Ruby's. I'll be back by midnight, I promise."

I took a deep breath.

"I swear, Pyper…" Ethan started.

"Dad." She drew it out to at least three syllables. "Promise. Love you. Thanks for coming." Pyper gave him a kiss on the cheek and started to walk away,

"Pyper, say bye to your mom." Ethan snapped.

She came to give me a quick hug. "Love you, Mom." I squeezed her tight and off she went to find her friends.

I looked around at Ethan.

"You okay?" he asked. "It's okay if you're not. It can't be easy watching her go off with her friends after a play she was just in—"

I cut him off. "I'm fine." I turned to watch her walk away. I could make out her curly hair dancing as she laughed with her friends.

The way I never had.

I was so proud.

I smiled. "She's got this."

Acknowledgements

Daddy!
My favorite person in the world. I don't even know where to start with this acknowledgment. This whole book is based on the level of love I have for you. You're sitting right next to me. Thank you for always just simply being there, like you are now.

Michael, my OG therapist - for making me realize I'm not too messed up for help and reminding me that I am a living miracle and mental illness doesn't have to define me

Tatiana Amaro - one of the only friends that survived the wreckage that my mental illness caused and not judging me at all. At all. Even through the weird parts.

Melanie Lewis- for saving my life and showing me a new design of living.

Talia Ballig- for introducing me to Melanie and calling me a Uber when I was in New York for the first time trying to get this book published, having a mental breakdown because there was no way I could hail a taxi.

Allie Senfelds- for always willing to help me when I'm down and out.

You worried way too much about me and I'm so happy you get to see me be better.

Merisa Bambur - my trudge buddy. My road dog. You were the first person I called when I got the offer email. I was screaming and crying. You were screaming in your office. It was one of the best moments of my life and I'm so glad I got to share that moment with you. I will always love you. Know that.

Jayda Knight- one of my longest supporters- for being the friend that is just UNCONDITIONALLY there for you no matter how much I cry wolf and say the same old stories. And being the friend I randomly send very important things to so you can look over - resumes, books, professional emails, sample chapters, pitches. You have everything to do with my success today.

Mrs. Foley- for being the first writer I can see in real life and look up to. For birthing Rebecca Foley - my very first friend. You were there when my writing started in 1997 and both of you hold a special place in my heart.

Tyler Van Zeeland- for paying for my plane ticket to New York. You saw potential and a dream in a very poor girls heart. Thank you for believing in me!

Sage Griffin- for coming through for me as a friend these past few months. You have no idea how much you've helped me feel not alone. You remind me that we all feel insecure sometimes and it's ok. You help me not be hard on myself. Thank you. I love you.

Writers Digest- for hosting Pitch Slam at your annual conference, giving new authors the opportunity to share their work with agents and editors. Making dreams come true!

YA Group Attendees of the conference- there was a lot of you to name but you guys saved me with your honesty and helped me redo my pitch because my first one was trash and probably was not going to get me noticed. So thank you!

And if it wasn't for the following people, this book wouldn't be happening so I appreciate you. I love you. And thank you for everything you do!

Camille Taylor
Mara Zobava
Christina White
Marisa Veys
Pete Mills
Eric Urbiztondo
Dean Grosbard
Rick Steadman
Jake Marin
Ryan O'Connor
Tony De Marco
Amy Dresner
Shaun Barger
Megan Holiday
Breanna Webb
Calli Heussler
Elliott Paulson
Jim Woods
Caleb Pennypacker

And of course Chantelle, Jason and everyone at Agora for letting my voice be heard!

If you or anyone you know are struggling with social anxiety or any other mental health issues, there is hope!

NAMI Crisis Line (844) 549-4266

ADAA (Anxiety & Depression Association of America) (240) 485-1001

SAMHSA Treatment Locator (800) 662-4357

American Trauma Society (800) 556-7890

A portion of the proceeds of REMEMBER will be donated to Hope for the Day which achieves proactive suicide prevention through outreach and mental health education. Learn more at www.hftd.org.

About the Author

Patricia Shanae Smith was born and raised in Los Angeles, CA. She wrote *Remember*, her debut novel, after dealing with depression, cutting, eating disorders, addiction—she wanted to be part of the author club where you can save lives with words. She always says, "writing is not what I do, it's who I am". You can always find her at pop punk shows and coffee shops. Follow her on Twitter at @pssmith92 and Instagram at @patriciashanae.

She also hosts an open community where people who are going through a hard time can submit their troubles, secrets and express how they're feeling without judgement at www.tell-patricia.tumblr.com.